THE FARMERS' SON

G.A.HAUSER

G. A. HAUSER

*Special thanks to my three muses
Angelina, Trish, and Rachel*

The Farmer's Son

G. A. HAUSER

THE FARMER'S SON

Copyright © G.A. Hauser, 2013

Cover design by Charlie Mosby

© Cover Photography by Dennis Dean Images

© Original Cartoon Illustration by Arlen Schumer

Edited by Stacey Rhodes

ISBN Trade paperback: 978-1484-0185-1-4

© The G.A. Hauser Collection LLC

This is a work of fiction and any resemblance to persons, living or dead, or business establishments, events or locales is coincidental.

All Rights Are Reserved. No part of this may be used or reproduced in any manner whatsoever without written permission, except in the case of brief quotations embodied in critical articles and reviews.

WARNING
This book contains material that maybe offensive to some: graphic language, homosexual relations, adult situations. Please store your books carefully where they cannot be accessed by underage readers.

© First The G.A. Hauser Collection LLC publication: April 2013

The Farmer's Son

WARNING:
"The unauthorized reproduction or distribution of this copyrighted work is illegal. Criminal copyright infringement, including infringement without monetary gain, is investigated by the FBI and is punishable by up to 5 years in federal prison and a fine of $250,000."

ABOUT THE PHOTOGRAPHER

Dennis Dean Images

Award-winning photographer Dennis Dean continues to make his mark as an internationally known photographer. He is credited for his creative abilities, strong composition, and dramatic lighting. Dennis specializes in state of the art digital photography for fitness, fashion, and fine art.

Dennis published his first art book, "Within Reach" to rave reviews, which led to his work being showcased in a plethora of art publications, fitness magazines, calendars, greeting cards, as well as countless exhibitions, including two in London at the Adonis Art Gallery.

He is the founder of Dennis Dean Images and creative director and photographer of Five Star Monkey's Ruff Riders and Live Free Be Strong brands. He is also the editorial photographer for *Mark* and *Passport Magazines*, having shot countless covers and fashion layouts.

Dennis is proud to be partnering with Fort Lauderdale's Royal Palms Resort & Spa showcasing his work in all the rooms, bar and grill, the spa and fitness center. Stop by the resort to see Dennis' work, or make an appointment for a photo session at 954-240-8307.

Be sure and check out www.DennisDean.com &

www.RoyalPalms.com.

THE FARMER'S SON

ABOUT THE ILLUSTRATOR:

Arlen Schumer is a member of The Society of Illustrators, creating comic book-style illustrations for advertising and editorial usage, and one of the foremost historians of comic book art—his book *The Silver Age of Comic Book Art* won the Independent Publishers Award for Best Popular Culture Book of 2003.

www.arlenschumer.com

G. A. Hauser

Chapter 1

It was four a.m. and twenty-three year old Ayden Solomon was already sitting at the kitchen table in the country farmhouse on his family's almond orchard in California's Great Central Valley.

His mom, Helen, fried up fresh barnyard eggs from their own chickens, and bacon sizzled in a black iron skillet, making the whole home smell like a smokehouse.

His older brothers, Jacob, Jeremiah, and Levi, devoured the homemade cinnamon rolls and sipped black coffee, seated at the large rectangular table.

Fifty-five year old Josiah, Ayden's father, appeared grim, looking worn out and angry ever since his heart attack. The man was used to doing all the physical work himself, and now was made to slow down, like Granddad Tony. At eighty, Granddad was a World War II vet, and loved to tell his stories whenever the opportunity presented itself.

Though his brothers appeared jovial, laughing and teasing each other, Ayden had never felt connected to them. Living in the Valley, he had a sense of being isolated and stuck in the 'small town' mentality as well as the location.

Ayden was miserable.

After getting a cup of coffee from the pot, Josiah sat at the head of the table. "We need the tractors fixed. Jacob, you tend that, and you other boys, go about getting the day-workers to get that pruning done. No horsing around."

Levi punched Ayden in the arm.

Ayden flinched and gave him a dirty look. "Cut it out." Levi, who was two years older than Ayden, was the husky one of the four of them, with short cropped hair and a beard. Levi always picked on Ayden when he had the chance.

Jacob, the oldest, his head shaven and long bushy sideburns, didn't talk to anyone much, but since he was the first born, he shouldered most of the responsibilities.

Jeremiah, unkempt with a habit of packing his lower lip with chewing tobacco and spitting brown goo, seemed to support anything Jacob or Levi suggested, and that included bullying Ayden when they were drunk and looking for sport.

Helen brought platters of fried eggs, a stack of bacon and another huge plate of buttered toast to the table. Ayden stayed put until the swarm of hungry men subsided. They were like jackals on a carcass and Ayden knew if he reached for the food, he'd either get another punch or his hand would be poked with a fork.

His mother gave his father and grandfather their own stacked-high plates. No way Josiah or Granddad were going to compete for a meal. After the frenzy died down, Ayden took two fried eggs and a piece of toast. When he stood to get more coffee and returned to the table, his plate was empty and the boys were snickering to themselves.

"Fer cryin' out loud!" Ayden was sick of them picking on him.

"Here, Ayden." His mother replaced the empty platters with more food, and Ayden took his share once more. *Fucking hate it here! Hate it!*

"Where's Paw-Paw?" Jeremiah asked, his cheeks stuffed with food.

"He's on his way," their dad said, "He moves slower now that he's turned eighty."

Ayden ate his eggs with toast, thinking about how his dad moved just as slow as his grandfather since the heart attack and surgery.

Jacob was the first to finish. All the boys ate their food so fast, Ayden visualized them as sharks going after chum.

His oldest brother stood from the table, wearing a red plaid flannel shirt and baggy jeans, and walked out of the room. And as if the first born was a mother duck with her chicks, the other two quickly gobbled the food and followed him out.

Ayden peeked at his dad, knowing he was not earning brownie points by hating being where he was and having no desire to stay, but what he really wanted was to go to art school.

No chance in hell of that.

His mother had borne sons, and sons took over the family orchard. That's just how it worked at the Solomon household, and Ayden was certain it was the same for every other family farm and orchard in California.

Almonds. It was their life's breath and work. It paid very well. They weren't starving, had a big six room farmhouse, a barn, outbuildings filled with enormous equipment, a huge staff of day-workers when harvesting season came... It was a good business to be in, and his brothers loved it. The other three were content that they didn't have to be in college or working in an office.

Why Ayden was not, he couldn't explain. He was just different. He didn't even look like his brothers or his dad.

He finished his food and when he went to help his mother clear the table, his father said, "Leave that. It's woman's work. Get out there and help your brothers."

Ayden turned to look at his mother. She didn't react, still at the stove cooking. Knowing nothing he did would ever be right in his family's eyes, Ayden left the room. He passed the hall that led to his parents' and grandfather's bedrooms and noticed the old man crossing it to the bathroom opposite his door.

Ayden didn't say anything in greeting, headed to his bedroom and grabbed his fleece-lined denim jacket and a baseball cap. January in the valley—cold, damp and windy. Not to mention, rainy. *It never rains in California? Sorry. It does.*

He sat on his bed and laced his boots, trying to deal with the day, like every other day. It was a seven day work week. This wasn't an office, not a retail shop that closed up for the night or a holiday. This was a high production orchard, and the work never stopped.

Standing, making sure his gloves were in his pockets, Ayden took a peek at himself in his dresser mirror. His hair was long enough to brush his jacket collar, he was clean-shaven, and his eyes were piercing sky blue. At six foot three inches, he was taller than everyone else in the family, including his oldest brother, which infuriated Jacob. Why, when Ayden could do nothing about their maximum heights, Ayden couldn't guess. Everything he did upset the family.

Ayden adjusted his ball cap and left his room, heading straight to the barn since he knew he was the best at the mechanics and fixing the machines. The other boys were capable, but less patient. When things did not work right, they tended to throw tools or snap bolts.

Outside the fog was so thick, Ayden couldn't see from the farmhouse to the barn. Tule fog. Notorious for blocking out the sun for days.

And without that California sunshine, it stayed very damp and cold. Head down, Ayden walked the gravel and mud lane towards a light inside the outbuilding, shining like a small beacon in the gloom. Sunrise wouldn't hit for a couple hours, so he prepared himself for another long day.

He spotted Jacob behind the tractor, already working on it. Ayden stood beside him to see what he was doing. As usual, Jacob was flying by the seat of his pants, when every year at this time, after the harvest, they had to keep the machinery in good working order.

Figuring telling Jacob how to do the work would create a bad reaction, Ayden walked on. He knew where the owner's manuals were kept for each piece of machinery. He pulled open a metal drawer of the top of a tool cabinet and located the correct one, flipping through it quickly, refreshing his mind from when he did this same chore last year.

The tractor was getting older, but if maintained correctly they were built to last.

"Fuck!" he heard Jacob shout in pain and turned to look. His brother was shaking his hand in annoyance, as if trying to rid the sting of whatever he had done to himself. Working with cold fingers was not easy and usually meant skinned knuckles.

Ayden approached him, the manual in his hand. "Is it leaking oil?"

"Yeah." Jacob wiped his palm on his pants and kept fussing with the tractor.

"Can I just look at one thing?"

Jacob gave him a frustrated glare and dropped his arms, indicating *yes*.

Ayden placed the manual on the tractor's seat and inspected the lines. "It's cracked. You see here?" He showed Jacob the chafed line. "I have replacements."

He heard Jacob exhale loudly as if he hated knowing Ayden was right, but he listened and waited.

Ayden resisted the urge to shake his head since because he was the youngest, they assumed he was stupid. He was far from stupid. He retrieved a replacement hose from the cabinet and brought it over, dropping his gloves on the floor and removing the old worn out line as Jacob silently watched.

~

"Wade?"

"Yes, Cassandra?" Wade Reed looked up from his desk in his environmental planning office, which overlooked the downtown LA skyline.

"You're taking a few days off for a long weekend, right?"

"Just tomorrow. My brother has a parole hearing." Wade tried not to feel embarrassed. Just because his brother was a fuck-up didn't mean anyone else in his family was.

"Oh. Sorry." Cassandra made an exaggerated expression of remorse. "My bad. I didn't know. I was thinking you were taking a nice break."

"If I was going to have time off for a nice break in January, I'd be headed to Hawaii." He smiled at her.

"What prison is he in?"

"Corcoran." Wade rolled his chair back slightly from the desk, straightening his tie. "My guess is he'll be denied. He was convicted of armed robbery."

"Sheesh!"

"No kidding. But he had a bad dope habit. He's clean now, but to be honest, I still think because of what he did, he's stuck where he is for a while."

"Do you dread going?"

"Yes. But I owe it to him. No one else in my family gives a shit." Wade ran his hand through his hair, staring at the computer and the work he needed to do.

"Well, then don't worry about tomorrow. I don't think there's anything pressing that can't wait until Monday."

"Neither do I." Wade scooted closer to his desk and read over the letter he was composing for compliance documentation. After rereading the regulation for noise and air restrictions for a building project, he printed it. He had quite a lot of work to do today, but could certainly get it done.

"Okay, Wade, well, if there's anything I help with, just call."

"Thanks, Cassandra, but I've done this before. I'm not that emotionally invested in my brother's fucked up life. You play, you pay, ya know?"

"I do. Sorry, Wade."

"It's okay. Thanks." Wade checked the time on his computer. He had the whole day ahead to get things done, and wasn't worried about missing tomorrow. He was owed time off and had accumulated enough to take long weekends when he needed it. But heading to a parole hearing was not his idea of a fun time.

He rubbed his face tiredly and continued to work.

~

Ayden used the forearm of his jacket to wipe his face. His hands were a greasy mess. They had managed to get the tractor running smoothly and maintained for the winter, but that was just one machine. And Jacob had left Ayden to deal with it by himself, since Ayden knew what he was doing.

Nothing frustrated Jacob more than being 'shown up' by him. So while Jacob joined the others to help prune back the trees, Ayden continued to grease up and repair the equipment.

As the morning waned, he grew hungry. Using a worn out rag, he wiped his hands and noticed they were cracking from the cold. Calluses had formed on his palms and knuckles—the hands of a worker, not a pampered pet. Ayden couldn't get all the grease off with just the rag so he gave up.

Walking back to the farmhouse, he could see the trucks belonging to the day-workers parked on a long lane. On either side of the main entrance to their property, tall palm trees stood like sentries, making the rugged road appear stately.

THE FARMER'S SON

When he arrived at his front door, his grandfather was seated inside by the fireplace, staring at the flames, as if either deep in thought or daydreaming.

Ayden removed his shoes and jacket at the door, smiling to himself at his affection for the octogenarian. He and his grandfather got along well. At times it appeared his brothers didn't want to be bothered with Granddad, but Ayden sat with his dad's dad and listened to his stories, mostly about the war.

Through his spectacles, Tony looked up when he heard Ayden enter.

"Hi, Granddad." Ayden smiled as he walked through the room towards the kitchen, the aroma of cooked food luring him closer.

"Hello, Ayden. Is it still foggy outside?"

"A little. Not as bad as this morning." He paused. "Mom have lunch ready?"

"I'm not sure." Tony gave an effort at standing up from the sofa. Ayden raced to help him but looked down at his dirty hands in dismay. He offered his grandfather his arm instead. "Hang on. I'll haul you up."

Tony smiled and gripped Ayden's forearm through his sleeve, a strong hold for the shell of what had been a very powerful man in his prime. Ayden got him to his feet and they walked together to the kitchen. "I fixed up the tractor."

"Good boy. I know your father appreciates it." He patted Ayden's back.

Ayden doubted it, but smiled. Once they entered the kitchen he found his mother, as usual, up to her neck in pots and pans.

Standing at the sink, Ayden used a strong cleanser and rough sponge, one they kept just for the purpose of scrubbing off grease from their hands, and worked on getting all the oil out of his nails and cuticles.

One by one, the others showed up, their stomachs drawing them back for a hot meal, rosy cheeks from the cold and hard work, and the scent of dried sweat and mud permeating the tantalizing aroma of baked ham and potatoes.

Once his hands were spotless but raw from the scrubbing, Ayden tossed his ball cap onto the sofa in the living room and ran his hand through his flattened long hair.

"Get a haircut," Jeremiah said, "it's so much easier."

"I know." Ayden sat down beside him at the table and took a roll from the basket, buttering it.

When his father walked in, appearing grim as ever, Ayden said, "Got the tractor working, Dad."

"Good." He nodded and sat down at the table as Ayden's mom brought his dad a cup of coffee, setting the pot down for the rest of them.

Ayden poured a cup, passing it to Jeremiah, who did the same. "Do you want me to pour a cup for you, Granddad?"

"I can." Jacob appeared to have a chip on his shoulder about the tractor. He filled a second cup and set it in front of the old man.

"Jacob," Ayden's dad said, "I want you to help me with the paperwork this afternoon."

"Have Ayden do it." Jacob stuffed half a roll into his mouth.

Ayden was about to say he'd be happy to help, when Josiah snapped at Jacob, "I asked you. You're the oldest. You need to do the damn books."

"I hate that shit." Jacob shook his head, his hands still showing signs of grease, though Ayden knew he must have washed them. But to get all the oil off took time. And not just soap and water.

Grandpa Tony laughed and replied, "Sometimes, son, you have to do what you hate in order to get what you want."

THE FARMER'S SON

Ayden knew that was the truth. He was living it. He simply had no idea how to get what he wanted. At twenty-two, his only source of income was his family's pay, and of course living at the farmhouse was a free room and food. If he left? What then?

None of them had gone to college, since the idea was for all four boys to inherit the orchard and almond business. It had been in their family for four generations, and Ayden knew that was how it was going to be.

Even though it was controversial, Ayden said, "I can help with the books, Dad."

"I didn't ask you."

Helen brought to the table a baked ham surrounded by roasted potatoes and onions, on a platter. "Carve this, Josiah." Once she set it down, she walked away then returned with an electric carving knife and handed it to her husband.

Ayden watched as the soft meat sliced easily, and he knew the minute the food was handed out, his brothers would knock him over for their share.

His stomach growled but he waited patiently, finishing the roll, wishing, hoping, something good would happen and he could change things. But that wasn't likely.

His fate had been set before him, and he had to accept it.

G. A. Hauser

Chapter 2

The daylight vanishing, twelve hours of physical labor behind him, Ayden made sure the chickens were fed and heard the pickup trucks of the day-workers starting up as they left for the night. The fog was back and he couldn't see anything through the gloom but their headlights, which reflected the thick mist instead of penetrating it.

The same routine he did nightly, awaited him. He entered the house, took off his boots and jacket and instead of just washing his hands before dinner, he headed to his room, stripping for a shower. The farmhouse had six and a half bathrooms, so at least he had his own, and didn't have to fight with his brothers to shower or piss.

Though the bathroom only had a small shower stall, it was more than adequate for Ayden. He made sure his bedroom door was locked, dropped his dirty clothing on the floor and stood naked in his room, feeling the cool air but hearing the central heating kick in.

He moved slowly, walking to his closet and opened the door. Behind that door was a full length mirror.

Ayden stared into his eyes first, then inspected his hairless torso and tiny erect nipples. He flexed his chest and watched his pectoral muscles swell. His biceps were large and rounded, like his shoulders. Ayden lowered his gaze to his six-pack abs and the treasure trail, then to his dark pubic hair and circumcised

THE FARMER'S SON

cock and the soft balls underneath. After a quick peek at his dirty hands, Ayden imaged he was not looking at himself, but at a lover. Another man.

Keeping his eyes on his groin, he fantasized how it would feel to touch a man and have a man touch him. Moving closer to the mirror, Ayden rested his forehead against it, staring at his own body, craving a man so much he was in agony. But he didn't dare. Didn't dare let his gaze linger too long on any of the day-workers, didn't dare go into town and try to pick up a man. Didn't dare.

With his cock becoming engorged as he imagined a man to touch, Ayden headed to the bathroom and started the shower, waiting for it to heat. He glanced at the sink vanity mirror behind him at his own ass, seeing its tight round firmness and his long muscular thighs.

Holding the shower door as he let his imagination take wing, Ayden stood under the hot spray and pulled the glass door closed with a 'click' behind him. He scrubbed his hands first, then shampooed his hair all the while, imagining kissing a man, holding one, tasting his skin, his sweat...

Once he had finished washing, Ayden used the soap to lather up and leaned on the tiled wall, spreading his legs. He closed his eyes and visualized a strong older man, dominating him, guiding him gently into the art of man on man loving.

His lips parted and the water cascaded down his legs as he fisted his own cock quickly. Resting his head against the wall behind him, Ayden reached to touch his own rim and pushed his finger inside himself. He came and coughed on the intensity, milking his cock to make the pleasure last.

After the climax had subsided, he washed his hands and groin and shut off the water, catching his breath as he recuperated. If he didn't leave this orchard, he would never know what being with a man was going to be like.

His brothers, and his dad, would lynch him if they even knew he had homoerotic thoughts. The water shut off, standing dripping, Ayden opened the glass door and used a towel to wipe his face, trying not to allow his dilemma to bring him to depressed state. But it was hard.

~

Wade checked the time. It was nearing five and he realized he wouldn't get everything finished to his satisfaction before he left for the night. It was a three hour drive to the prison from LA and although Wade had done it in one day previously, since this time the parole board hearing was in the afternoon and not in the morning, he planned on staying at a local motel and heading out early on Saturday. That area of California was so low key, Wade didn't even feel the need for reservations at a hotel. Along Interstate 5 there were plenty of accommodations.

Even though he earned a good living, he'd come from barebones and never turned up his nose at a cheap motel if all he needed was a clean bed for the night.

He got a text message from an ex whom he had remained good friends with. Simon Dabney. He picked up his phone and read, '*Movie tomorrow night?*'

Instead of trying to answer over text, Wade called him.

"Hi. I didn't expect you to drop everything and call," Simon chuckled as he spoke.

It made Wade smile. Yeah, even though Simon was a handsome young man, the spark wasn't there. They'd both acknowledged it after a few months of trying to force feelings of intimacy that simply didn't exist.

"I know. But I'm about to leave the office and head home."

"So? Interested in a movie with me and Michael?"

"I am, but not tomorrow. I'm headed to the prison to be present at my brother's parole hearing."

"Shit. That sucks."

The Farmer's Son

"Tell me about it. Fucking armed robbery. I could kill him for being so stupid." Wade ran his hand over his hair tiredly.

"Think he'll be let out?"

"No. The victim and his family show up each time he's up for parole and reminds the board of his injuries with gruesome photos taken at the hospital. And ya know what? I'm not sure the dipshit should be let out. He was given twenty years, let him fucking serve them all."

"You sound like you can use a drink."

"I fucking can." Wade looked at his computer again. "Screw it. See you at La Cabana in twenty."

"I'll be at the bar. Michael is working late."

"Okay." Wade disconnected the call and saved his work on the computer. He stood from his desk, straightened the paperwork, dropped his pen into his top desk drawer and put his suit jacket on.

A co-worker poked her head in. "Heard you were taking a long weekend, headed to your brother's parole hearing. Have a good one if ya can. And wish him luck for me."

"Thanks, Abby." Wade loosened his tie and opened the top button of his shirt.

"See ya Monday!" she said as she walked off.

Wade patted his pocket for his keys and nudged his chair under his desk. He walked out of his office, shutting and locking his door, since many of his files were confidential.

"'Night, Wade!"

"'Night, Cassandra." He waved at her and left the office, closing the exit door from to the hall behind him and walked the corridor to the elevator. Thursday evening in January. The rush and bustle of Christmas and New Year's behind them, Wade felt as if he could breathe again. His parents, Pat and Doug enjoyed big family gatherings with loads of very energetic boisterous aunts, uncles and cousins—his cousins—all of whom had children. The questions about why Wade, at forty, still had not found Mr Right, were many.

Because he had stopped searching.

Every avenue Wade had to meet quality men had been tried and if he were honest with himself, he wasn't sure he wanted someone whose demand for living an A-list dream and LA nightlife-lifestyle drained him.

He'd done all that in his twenties, calmed down and dated seriously in his thirties, and now? At forty? What was so bad about being single?

He had a great group of friends, liked his job, had a good income and a supportive family. Life could be worse.

~

After their meal, the three brothers took off for the local tavern, never even asking Ayden if he wanted to go. And he didn't.

His grandfather was napping in front of the fireplace, his mother was still washing pots and pans and his father was in his home office with the door closed, owning the only computer in the house.

Ayden knew all about the social networks and email, he wasn't a moron. But he hadn't managed to get out and buy a computer or smartphone of his own yet. If he wanted to use a computer to surf the net, he used the one at the local library. He was saving up for a smartphone, and knew owning one would be questioned by his parents, since the monthly bill would come to the farmhouse.

He wanted to be connected to other men like himself. But laptops were expensive, and Ayden knew if he owned one, somehow his brothers would gain access to it and see everything he looked up or bought. Again, leading them to a conclusion he couldn't possibly allow.

THE FARMER'S SON

So, if he didn't feel like hanging with his parents and watching television or playing cards with his grandfather, Ayden lay across his bed with his sketchpad and drew...superheroes.

Ever since middle-school Ayden was into art and cartoon drawing. He could draw Batman, Robin, Spiderman...any character published in comic books, freehand.

But he enjoyed creating his own superheroes the most.

One of the cartoon creations was his likeness, maybe cuter, with large bulging muscles and a mask covering his eyes. Although in his mind this hero saved gay men and women from bullies, he knew better than to allow anything incriminating that could be discovered by his family. The homoerotic and gay superheroes were hidden. It was bad enough everyone knew he drew cartoon heroes. He didn't have to make it so obvious that everyone figured out he was totally gay. Those were tucked away.

So, his hero was named Neo-Magnay an anagram for 'One Gay Man'. And on his chest was the letter 'N'. Ayden called him 'Neo' for short and of course Neo had his trusty side-kick, Booverly, which again was an anagram of 'Lover Boy'. These two men, Neo and Boo were never apart, even out of their crime-fighting outfits, which didn't include a cape, but certainly hid their features for all the mere mortals out there.

Chewing his lip as he sketched in blue pen, making a series of action drawings depicting how he and his handsome partner would rescue young gay teens from bullies, and even suicide, Ayden saved the world.

He had the two men living together in a mansion in Beverly 'Mills', patrolling the streets of a big grimy metropolis, heavy with smog and litter, noise of helicopters and traffic, highways that roped like veins around the city, and men who could use both their brains and brawn to combat ignorance.

The villains resembled his brothers...although he tried not to be too detailed since his artwork was exceptionally good and he knew they would recognize themselves easily.

But as a group of thugs, these homophobic morons would hunt for fragile gay victims to torment until Neo and Boo arrived to 'Bam!' 'Wham' and "Ka-bam!" them into oblivion.

As he looked at his work, chewing the pen cap, he added balloon dialogue, enjoying living in his fantasy world.

~

"So," Simon asked, sipping a margarita, "Why are you the only one in your family to go to your brother's parole hearing?"

Wade dabbed his lip with a cloth napkin and dipped a tortilla chip into salsa. "Location and apathy." He ate the chip and finished chewing before he added, "He made me look like the 'normal and acceptable' one of the family. I owe him."

"Shut up." Simon laughed.

Wade smiled at him and remembered the attempts they had made at a relationship. Simon was in his young twenties when they met yet the age gap hadn't proved the downfall. They were both top dogs in bed, and neither would give in. They tried other methods of sexual gratification, but in the end, they mutually agreed, it just wasn't going to work.

At the moment Simon was dating another man closer to his own age: Michael, but Wade had decided to take a break from the social scene. He picked up his margarita and took a swig, licking his lips after. "Your turn. How's Michael?"

"I wish I could meld the two of you into one guy." Simon ate a tortilla chip and then said, "You and I get along better as friends, but he's good in bed."

"I was good in bed."

"Not in my book." Simon winked.

The Farmer's Son

"I should have just taken it up the ass for you. I was a fool." Wade missed having a boyfriend, especially one as young and fit as Simon.

"You're so full of crap. You know it wasn't just that. And..." Simon leaned closer as he said, "We would have other issues."

"Expand on your theory."

The waiter brought over two plates of food, holding them with towels. Wade sat back as his combo meal was set before him.

"The plates are very hot, be careful." The waiter stated the obvious as even he wasn't touching them and they steamed.

They thanked him, asked for a refill of their drinks and after the waiter left, Wade leaned closer again, waiting for Simon to answer his question.

Simon glanced around and then mirrored Wade's posture. "You want someone who needs you."

"Doesn't everyone?" Wade was surprised.

"No. I mean, less independent than you. *Needs* you."

"I think I was just insulted." Wade tore a piece of soft tortilla and piled beans and chicken on it before he ate it.

"No. It's not an insult, just an observation. I think that's one of the reasons you're attracted to younger men."

"I'm attracted to younger men because they're more exciting. They want to hump for hours in the sack. But the drawback is, the young men from LA all want to be out in the clubs all night. I am so past that. I'm too old for that shit."

"You're not that old, Wade. Other men in their late thirties and forties are good in bed as well. And not everyone wants to do the club scene."

"The men my age that are gorgeous go for younger men. You see the dilemma?" Wade blew on the food before he ate it.

"But you have no problem attracting boy toys. You hot fucker."

Wade blinked. "Yeah? You think I'm hot? I'm surprised. I thought I was a little past hot, and working towards decrepit."

Simon gave him a gape of exaggeration. "Do you know how jealous Michael gets when I tell him I'm going out with you?"

"Ask him along. I never mind."

"I want you to myself." Simon ate his food and looked up as the waiter brought two fresh drinks.

"Anything else?" he asked before he left.

"I'm good." Wade smiled and Simon shook his head no. Once they were left alone, Wade said, "You want me to yourself? That's why you make Michael jealous. I like him. I don't mind if you bring him."

"You don't mind being the fifth wheel? Huh. I would."

"I'm not you. I don't harbor any jealousy about you two. I'm happy for you." Wade blew on his hot food before eating it.

Simon smiled at him. "You're one in a million, Wade. I hope you do eventually find a great guy."

"Eh. Whatever. I'm good how I am."

Simon grinned at him and they continued to eat their meal.

~

Ayden heard the noise of the front door slamming loudly, followed by his brothers' guffaws of laughter and roughhousing. He hid the drawings under his bed and checked the time. It was nearing ten and because they woke so early, it was rare anyone stayed out very late.

Ayden shut off his table lamp and drew the covers up, staring at the door to his room. It had a lock on the knob, but he rarely used it. The obnoxious voices grew louder as his brothers walked by in the hallway. He could overhear them talking about a woman—a waitress? Barmaid?—'Teresa'.

Levi was teasing Jacob about a woman named Teresa.

"She was hot for you! Why didn't you ask her out, ya dork?"

"I don't wanna ask her out. She's not my type."

The Farmer's Son

"Then what's your type?" Jeremiah asked. "Are you a homo like Ayden?"

Ayden cringed.

"Shut the fuck up, douchebag!" Jacob reacted angrily and Ayden could hear them fighting physically as they landed on the wall near his door.

His father's voice boomed as he yelled, "Be quiet! Go to bed!"

The noise stopped immediately.

Ayden curled on to his side and stared at the moonlight coming through the slatted blinds. He had nothing in common with his brothers, and had no idea why.

~

Holding the mail in his hand, Wade entered his apartment and turned on a light. It wasn't late, but he felt tired. Sorting through the junk fliers and the bills, Wade opened a few to pay in the morning, and then headed to his bedroom to change. He removed his business suit and hung it up, yawning and knowing he didn't have to wake up early the next day. He washed up for bed and got into comfortable clothing, sweat pants and a T-shirt, and sat in the living room with his laptop. The television on, Wade reread the directions to the prison since he had not been there in ages, and rubbed his face tiredly at the thought of sitting through this board, and knowing the outcome would be the same.

His thoughts growing too dour for his own good, Wade caught up on his emails and social contacts, watching the news in the background and trying to not think about tomorrow. He'd go, do his best to be supportive of Cole, and that would be it.

Chapter 3

By six a.m. Ayden had already had his breakfast and repaired a chainsaw. His hands were ice cold and even in the barn it felt damp and chilly. He blew on his fingers and shook out his hands, trying to work with small screws and washers, seated on the cold cement floor.

A brown rooster wandered into the barn, stopping to stare at him.

Ayden watched him for a moment. They locked gazes, making Ayden laugh. "What do you want?"

The rooster raised one foot up, as if undecided whether to continue walking closer.

Ayden shook his head and kept working. As he did the bird seemed to relax and pecked at the hay and dirt as if realizing Ayden was not a threat.

He enjoyed the company, however strange it was, and finished putting the saw back together. A scrape of boot made him look up. Jacob was there, and the rooster flapped its wings at being startled and scurried off.

"Ya done?"

"I think so." Ayden stood, stiffly from sitting on the cold floor and readied the saw to start, pointing it downwards. He pulled the short cord and it buzzed loudly. He revved it up, then shut it off. "Here."

Jacob took it and walked off.

The Farmer's Son

"You're welcome," Ayden said under his breath and put his gloves back on, headed out to see what needed tending next.

~

Wade rolled over in bed and noticed the time. He rubbed his face and sat up, knowing he had to get going sooner rather than later. Tossing the covers off, he headed to the bathroom and stood at the sink vanity. After he loaded up his toothbrush he decided he needed a shave, maybe to show the parole board Cole wasn't from a family of degenerates. He owed Cole at least that.

Brushing his teeth and shaving at the sink, Wade then entered the shower and scrubbed up. His thoughts were many, and having no one to go with—not his mother, father, or any family member to help support Cole—Wade was growing angry.

Fuck it. Just go. Who cares if it's only me?

He finished showering and brushed his hair in the mirror, seeing just a touch of gray at his temples. Vanity wasn't too high on his list, and Wade knew he couldn't compete with men twenty years his junior, so he didn't. He kept fit and clean-shaven, still had a full head of hair, and earned good money. That's who he was. Take it or leave it.

Over the years he'd become comfortable in his own skin and if he found a man who he enjoyed, he would be open to it. But they had to accept him for who he was. At his stage in life, he wasn't interested in changing for anyone.

Wade decided to wear a suit and tie. It just seemed appropriate. He couldn't show up in jeans. He did pack them, however, to change into once the hearing was finished and he had found a hotel.

His bag loaded and by the door next to his wool coat, Wade made toast and coffee for his breakfast, even though it was nearing eleven, and stood eating the toast over the sink. He finished one cup of coffee and poured the rest from the pot into a travel mug.

Looking around his unit after putting on his coat and a white scarf, he shut off lights, made sure he had everything he could possibly need, including his laptop to use in the hotel room, and left. Staring at his phone as he headed to the parking area of the condo complex, Wade dialed his parents' number, just because.

"Hello?"

"Mom."

"Wade. Is everything okay?"

"I'm on my way to Cole's parole hearing." He waited. She didn't reply. "Mom? Come with me."

"What can I say, Wade? I'm not going. Neither is your father."

"He could really use to see us all there. You know he could." Wade opened his trunk with his key fob, putting his overnight bag into it, then closed the trunk.

"I'm sorry, Wade. Your brother made some awful decisions and we simply don't care."

"How can you not care?" He took off his wool coat, placed it on the passenger's seat and sat behind the wheel. "He's your son. You haven't seen him in sixteen years."

"Look, Wade, we're not going. I don't know why you keep asking. We haven't been to visit him once since he was stupid enough to get thrown in jail."

"I know that. You think he doesn't know that?" Wade started the car and lowered the music he had playing from the night before. "He knows he fucked up. But maybe he's changed."

"Goodbye, Wade."

"I hope you don't feel that way about me when I'm not around." He grew bitter. "I hope you don't think you fucked up twice; once with a gay son and once with—"

The line went dead. Wade looked at his phone and shook his head. "Unreal. No son of mine would be abandoned like that." He put the car in reverse and backed out. "And did you two ever wonder what you did to make Cole a drug addict in the first place?" He tried not to be too critical. Both his parents were very supportive of him, and members of PFLAG. So he couldn't whine too much, in reality.

Wade turned on his navigation system and headed to the highway to connect with Interstate 5 North. He had a long drive ahead of him. The sky was overcast and gloomy, which was appropriate for his mood.

~

Ayden sat at the large dining table and ate, keeping to himself. It was Friday but that didn't mean he had the weekend off. They never did. If there was something going on—like a family wedding or funeral—maybe then everyone would take a break from working and go. But normally, life was the same day to day, and the tedium was about to drive Ayden insane.

"Jacob," Josiah said with his mouth full of meatloaf and mash potatoes, "The accounts need to be updated."

"Let Ayden do it."

Ayden sat up, happy to help, but his father didn't even make eye contact. "I asked you! Why, Jacob, every time I ask you to do something do I get lip?"

Jacob shoved out his chair, stood, and left the room in a huff.

"Dad," Ayden said quietly.

His father cut him off by holding up his hand, then kept eating.

Ayden looked at his grandfather, who was offering him a sympathetic smile, but no one spoke out loud to defy Josiah. One by one, the boys went back to their work in the orchard. Ayden picked up all the empty plates to stack and brought them to the sink. "Thanks, Mom." He kissed her cheek.

"You're welcome. Go get busy. It's going to start raining soon."

Nodding, Ayden left the kitchen and put his boots back on, then his coat and hat, lastly, his gloves. He opened the front door and the Tule fog had moved in quickly, making afternoon look like night. His head down, fending off the chill, Ayden kicked at the gravel on the driveway and frowned. He could hear chainsaws whining in the distance and hopped into a pickup truck and started it up. He blasted the heat and could barely see down the long lane in front of him. There was no wind, and that usually meant they were going to be socked in for the night.

After driving a few miles to the northern edge of their orchard, Ayden parked.

The last thing Ayden wanted was to be around his brothers. If he even acknowledged one of the young men who worked for them, he'd never hear the end of it. So, he went on his own to do work elsewhere. Their property was so vast, Ayden couldn't even hear their chainsaws from where he was.

Ayden sat for a more moment, enjoying the heat coming from the truck before he shut off the engine and climbed out. The oldest trees were being cut down, replaced with saplings, and the rest were being pruned so they would reap the best almond harvest possible in the coming year. After a moment to reflect on what he needed to do, Ayden stepped out of the truck. The silence was eerie. Because of the dense fog, it felt as if he were in a domed realm of silence. But soon he would break that calm.

Ayden opened the tailgate and removed a chainsaw, carrying it to marked trees, walking through the gray gloom. He rested the chainsaw against his leg, and tucked his gloves under his arm. From out of his coat pocket he retrieved earplugs and pushed them into his ears, next he placed safety goggles over his eyes. Then, with the chainsaw resting on his shoulder, he walked to the nearest marked tree to be cut down and started the saw up. It revved high and he sliced wedges into the thick trunk weakening it on either side until it fell over and could be sliced up.

The Farmer's Son

~

In a female voice that got on his nerves, Wade's navigation system said, '*Make a left turn...ding!*'

Wade struggled to see through the thick fog and didn't even find an exit or road.

'*Make a left turn...ding!*'

"There is no left turn!" Wade snarled and looked in his rear view mirror. No one was behind him so he slowed down.

'*...when possible, make a U-turn. Ding!*'

Wade crawled slowly along the single lane roadway with barriers on either side. He had left Highway 99 ages ago, and assumed he was on State Route 144. Or maybe Highway 43?

'*When possible...make a U-turn. Ding!*'

"Shut up!" Wade yelled at the machine and looked for a spot to turn around.

'*Make a U-turn...ding!*'

He pulled over to the shoulder of the narrow highway and tried to get his phone to work so he could see where he was. There was no signal. "Are you kidding me?" He looked around and saw nothing but trees...and fog. Giving a good check of the limited visibility on the roadway, Wade made a U-turn and hoped no one was coming barreling his way. He waited for the navigator to re-negotiate his change of direction and headed back.

'*In five hundred feet, turn right...*'

Wade drove slowly in the dense haze. His high beams made the fog worse, so he shut them off and used his regular lights as well as his windshield wipers to try and keep the mist at bay.

'*In one hundred feet, turn right...*'

For the life of him, all Wade could see was a metal barrier and a field, no street.

'*Turn right...bing!*'

He slowed down, nearly to a stop. Nothing was there. No exit, not even a driveway. "Are you shitting me?" He drove on, and the navigator said, '*When possible make a U-turn...bing!*'

He turned off the navigator since he was about to toss it out the window, and kept driving trying to figure out where the hell he was. Dim lights approached from the opposite direction but it was so foggy, he couldn't even see what kind of car it was even as it passed. He stopped when the shoulder of the road opened enough to be safe. He tried his phone again. No service.

Struggling not to get angry, Wade checked his watch and was worried he was going to be late if he couldn't find his way. In his mind he reconstructed how he had come so far—I-5, 99, SR144...he should be on Highway 43, and he should have been headed in the correct direction.

Having a good look again up and down the roadway, Wade once again made a U-turn and kept going the same direction, knowing the opposite way was truly wrong.

"Whitney Ave...right?" he asked himself, driving slowly, looking for a sign, anything...to let him know where he was.

A car came up quickly behind him, since he was crawling. Wade put his right blinker on and tried to move to the shoulder. The vehicle, a pickup, veered past him, acting enraged, and took off as if it wasn't zero visibility. He shook his head and kept driving, struggling to see as the winter afternoon turned into winter night, even before four p.m.

"I'm late. How did I get late? I left early, didn't I?"

But he didn't anticipate fog. Not like this.

An opening in the metal barrier appeared on his left, the same direction his navigation system had told him to go originally. He turned onto the lane, but didn't see a street sign. "Where the hell am I?" His tires making crunching noises on the gravel, Wade believed he had to have made a wrong turn. This road wasn't even paved, and if he remembered right, there were no dirt roads on the way to Corcoran. He kept going a little more, in an effort to find a home, a shop, or someone he could ask for directions. When the length of time he was driving felt unreasonably long, and he knew again he was off course, he began looking for a place to turn around.

The small roadway was a single lane and no turn around area existed. He reluctantly drove another ten minutes and a small lip of dirt was his only option to turn back. He drove the BMW into it and reversed, trying to make a successful three-point turn. He felt the car dip sharply on his left driver's side rear and panicked. "No way." He put the car in drive and the wheel spun. "No fucking way!"

He drove back a few inches and the car dipped even deeper. "Fuck!" Wade threw it into park and got out. His car was wedged inside a drainage ditch…in mud. And it was beginning to rain.

He looked down at his designer suit and balled his fists. Taking out his phone, he tried for a signal, walking up and down the one lane road and about to throw the phone into the scrub in frustration. Beginning to freeze, he got back into his car, put on his wool coat in the tight space, and kept trying his phone—no text, no signal, no nothing.

He had a half a tank of gas and had no clue if he got out and walked if he'd be going nowhere into the Central Valley and end up cold, wet and more lost.

Hoping for help, he put his emergency flashers on and punched his fist into the dashboard in anger. Shutting off the CD and trying radio stations, he was astonished nothing but static came through the radio, AM or FM.

"Where the hell am I?" Wade ran his hand through his hair and had no idea there was an area in California that felt so isolated and secluded. Not to mention, blind with fog. He was an

LA boy, born and bred, and this kind of thing was slightly unnerving to him.

He ran the car heater on high, having no way to let Cole know he was on his way. *You're going to think I abandoned you. Like everyone else in the family. No!*

He put the car in low gear and rocked it forward and back to try and get out of the ditch. But every time he reversed, the car tilted upwards in the front even more. He dialed 911 on his phone and could see nothing was happening. No connection whatsoever.

Wade ground his jaw and took off his tie. He put the car in neutral and threw open the door. Looking at the angle of the car, he knew it was useless but had to try. Walking down the incline where the wheel was wedged, Wade stood at the rear bumper and pushed. It was absurd. He couldn't even rock the car, let along move it. "My luck it'll roll back and flatten me." He cursed as his shoes slid on the slick mud and he returned to the driver's door. He sat back down, putting the car in park, with the emergency brake on to prevent sliding even farther backwards.

He looked down at the caked mud on his leather shoes and rubbed his face in frustration.

~

Ayden used the chainsaw to cut up a trunk of a tree. His arms and back fatigued, he shut the motor, stopping the noise. He set the saw by his feet, taking off his gloves. It was nearly dark out and the fog was so thick he couldn't see across the lane from where he stood. Ayden took the earplugs out, and the goggles off his face, and stuffed them into his pocket. He removed his hat and ran his hand through his hair tiredly. Gloves and hat back on, he picked up the chainsaw and put it in the bed of his truck, closing the tailgate. His stomach began to grumble and he suspected his brothers were probably already on their way back to the farmhouse to eat dinner.

THE FARMER'S SON

It felt late, but he didn't wear a watch. He had no clue the time, since the fog had obscured the sun since after noon.

Drizzle fell, heavier than an hour ago, making everything damp and the drops made popping noises on the dry dead leaves on the ground.

He looked up at the sky and felt the dewy moisture on his face, not wanting to go back to the farmhouse yet, enjoying the solitude. Once all the noise he had created stopped, Ayden heard a whining sound off in the distance. Glancing back at the direction of the day-workers, he wondered if it could be them. He waited and again heard the noise, but it was coming from the wrong direction and couldn't be the hired help. It sounded like a car tire spinning in mud to him, but could possibly be from a neighboring orchard or cotton farm. The foggy gloom played tricks on sound and sight. Ayden climbed into the cab of his truck and started it up, his headlights doing nothing in the white mist, but reflecting back.

He tossed his ball cap on the seat beside him with his gloves and ran his hand through his hair. After working with the chainsaw, he was hot and craved a shower. Headed down the long lane before he was able to make a U-turn and return to the farmhouse, Ayden didn't mind the solitude, he craved it.

He lowered the window and leaned his arm on the frame to cool down, driving slowly along the deserted gravel lane that was his family orchard, their property…acres upon acres of trees…

Finding the spot he always used to turn around, Ayden backed into a small opening and noticed very dim flashing lights way out in the distance. It was so foggy out he couldn't figure out what they were coming from. He stopped the truck and stared at them curiously. They were definitely in the wrong direction to be his crew. It was the opposite area from where everyone came and went to their home. The utility road behind the property was nearly impassable in the rainy season because it was rutty and unpaved. No one used it.

He narrowed his eyes to see more clearly and couldn't figure out what it was. If it was a car, the lights were pointing too high as if it were angled strangely.

Since it was on his parents' property, Ayden drove the slushy dirt road, using his four wheel drive, and crept his way to figure out what it could be.

~

His gas gauge beginning to run low, Wade shut off the car and his headlights dimmed slightly. He kept his emergency flashers on and pulled his wool coat around him, leaning against the driver's door and trying not to fume. Hours had passed. Literally hours. He wondered if he kept his headlights on all night, if he'd wear his battery out as well. He shut them off but kept the emergency flashers on.

"This is absurd! How could not one car pass me? What the hell? Where am I?" He thought about getting out and walking the roadway, but knew that was just stupidity. It was so foggy he couldn't see two feet in front of him. Resting his head on the window, hoping the light of day would change his miserable existence, Wade closed his eyes and figured he'd be sleeping in a car instead of a hotel. He'd missed the parole hearing, let Cole down, and now had to figure out how to get help…in the morning.

He was just dozing off when he heard something. Blinking, sitting upright, through the impenetrable fog, he spotted a set of headlights far in the distance. He instantly turned his headlights back on, flashing them, honking the horn. "Thank fuck!"

The vehicle was moving towards him at a crawl, and Wade waited as it approached, barely making out the lights, like two white, dim eyes in the dense fog.

The Farmer's Son

He grew excited and figured the person had obviously seen him, so he stopped honking and flashing and watched it make its way closer, very slowly. Wade knew the road must be a muddy slippery mess. He had the slop on his shoes to prove it.

It started to rain harder. Wade waited impatiently for the vehicle to come approach. In what felt like a time warp, it took forever until Wade realized just how slow it was moving. He stepped out of the car and shielded his eyes from the rain, waving to make sure the occupant knew he was there, and it wasn't just an abandoned car with the alarm going off. In the thick white gloom, the headlights gradually became clear but Wade wondered if the driver could even see him yet.

Finally Wade could tell it was a pickup truck. It stopped and the door opened and legs in jeans were visible as they crossed in front of the truck's headlamps.

"Thank God! I've been stuck for hours. Can you help me?" Wade tried to see this man from beyond the bright halo of headlights which made him appear shadowy—a silhouette with a heavy coat and ball cap.

"How on earth did you get on this road?"

"No clue. I blame my navigator." Wade noticed the man look into his car. "My satellite navigator. I'm alone." Wade laughed nervously, thinking of horror movies and wondering how vulnerable he was out here in nowhere's-ville.

When the man began to investigate the state of Wade's car, his own headlights shined on him. Wade could make out his features in the dim gloom. *Holy shit! Are you kidding me?*

Horror film instantly turned into gay porn film in Wade's mind. Tall, at least six-two, and young, maybe early to mid twenties? Strikingly beautiful with long dark hair coming out from under the ball cap, wet and dripping on his coat's upturned collar.

"I can try to haul you out."

"That would be very kind of you. I have no cell phone reception here at all."

"No. There's none in this area. I know that." The young man smiled. "Let me see if I have some rope in the truck."

"Thanks, seriously. I really appreciate it." Wade rubbed his cold hands together. Getting drenched in the damp mist, Wade wondered if it would seem rude to sit behind the wheel of his car while this hunk helped him out. He watched him walk back to the truck, staring at his tight jeans and work boots. *Damn!*

Wade wanted to let his fantasy run rampant, but tried to keep a lid on it. After all, this was not LA, and it was bad enough he was a 'city slicker' with his suit, wool coat and BMW. Last thing he needed was for this guy to think he was gay.

~

Ayden was trying not to pant in excitement. His hero fantasy, helping someone in need, helping handsome men? Men in fancy black cars wearing business suits? *Oh yes! Neo is here to save you!*

He opened the toolbox in the bed of the truck and hunted around for something to use to haul the guy's car out. The rain was increasing and with it the blinding fog and darkness. He had a piece of fencing wire, no rope. He hopped out of the truck bed and slid on the slimy mud, catching himself on the pickup and trying to figure out how to hook this guy's car up and drag him out of a ditch, something he had never done before. He headed towards the man, seeing him waiting in his long wool coat, his chiseled model features and his wet head of hair. "You don't have to stand out here. Get in your car."

"No. It wouldn't be fair. Tell me what I can do."

"I only have this wire. I have no idea if it's going to hold. I can head back to the farmhouse and get something better, but it'll take a while."

"Up to you. I'm no expert."

The Farmer's Son

"Let me give it a try." Ayden knelt down in the mud and tied the wire connected to the axel of the BMW. He tugged it, securing it, and stood back up, wiping his muddy hands on his jeans. "Right. Let me pull the rig up, and I can tie it to the trailer hook."

"Okay."

Ayden headed back to his truck, his cock thick in his pants from the handsome looks of the man. He wanted to invite him for coffee at a café...maybe have five seconds to get to know him. Get to know someone who wasn't from the orchard, someone who had a damn brain and could talk about *things*. Things other than work or sports. Someone who would take the time and actually have a conversation with him, without jeering and mocking.

Ayden drove the truck slowly passed where the man was standing, trying to position his rear bumper so he could secure the man's car to the hitch. He stopped and leaned out his open window to look. He backed up, angling the truck awkwardly across the soaked narrow lane. Then he hopped out again. Using the end of the wire, wearing his gloves this time since the wire was sharp, he wrapped it up and tugged it. "Okay. Let's see if I can get you out."

"You have no idea how much I appreciate this."

Ayden smiled and wondered what color this man's eyes were. They looked light. Blue? Like his? The guy was tall, nearly his height, and Ayden would pay money to see him naked. At this point, he'd pay to have any man naked in front of him.

He climbed back into the truck and began to drive, trying to pull the car from the ditch. His truck skid in the slick mud with the extra weight, so Ayden slowed down and put it into the lowest gear. Even in four wheel drive, he couldn't budge the BMW and began sliding sideways. He stopped the truck and tried to think. He really needed to be a hero and save this guy.

He put the truck into first and pushed down on the gas harder, trying to use brute force and heavy horsepower. The tires spun and his truck moved forward a few inches, then lurched completely sideways and into the same drainage ditch he had been trying to pull the BMW out of. "Shit!"

The man rushed to Ayden's open window. "Stop! You're getting yourself stuck! Just drive me to a phone and I can call a tow truck."

"Okay." Ayden climbed out and began unwinding the wire. Once he removed it from his trailer hook, he climbed back into his truck and tried to rock out of the ditch. Now he was stuck. He couldn't believe it. He rolled forward and back, sliding off the side of the road even worse than before. "No way! This truck never gets stuck!" Ayden spun the tires and began to inch sideways. He stopped and the man again stood at the door of his rig. "Don't. Seriously. You're going the wrong way. All you're doing is sliding into the drainage ditch with me."

"You have got to be kidding!" Ayden was dying of embarrassment.

"How far a walk is it to the farmhouse you were talking about?"

"Miles." Ayden took off his glove and rubbed his forehead, then realized his hands were dirty too.

"Really? Too far to walk? Seriously?"

"Nothing's too far to walk, but I figure it's going to take us a few hours. Do you have a flashlight?"

"Uh no. Do you?"

"No." Ayden shook his head. "At least get in here. You're going to freeze."

"Okay. Let me shut off my hazard lights so I don't drain my battery completely."

Ayden watched him go and rolled his window up, putting his heater on high as he cooled off. He wondered once his family figured out he was missing if they would even think of looking for him here. He wouldn't. It would be the last place he would look.

The passenger's door opened and the man climbed in.

"Hi. I'm Wade Reed. Thank you so much for trying."

Ayden looked down at the man's hand. "I'm Ayden Solomon. Sorry I couldn't pull you from the ditch."

They shook warmly and Wade laughed. "I'm to blame now. I got you stuck with me."

Look at that smile! "I...I don't mind being stuck with you." Ayden blushed to the ears.

Wade inspected him closely in the dim interior of the truck. With his index finger poking the overhead dome light, Wade turned on one of the interior lamps. "I like to see who I'm stuck with."

Ayden felt shy to the handsome man's gaze. "Just me." He smiled meekly. *Blue. Your eyes are sky blue, and you are the most amazing looking man I have ever seen!*

"Just you." Wade grinned warmly.

Chapter 4

In the illumination of the dome light, Wade couldn't believe what fate had brought him. He examined this masculine stud from his mud-smeared cheek, his bright blue eyes and smooth skin, down to his denim and fleece jacket, dirt caked blue jeans and equally muddy work boots. Fucking gorgeous!

"You work someplace around here?" Wade asked.

"My family owns this property. We have an almond orchard."

"Nice. I'm sorry I'm trespassing." Wade wanted to wipe the smudge of dirt from Ayden's cheek, maybe just to touch him.

"You're not trespassing. You're lost in nowhere land."

Ayden's shyness was making Wade an inferno. He glanced down at himself and realized he was as muddy as Ayden was. He looked at his hands and sighed.

"Why are you here in this area?"

"My brother is in the Corcoran prison. I was trying to get to his parole hearing." Wade lowered the visor and inspected his face, wiping at a dirt streak on his cheek.

"You should have taken Whitney Ave. I think it's Whitney to Otis. Something like that."

"Ever been there?" Wade flipped the visor up.

"No. I don't get into trouble. But I know where the place is."

Wade leaned over to see the gas gauge. Ayden stiffened up his posture as if he were nervous he'd be touched. "I was just checking to make sure you didn't run out of gas. I won't do anything to you. Believe me."

"Oh." Ayden actually sounded slightly disappointed. "I've got nearly a full tank."

Wade leaned against the passenger's door, bending one knee so he could look at Ayden as they spoke. "How did you find me? Did you see my lights?"

"Yes. I was cutting down some old trees and spotted something blinking. I'm glad it wasn't a UFO." He chuckled.

Wade laughed too, shaking his head. "So, what's the plan?"

"If you want to try to walk in the dark, we can head to the farmhouse now."

"Who lives at the farmhouse?"

"My parents and brothers."

At the intense frown that accompanied that statement, Wade asked, "Why when you said that did you look upset?"

Ayden shrugged. "I don't know." He glanced down at his muddy hands and tried to wipe them on his jacket.

"You don't have to tell me about dysfunctional families. I wrote the book."

Ayden chuckled softly and met Wade's gaze. "I don't get along well with them."

Wade nodded, loving to stare into this young man's blue eyes. "It happens."

Again Ayden shrugged. "I can't imagine being here my whole life. I'd rather do something else."

"Like?"

"Like anything else. Just not being here." He tilted his head towards the farmhouse. "I mean there."

"How old are you?"

"Twenty-two."

"Did you go to college?"

"I wanted...want to. But my father pretty much said everyone has to work the family business, so..."

"That doesn't seem right. I mean, you sound like a very intelligent young man. Can't you go on your own? Apply for a loan and just go?"

"I guess I should, huh." Ayden looked down at his hands again.

"You should if you want to."

"I feel like they have me in a stranglehold."

"Why?"

"Oh, God. It's so complicated." Ayden rubbed his forehead.

"Don't do that. You're already a muddy mess." Wade reached out his hand to stop Ayden.

When Ayden turned to look at him his eyes seemed glossy and red.

Wade reached into his pocket and removed a tissue. He tried to wipe the mud off Ayden's face and Ayden seemed to go limp as he did.

~

Touch me. Oh, God, touch me.

Ayden was so starved for physical affection he was growing emotional. He closed his eyes and allowed Wade to clean his cheek. It was so kind, he never wanted them to get out of the truck, didn't want to walk back to the farmhouse...ever.

"I think I got most of it."

Ayden opened his eyes and stared at Wade. He bit his lower lip in longing. "What...uh... What do you do? For a living, I mean."

Wade stuffed the tissue into his coat pocket. "I'm an environmental planner. Boring shit."

"Do you like it?"

The Farmer's Son

"I do. It's okay. I don't hate it. If I hated it, I would do something else." Wade paused and touched Ayden's leg lightly. "Life's too short to do something you don't like."

Ayden glanced down at the touch but it soon withdrew. He tried to estimate this man's age, and came up with mid-thirties. It was his best guess in the dim light. "Where do you live?"

"LA."

"I've never been there. I've always wanted to go."

"It's a crazy place. Over-priced and too full of itself, but I love it."

The smile was dazzling and Ayden imagined what kissing him would be like. "Are you married?"

"No." Wade chuckled and looked shy, lowering his head.

"Why not? I mean, you're really…uh…" Ayden shut up, not knowing if telling this man he was handsome was appropriate.

As the interior of the cab warmed from the high blasting of the heater, Wade shrugged off his wool coat and Ayden could see his suit jacket and cotton shirt, the top button open, and no necktie.

"Just never met the right person." Wade tugged on his cuffs and settled against the passenger's door again.

Person? Not 'woman'?

Ayden shrugged his jacket off as well, growing hot, and not sure if it was from the truck's heater making him an inferno or it was his attraction to Wade. "You got your nice suit dirty."

"I know." Wade stared at his pant legs. "I brought a change of clothing. It's in the trunk of my car. I imagined I'd be in a hotel overnight. Not quite, huh?" He laughed. "So, will your family panic when you don't show up?"

"Panic? No. They're not the type to call the police or anything. I figure they'll give a look around the property and then assume I headed off someplace to be on my own."

"Really? No one will freak out if you don't show up overnight?"

Ayden wondered if they would. "Maybe. My mom may wonder what I'm up to."

"Do you go out much? Hang out with friends?"

"Not really."

"Do…do you have a girlfriend who'll miss you?"

"No." Ayden stared directly into Wade's eyes. "I'm not into girlfriends."

Wade's expression changed slightly. "Too young to get into a committed relationship?"

"No, it's not that…I…" Ayden couldn't say it. He wanted to, but couldn't.

"What kind of work were you doing today?"

"Cutting down old trees." Ayden looked at his dirty hands again. "I stink. I need a shower." He tried to rub the dirt off his palms. "How bad do I smell?"

Wade smiled. "I don't mind the smell of a man's sweat."

"Huh?" Ayden perked up and his cock grew thick. "Did you say you don't mind the smell of a man's sweat?"

"I did."

Ayden didn't know how to answer.

"Did I offend you?" Wade asked.

"No!" Ayden struggled with how to interpret that last comment. "Are you…?"

"Gay?" Wade finished his sentence. "If I say yes, will you kick me out of your truck and not help me? Or worse?"

"Oh my God." Ayden couldn't believe it. He looked up and said, "Thank you."

"Who are you thanking?"

"I don't know. But…" Ayden slouched in the seat and blew out a breath. "You have no idea."

"Nope. None, until you tell me what's in your head. I don't."

THE FARMER'S SON

Ayden thought of his cartoon character 'Neo' and faced Wade on the seat. "I'm gay."

Wade tilted his head. "*You're* gay?"

"I am. Like totally."

"Well! My lucky night." Wade interlaced his hands on his lap. "How did I find a gorgeous gay angel to come rescue me in the dark?"

"I didn't do a very good job rescuing you." Ayden blushed, and felt his hands go clammy.

"You did. I couldn't run the car all night and would have frozen my ass off. Besides, your company is wonderful. I'm enjoying talking to you."

Ayden brightened up. "Me too. I can't tell you how nice it is to have someone intelligent to talk to. My brothers are well…" He rolled his eyes.

"Family. Like I said." Wade threw up his hands. "Cole, my brother, is in jail for armed robbery."

"Wow. That's serious stuff."

"It is. He was an addict and that's what drove him to commit crimes. My missing his hearing is going to crush him. But what can you do? I tried."

"My brothers already call me a fag. I get the cold shoulder mostly. That's why I was working on my own away from them. I'm the youngest and they treat me like I'm either a pest or have a disease."

"I'm sorry, Ayden. Truly."

"I haven't come out or anything. They just don't get me. *I* don't get me."

"What's to get? You are who you are."

"I know that. I can't change who I am. But they're real good ole boys. I know they'd kill me if I actually came out and admitted it."

"You wouldn't be the first or the last young man to deal with ignorance. I've heard it all."

"Why, Wade? Why should they care?"

"I don't know. I can't answer that question."

"Does your family know you're gay?"

"Yes. But I don't live with them. You do."

"I don't want to live with them. I want to go to college."

Wade shifted on the seat, his hands interlaced on his lap again. "What do you want to study?"

"Art. I draw cartoons." When Wade raised his eyebrow, he added, "Superheroes. Gay superheroes."

"I love it." Wade laughed. "I would love to see your work." He looked into the dark rain. "If we ever get out of here."

"I don't want to get out of here." Ayden smiled shyly.

"Me neither." Wade touched Ayden's knee with the tip of his index finger teasingly.

"Can I ask you something?" Ayden lowered the heat blower since he was now boiling.

"Sure. Anything."

"Have…have you been with a lot of guys?"

Wade looked down at his hands first and asked, "What's 'a lot'?"

"I don't know."

"Have you?" Wade turned the point.

"No. Not one."

"Not one? Not even to experiment with?" Wade appeared surprised.

"Nope. Crazy huh? Going all this time without touching a guy."

"I suppose if you come from a family that will kick your ass, I don't blame you."

"I fantasize all the time."

"I can imagine."

The Farmer's Son

"Kissing a man. Touching one. Being naked with one." Ayden felt embarrassed but what did he have to lose telling Wade everything he felt? It was nice sharing his feelings without the threat of retaliation hanging over his head.

"Oh, babe. You can't keep going like this. You have to find a way out so you can get affection."

"How? I really am stuck. They pay me very little since I live and eat home. I have some savings but I can't afford LA."

"It doesn't have to be LA. You may be able to afford something in one of the suburbs. And you can share an apartment, look for a job someplace. There are always ways out."

"I know." Ayden nodded, looking at the rain running down the windshield. "You're right. I should just pack up and hit the road."

"Do you own this truck?"

"No. It's my family's but I would just take it. They have quite a few vehicles."

"I know it would be scary for you, and not an easy decision to make."

"It is hard to do. Once Mom and Dad die, the business will pass to all of us, and believe me, almonds are big business. My parents are very well off."

"Huh. Really?"

"Yes. Really."

"So you'd lose out on your inheritance?"

"Not like in cash, but in assets. Yes."

Wade nodded and he too stared out at the rain. "Life's not easy for anyone. It's about choices."

"Yes. I know." Ayden glanced at Wade.

Wade caught him staring and looked back.

"So?" Wade asked, "Are we here all night or are we going to try and walk in the dark in the rain?"

"Without a flashlight?" Ayden didn't want to go back. Not at all.

"Yeah. My vote is to stay here until morning too. I think I may have a few power bars in my overnight bag. Are you hungry?"

"You're going to go out in that rain for a protein bar?" Ayden laughed softly.

"For you? Yes. You crawled under my car in mud. I owe you."

"Sure." Ayden felt his cheeks blush again and wanted to hold Wade's hand.

"Be back." He pointed teasingly. "Don't go anywhere."

"I won't. I can't!" Ayden laughed loudly.

"Good." Wade winked and opened the truck door.

As Wade raced out in the downpour, Ayden reached into his pants and adjusted his cock. He was hard as a rock.

~

Wade used his key fob to open his trunk and dug through the outer pocket of his overnight bag for where he knew he'd stuffed snacks. He grabbed a handful of protein bars and then looked down at his trousers. "Fuck it." He unzipped the overnight bag and removed the jeans as well. Taking them with him, jogging back to the truck, Wade climbed back in and put the handful of protein bars on the seat between them. "Now we won't starve." He laughed and placed the pants on his lap.

Ayden picked one up and peeled the wrapper. "Thanks. I am hungry. One thing I have to say…Mom's a good cook." He bit into it and nodded. "It'll do."

"Look, uh… You mind if I change my pants quickly? I can do it in my car if you do."

Ayden stopped chewing and stared at him. "I don't mind."

THE FARMER'S SON

"Good. It's freezing in my car." He toed off his muddy shoes and unbuckled his belt. He caught Ayden look and then turn away quickly. "Ayden."

"Huh? You want me to turn the other way?" He made a move to face his back towards Wade.

"No. You can look. I'm fine with you checking me out."

"You are?" Ayden's eyes went wide as he held the protein bar close to his mouth.

"Sure. Ya poor guy. Have you even seen another man naked?" Wade unzipped his pants.

"Not for real. I mean, no."

"Well, here goes nothing. I hope I don't let you down for gay men everywhere." Wade removed his muddy slacks, showing his boxer briefs and tried to step into the jeans in the tight space. He managed to get them up his legs and zipped. "Sorry."

"About?" Ayden kept eating the bar.

"About not being a twenty year old gym junkie." He folded his muddy slacks and put them on right corner of the dashboard.

"You're kidding, right?" Ayden ate the last bite of the protein bar and chewed it as he stared.

"No, I'm not. I can't imagine what you look like under those clothes." Wade tucked his shirt into the jeans, feeling better to be out of his work pants. "But I bet I could sell tickets."

Ayden laughed and appeared shy. "You look great, Wade. I bet you work out."

"I do. I try hard, but still…I'm not twenty." Wade stepped into his shoes even though they were muddy, but what was the point of changing into his clean tennis shoes if they were going to walk in the mud tomorrow?

"Why do you want to be twenty? Believe me. I want to be older so I can make decisions like a man. I feel like being so young, I have no say on my future."

Wade picked up one of the protein bars and peeled back the wrapper. "It's a crazy world, huh? By the time you're old enough to have a good life and intelligent enough to know what you want, your body starts to go."

"Are you joking?" Ayden crushed the wrapper and put it into the side pocket of the truck's door. "You look perfect."

"Hardly."

"When I get the chance, I'll make you into one of my superhero characters."

Wade laughed in amusement. "Who will I be? The Moron-who-got-his-car-stuck-in-a-ditch Man?"

"No. Wade-the-Wonderful."

The smile on Wade's face fell. Thinking about this young man and how deprived he must be of kindness, touch, love… He felt so much pity for him, he ached. "Ayden."

Ayden met Wade's gaze instantly.

"When we get out of here, why don't you come to LA and spend a weekend?"

"Huh?" Ayden perked up. "For real?"

"For real."

"I'd love that. You have no idea."

"It's the least I can do." Wade finished the protein bar and placed the other two on the dashboard.

"Huh. A weekend in LA. Wow."

"So, does that mean you haven't traveled very much?" Wade stuck the wrapper into his coat pocket.

"I've been to a few places. Not like Europe or anything. But when we were kids we went to Disneyland. Stuff like that."

"I would think because of how well you say your family does, that you would get more vacation time."

"We don't. The orchard maintenance is so demanding we work constantly." Ayden looked down at his hands again.

Wade reached for one. At the touch Ayden appeared to melt.

The Farmer's Son

In the dim dome light, Wade inspected Ayden's hands. Working man's hands—callused and dry. He massaged his fingers gently, feeling affection for him.

"I usually scrub them up good. The oil gets into my skin." Ayden seemed embarrassed.

"I can't imagine how hard you must work." Wade used his thumbs to massage the pads of Ayden's palms.

A small whimpering sound came from Ayden and he shifted his legs on the bench seat.

Wade worked each of Ayden's fingers individually, squeezing them and giving each a little rub down. "The physical labor you do? Cutting down trees? That must take so much strength." Wade glanced at Ayden's crotch since Ayden looked down at his own lap. A bulge was visible under Ayden's zipper flap. Wade worked his way to Ayden's middle finger, and if their hands weren't so dirty, he would have sucked it.

Chapter 5

Ayden's cock was throbbing and getting his briefs damp with pre-cum. He swallowed a sound of longing as Wade's warm hands massaged his callused fingers and palm. Resting his head back on the driver's window, he shut off the dome light and his headlights. No way did he want anyone to discover him now. Uh uh.

Wade paused in the caress, as if waiting to see why Ayden had done what he did. "You okay?"

"Don't want anyone to find me now."

"Ah." Wade chuckled softly. "But I can't see a thing. And I want to see...see you."

Ayden brightened the intensity of the truck's dashboard gauges, giving them dim blue light to see each other by.

"Perfect." Wade inched closer on the bench seat.

Ayden's breathing became audible and he pressed his back into the driver's door nervously. "I..."

"Yes?" Wade released Ayden's hand and touched his thigh.

"I never kissed anyone."

"No one? Not even a girl in school?"

"Nothing more than a peck on the cheek. No."

"How could that be?" Wade cupped Ayden's jaw tenderly. "Ayden, you're so incredibly beautiful."

"Am...am I?" No one had ever told him that before.

"Yes."

The Farmer's Son

"I never felt beautiful. I always felt self-conscious and worried of what my family would think…and…" Ayden loved the touch of Wade's hand to his cheek. "I didn't want to kiss girls."

"No. Neither did I."

He could catch a scent of Wade's cologne and was embarrassed he hadn't had a chance to shower. Ayden could smell his own scent from working hard and was afraid it would be unpleasant to Wade.

"Can I kiss you?" Wade's breath was a puff on Ayden's chin.

"Please."

With the tip of his finger, Wade turned Ayden's jaw towards his and they met lips.

Ayden let out a low groan before he could prevent it and his legs relaxed and splayed out as he sank into the truck's bench seat. Wade kissed him a few times, lightly, and checked Ayden's expression.

"That was nice." Ayden couldn't catch his breath.

"Do you want more?"

"I do, Wade. Is that okay?'

"More than okay."

Ayden shifted on the seat so he could be closer to Wade. "I'm sorry I stink."

"You don't." Wade ran his hand over Ayden's neck, touching his hair. "You smell like a man. All man."

Ayden tossed his ball cap onto the dash and gazed into Wade's handsome features in the dim blue light. Nervous, terrified of venturing into the unknown—the forbidden—Ayden wanted to touch Wade the same way he was being touched. To cup his head, run his fingers through his hair, but he didn't know the rules. Were there rules?

Ayden looked down at Wade's jeans, trying to see if he was as excited as he was. That glimpse of the outline of Wade's cock and balls in his dark briefs when he'd changed pants was like a brand on Ayden's mind.

His jaw was tilted upwards and Ayden closed his eyes as Wade kissed him, kissed him so tenderly he was about to swoon and declare his love for this handsome stranger.

When he felt Wade touch his lips with the tip of his tongue, Ayden relaxed his jaw and allowed that tongue in. In a pure reflex reaction, Ayden reached around the nape of Wade's neck and drew him tighter, making the kiss stronger. The rain had soaked Wade's hair, but because the truck interior was warm, it didn't feel cold to Ayden's fingers.

His focus was drawn to the way Wade was using his tongue to slowly explore inside his mouth, touching his own tongue and making slow swirls around it. Ayden's cock began to pulsate and the urge to come became strong.

He moaned against Wade's mouth and scooted even closer, overlapping their knees on the seat, fogging up the interior of the truck cab.

Wade rested his head against Ayden's forehead. "You're a great kisser."

"I don't know how I can be." Ayden's skin was on fire. He interlaced his fingers behind Wade's neck and went for his mouth again. This time he used his tongue to enter Wade's mouth. When Wade sucked on it lightly, Ayden nearly came. He stopped kissing him and grabbed his own cock through his jeans to hold back a tidal wave of pleasure.

Wade patiently gave him the time he needed. Not rushing him. Not forcing him to do anything more than what they were doing.

And Ayden simply did not know what they would or could do.

He used his windshield wipers to make sure no one was creeping up on them in the foggy darkness, which was absurd since their cars were in an area of the property that was never used. Nothing was here but an old logging road which was obviously nearly impassable.

After he was confident it was indeed safe to continue, Ayden ran his hands down Wade's shoulders and stared into his handsome face. "Have...have you ever been with a man as inexperienced as me before?"

"No." Wade smiled. "I love it. You have no idea how much."

That surprised Ayden. "Why?"

"Because everything about you is so pure. So fresh." He brushed the wet locks out of Ayden's eyes.

Ayden was humiliated he was a virgin. Who was a virgin at twenty-two? He assumed none of his older brothers were, judging by their tales of marauding with the barmaids in the local tavern and the checkout girls at the market. "I've never been called fresh and pure before." Ayden laughed at the irony. "That's pretty funny."

"To me, it's sexy as hell. I have never been a man's first."

Ayden was so smitten with Wade, he stared deeply into his eyes, seeing nothing sinister, nothing mocking, demeaning. The only other person who looked that way at Ayden was his grandfather. "I feel so ashamed."

Wade backed off. "I'm sorry." He scooted back on the seat to make space between them.

"No. I'm ashamed for being so naïve. Not for what I want to do." Ayden reached out for Wade's hand. "For what I don't know. For being so inexperienced and lost."

"How were you to learn? Hm?" Wade ran his fingers through Ayden's hair. "Who was going to be your mentor?"

Ayden stared into Wade's eyes. "No one."

"Then there's nothing to be ashamed about."

"If that's true, why is this so hard for me?"

"Not just for you, for everyone. Even straight kids have a hard time getting through this part of growing up."

"I'm not a 'kid'. I'm a man." Ayden knew Wade wasn't trying to be insulting, but he was sick of everyone thinking he was stupid simply because he was the youngest.

"No. You're not. You're a man. A full grown, beautiful man."

Ayden went for Wade this time, leaning towards his mouth.

~

Not in a million years did Wade ever think on his way to his brother's parole hearing in the Great Central Valley, that his navigator would fail him and get him lost. Then found.

Found in the arms of a young man who was not only a gay man's wet-dream, he was so lonely and deprived of love, Wade was stunned at how desperate Ayden was for even a crumb of compassion...and *passion*.

The previous anger over his stuck car, his muddy clothing, missing Cole's hearing, all vanished with the timid touch of Ayden's tongue.

Wade wanted to ravish the young man. All he could think about was stripping him bare to see just what physique lay under the layers of flannel and cotton. Leaning across Ayden's lap in the confined space, Wade dug his fingers through Ayden's long, soft hair and went for a more passionate kiss. A low moan came from Ayden, and Ayden touched himself as Wade tried to determine boundaries. He pinned Ayden against the driver's door, climbing on top of him, urging him to spread out his legs on the seat.

Ayden's breathing grew deep and heavy through his nose while they kissed and he allowed Wade to manipulate him, positioning Ayden under him. As their kisses continued, with more tongue sucking and vocalizations of their attraction, Wade managed to get Ayden nearly horizontal across the pickup

The Farmer's Son

truck's bench seat, and lay on top of him, exactly as he wanted their contact to be.

Dominating a virgin? A farm boy? Are you kidding me? I can't even make this shit up!

Ayden seemed to be resisting at first, struggling to either submit or to simply fit across the truck seat with the limited space. Wade leaned up from their kiss since they were both panting to catch their breath. "Stop me if I go too far."

"I'm not stopping you." Ayden shook his head emphatically. "I've been waiting for this all my life."

The smile broadened on Wade's face. "Ya wanna move the seat back?"

"It's as far back as it'll go."

Wade glanced down at Ayden's long muscular legs as they stretched out on the seat under him. "You're a big boy, aren't you?"

"Six-three."

"Damn." Wade pressed his hard cock against Ayden's thigh.

Ayden ran his hand over Wade's hair, gently caressing him from his forehead to his neck. "What do you want to do to me?"

"Everything." Wade relaxed so their bodies were connected from the hips down, leaning on his elbow while they spoke softly.

"Wish we weren't in a damn truck." Ayden used the back of his knuckles to touch Wade's cheek.

Wade could feel how rough they were from years of hard work. He had visions of taking Ayden to all the best salons in LA, pampering him—manicures, facials, massages, sauna, pedicures…

"What do you want me to do to you?" Wade felt both their cocks throbbing at the teasing talk.

Looking shy, Ayden answered in a whisper, "Everything."

Wade fell on down on him and went for his mouth, digging his hand into Ayden's hair, cupping his head and raising him up to meet his hungry embrace.

Ayden hugged Wade, holding him around his back, rubbing his shoulders and caressing down to Wade's ass. With both hands Ayden grabbed Wade's bottom and ground his cock hard into Wade's crotch.

Wade broke the kiss and began pushing Ayden's shirt up his body. He had to see him, had to. In the dimmest of blue light from the dash gauges, Wade took his first look at Ayden's unbelievable build. Hairless, sculpted from his chest to his treasure trail… Wade lost all self control and began licking Ayden's skin, tasting the salt of his labor and chewing his way to his nipple.

A gasp of excitement came from Ayden and his hips jolted upwards, hard, into Wade. "You're going to make me…make me…" As he tried to tell Wade he was coming, Wade knew Ayden did. Wade felt Ayden's entire body tense up and the grip of Ayden's fists became so tight it was painful. Under his own throbbing length he felt Ayden's cock pulsate. Ayden choked on his climax and his legs jolted as if from an electrical charge.

The amount Wade wished that climax was either in his mouth or while Wade had his cock inside this stud, made Wade crazy. While Ayden recuperated, Wade lapped long licks against his skin, pushing his clothing higher, wedging his face into Ayden's armpit to inhale his musky masculine scent while grinding his own stiff cock against Ayden's thigh.

Ayden continued to catch his breath—open-mouthed huffing, and his body limp under Wade.

Wade sat up, staring down at what he could see of this Greek god, his shirt high on his chest, exposing his spectacular torso. Giving Ayden the chance to stop him if he wished, Wade opened the top button of his faded, muddy blue jeans.

The Farmer's Son

Ayden appeared anxious, as if showing his cock to Wade would be one of the scariest things he had done.

Wade paused, then held Ayden's zipper pull and moved it downwards.

He could hear Ayden gulp and his breathing accelerate once more. Wade parted the young man's zipper and touched his briefs, feeling how wet they were from his cum.

Scooting back on Ayden's thighs, Wade tugged Ayden's jeans down his hips, with his briefs, and began to see pubic hair.

The handsome man's cock was still hard, pointing upward, as if Ayden had shifted it after he had gotten excited. Wade kept taking down Ayden's pants until he could see the base of his cock. He leaned down and pressed his lips against it in ecstasy.

~

Ayden thought he would be humiliated he had climaxed in his pants. But...he was elated! He came with another man!

At this point he didn't care how or why, he just did!

Superhero Neo Magnay reigns supreme!

He couldn't wipe the smile from his face. As Wade stared at his body, Ayden could feel the admiration. See Wade's hunger for him. This man, this sophisticated Los Angeles businessman, was ogling *him! Look at my cock. Go on. Look at it.*

Ayden wanted Wade to take his pants down, wanted Wade to stare at him nude. Wanted it so much!

He raised his hips to allow Wade to tug his clothing lower. Wade gently released Ayden's cock from where it had been hidden. Still erect, poking straight up, Ayden peeked down at himself and then up at Wade for his reaction.

Wade wrapped his fingers around the base and held onto it.

Oh my God a man is touching me. Touching my cock. I'm dreaming.

"You beautiful creature." Wade's gaze swept up Ayden's body to his eyes. "You are spectacular."

Before he could comment or thank Wade, Wade leaned down and took Ayden's cock into his mouth. "I...I need a shower."

"Mm...mm..." Wade indicated no with his mouth full.

Ayden held Wade's head through his hair and focused on every new sensation and vibration, and felt as if he was having an out of body experience. It was his sexual awakening in the flesh.

Experiencing everything acutely—the low rumble of the truck's engine, the blowing from the vents of warm air—Ayden closed his eyes and wondered if this was all some wild dream. He couldn't figure out how he had gone from his daily routine, to having his cock inside a man's mouth.

Wade began to get vocal, whimpering as he moved to the floor so he could kneel beside Ayden. Holding Ayden's cock at the base, Wade sucked deep and strong, running one hand up Ayden's chest to his nipples.

He had never grown soft, and now the sensation that he could once again come began to rock Ayden.

In the silence of the surroundings, the rain, the low hum of the idling engine, Ayden added his grunts. He began thrusting into Wade's mouth, having never in his life been inside a hot wet, hole. Gripping the steering wheel with his left, Wade's shoulder with his right, Ayden fucked him orally and wished this night would never end. How would he ever be the same man again?

The pleasure of the impending climax making him crazy, Ayden heard the echo of his own rhythmic cries and didn't even recognize them as his. "Augh! Augh! Yes! Yes!" He arched his back and raised his hips high off the seat. Wade went for his balls and the root of his cock and Ayden fell off the edge of the cliff and into his second orgasm crying out loudly in the small space.

The Farmer's Son

Wade milked his cock and massaged Ayden's rim and under his balls until Ayden was delirious.

As if allowing Ayden the full pleasure of the receding waves, Wade took his time, slowing down his actions and finally resting his cheek against Ayden's pelvis, catching his breath.

Ayden petted Wade's hair and felt emotional. He couldn't imagine a better first experience if he tried.

The interior of the truck's windows were dripping with dewy condensation from their heat and the dampness outdoors.

Their breathing returning to normal, Ayden listened to the rain pelting the pickup and closed his eyes. He could sleep. Sleep and float into heaven.

Wade sat up and tucked Ayden's cock into his briefs for him, dressing him considerately, zipping and fastening his button, then tugging Ayden's shirt back down his chest.

Ayden opened his eyes, groggy and spent. Wade rested against the passenger's door, watching him.

"What...what about you...?" Ayden touched his chest, feeling his pounding heart.

"What about me?" Wade's voice was soft, kind.

Ayden struggled to sit up after two climaxes and growing cozy lying flat on his back on the seat. He ran his hand through his hair, not knowing what to say.

"You want to satisfy me?" Wade appeared slightly surprised.

"I can."

"But...you've never been with a man."

Ayden felt his cheeks blush. "So, you're not even going to give me a chance?"

"You want a chance?" Wade rubbed his own chin with his index finger. "With me? You sure? You can get some young—"

"Stop." Ayden held up his hand. "If you don't want me to touch you that way it's okay." It was not okay. Ayden turned forward in the seat and wiped the condensation with the ball of his fist so he could see out of the windshield.

"Ayden."

"What."

"The idea of you wanting to satisfy me is very flattering. You have no idea."

"Yeah?" He looked at Wade. "But?"

"You don't think I'm too old for you?"

"No!" Ayden lowered his voice. "No. I don't. I don't even want to know how old you are."

Wade faced him and gestured to himself. "Do whatever you want to do."

Ayden's heart quickened. "You actually want me to, right?"

"Are you kidding? If I had a rubber and lube I'd fuck your brains out."

"Wow." Ayden looked away bashfully and laughed. "Wish I had a rubber and lube."

"Would you…uh, let me take you that way if we did?"

Ayden met Wade's eyes. "Yes. I would."

"So…uh, you don't feel the desire to dominate…I mean, you know. Do the fucking?"

"I haven't thought about it. Ya know? I don't know what I want. I wish I had experimented enough to have that answer for you. But I don't."

"I…I prefer to top. To dominate. To…" Wade looked slightly upset. "To do the fucking."

Ayden shrugged. "I'd let you. I wouldn't stop you."

Wade again gestured to his body. "Play. I'm yours tonight."

Tonight? I wish you were mine forever.

THE FARMER'S SON

CHAPTER 6

Wade wondered if he was more nervous than this twenty-two year old virgin. If Ayden lived in West Hollywood he'd have the boys bowing at his feet to get a taste of him.

There was doubt in Wade's mind that it was unfair to Ayden to be this man's first anything. This young hunk should be up in a hayloft with a cowboy as strikingly handsome as he was. Not stuck in a car with a forty-year-old who was out to pasture.

As Ayden scooted closer, Wade held his breath, hoping he would not disappoint. Ayden opened the buttons of Wade's cotton shirt, his hands unsteady but not shaking too badly. Once he had them undone, he spread the material wide. Wade did not wax or shave his body hair, but he wasn't an ape either. Yet most vain men in LA craved youth, and with youth came smoothness, skin devoid of hair or wrinkles. Wade was who he was, graying temples and all.

Exhaling deeply, Ayden ran his hand over the inverted triangle of hair on his chest. The urge for Wade to keep apologizing that he was not LA prime cut was strong, but he shut up.

Ayden looked once into Wade's eyes, then pressed his mouth against one of Wade's erect nipples.

"Oh, Christ..." Wade closed his eyes and cupped Ayden's head in both hands, kissing his hair. While Ayden chewed on that hard nib, he opened Wade's jeans.

Wade tried to shift on the bench seat, allowing Ayden to remove his lower half of clothing, but the timing was awkward and neither man was discussing the act verbally. Finally Wade felt Ayden actually tug on his clothing. He raised his hips off the seat and watched his jeans draw down his thighs.

Ayden touched the treasure trail under Wade's belly button and traced it to the edge of Wade's briefs.

Wade continued to caress Ayden's hair, reassuring him and also loving touching him.

Ayden looked up at him. Those large light eyes framed by thick dark lashes, reflecting the blue dashboard lights, appeared to glow. Wade smiled sweetly at him.

As if he got the affirmation he needed, Ayden lowered down and kissed Wade's cock through the material. Wade closed his eyes and tried to spread his legs in the confining clothing.

Ayden flipped Wade's hard cock out of his briefs and Wade assumed Ayden was staring at it, since nothing was happening. He wasn't too large or too small, so he hoped he fulfilled whatever fantasy Ayden had spun in his head of his first encounter. When Ayden caressed his cheek with Wade's cock, Wade melted right into the seat below him at the tender touch. He was so used to men of experience who dove into sex hard, fast, and crazy, maybe this was a first for Wade as well.

Ayden ran the head of Wade's cock over his lips, across his jaw and along his cheek. A tug of his clothing coaxed Wade to lift up once more and his pants went to his ankles.

Outside, the wind blew the rain onto the truck, noisy tapping, pelting of the windows. Wade had an anxious moment—if someone did come looking for Ayden from the 'farmhouse' would Wade spot a shotgun pointed his way? But there was no way someone could creep up on them. Not on that rutty road. Not without headlamps.

THE FARMER'S SON

As these thoughts passed through Wade's mind, Ayden seemed enthralled with his genitals.

I suppose when you haven't seen or touched anyone but yourself, it must be overwhelming.

Wade tried to relate, but growing up in LA, in WeHo, it simply was okay to play. And he did. Even as a youth, at fourteen, he had his first experience with a study-buddy. How did he feel the first time he touched another dick? He thought hard to try to recall.

Relaxing, caressing Ayden's hair and arms as he explored, Wade found his touch very gentle and soothing, keeping him hard and interested.

His balls were explored, cupped, held in the palm of Ayden's hand, his inner thighs were kissed, nuzzled. After a few minutes of Ayden investigating the equipment, he brushed the head of Wade's cock across his lips, opening his mouth for a taste.

Wade let out a low exhale and closed his eyes.

"Okay?" Ayden looked up.

"Oh, hell yeah." Wade cupped his cheek. "But if you go for it, be ready for a mouthful."

Ayden laughed and looked at Wade's cock as he touched it lightly. "I used to try and look at other boys in the locker room. But I was terrified I'd get a hard on. So…"

"What about the internet?"

"Nope. Dad's computer. I wouldn't dare. And if I get my own? I'd have to buy a safe to padlock it."

"Jesus."

Ayden gave Wade's cock a lap under the head. "I like it."

"I had a feeling you might." Wade smiled and relaxed again against the truck door. "Take your time. I have nowhere to go."

"Ha." Ayden grinned at Wade at the comment and continued to play with his cock as if it were a brand new toy on Christmas morning.

~

There was no doubt in Ayden's mind that Wade was the most beautiful man he had ever met. He looked good...he smelled good...and he tasted...divine.

Getting into a better position in the cramped cab of the truck, Ayden shifted his legs to the driver's side floor and rested his arms on Wade's thighs. From that position, Wade was able to spread his legs, allowing Ayden to explore between. He traced the root of Wade's cock, feeling how hard it was under his balls, to his rim. Ayden tried to see Wade's details in the dim light, but with his back facing the dash, he blocked most of it out. Using his fingertips, he felt the globes under the soft wrinkled skin and pressed his nose and lips against them to sniff and mouth. The musky scent mixed with either cologne or masculine soap made Ayden's groin tingle.

With his own drive revving up again, he sank the head of Wade's cock into his mouth and held it there, humming in delight. Wade's petting of his hair and shoulders grew more amorous and he made low whimpering sounds that Ayden loved.

One hand on Wade's balls, the other the base of his cock, Ayden began sucking in a rhythm, wanting Wade to come, craving tasting him. He knew how to jack-off, so it wasn't rocket science. He manipulated Wade's balls with his fingertips and fisted his cock into his mouth. The act excited Ayden so much, he was stiff again in his pants, which were already damp from coming in them.

"Oh, babe...just like that. Just like that..." Wade moaned and his legs tensed.

Ayden slurped in excitement, getting his own saliva on his fingers to make the grip slick. Closing his eyes, he lost himself on the act, wanting to do this every night, every day, every moment...wanting Wade.

The Farmer's Son

Wade's body jerked and he held tightly to Ayden. "I'm getting close. If you don't want to swallow…"

"Mm!" Ayden did. He increased his speed and sucked strong, long pulls of his mouth. He used one finger to brush over Wade's rim and immediately Wade came, filling Ayden's mouth with cum.

Although he wanted it, Ayden wasn't truly prepared for the taste or quantity. He swallowed down the mouthful and as he went to stop sucking, another blast hit his tongue. His eyes sprang open in surprise and he swallowed that too, waiting a moment before releasing Wade's cock. He did and caught his breath, wiping his mouth with the back of his hand. "Whoa."

Wade attempted to cover his laughter, but couldn't. He began cracking up, trying to stop.

Ayden watched his expression and Wade's laughter became contagious. "Wow. I didn't know what to expect."

"I had a feeling you didn't." Wade dabbed at the corner of his eye at his hilarity. "Hey, ya didn't spit it out. I give you credit for that."

"No. I wasn't going to do that." Ayden tried to climb back into the driver's seat.

Wade tugged his jeans up and fastened them, sitting correctly on the seat to give Ayden room.

"Wow." Ayden shook his head in amazement. "I sucked a man."

"And swallowed."

"And swallowed." He laughed and felt shy.

"Want a protein bar?" Wade held one up and kept chuckling. "To get the taste out of your mouth?"

Ayden thought about it. "No. I think I want the taste in my mouth for a little longer."

"Yeah?" Wade appeared impressed.

"Yeah." Ayden grinned wickedly at him.

When Wade dove on him to kiss, Ayden was nailed to the driver's door with a thud and opened his mouth. Wade seemed to be trying to taste his own cum from Ayden's tongue. It turned Ayden on so much he gripped Wade by his shirt and dragged him closer, running circles around Wade's tongue with his own.

After parting from an amazing kiss, Ayden gasped. "Is this what it's like with all men? Or are you spoiling me rotten?"

"Spoiling you rotten." Wade's grin was full of mischief.

"I swear, Wade. Wow. I mean, what a night." Ayden held him close, sniffing his hair.

"No kidding. I can get hooked on a guy like you."

You took the words right out of my mouth. Ayden closed his eyes and held Wade tight.

~

Tired, Wade rested on Ayden's chest. After the long drive, the aggravation of missing the parole hearing, getting stuck, and now a climax? He was ready to sleep.

Sitting up so he could see Ayden's face, he noticed he too had his eyes closed. "How could your family not panic if you don't show up?"

"They're not the panic kind." Ayden tried to draw Wade back to his chest.

"You work with a fucking chainsaw. Are you kidding me? If you were my"—Wade stopped himself from saying 'son'—"family member, I'd send out a search party."

"Look..." Ayden ran his hand over Wade's hair and gazed into his eyes. "They will discuss where I am over dinner. My oldest brother Jacob will tell everyone he hopes to hell I ran away, my second oldest brother, Jeremiah will tell everyone I'm probably at someone's ranch fucking sheep, and Levi, the brother who is only two years older than me, won't even comment."

"Your mom? Your dad?"

"Dad won't give a shit and will assume I decided to sleep in the truck someplace to get away from the constant bullying, and my mother may worry but nothing she does or says matters in that house."

"I can't believe that. How can they not care if you don't show up after the kind of work you do?"

Ayden shrugged and dragged Wade back to his embrace. He kissed Wade's hair. "They don't. I sometimes wonder why Mom had another kid after Levi. I don't even look like my brothers."

Wade blinked and had a thought. Maybe there was a reason Ayden didn't look like his siblings. Maybe his mom had an affair.

"Do your brothers look like each other?"

"Yes. Man, totally. They're all short and ugly." Ayden laughed but Wade could tell the family situation was making Ayden miserable. How could it not?

"Have you ever been out all night before?" Wade sat up, putting his hand on Ayden's leg.

"Yes. Sometimes. If the abuse gets too much. Lately they've let up on me a little."

"Why? Why do they torment you?" Wade hated bullies. Hated them.

"I don't know. Maybe because I'm taller than they are? I know Jacob hates it. Being the oldest he thinks he should be the tallest."

"And my guess is you're smarter than they are too."

"Probably. Dad keeps asking Jacob to help him with the books, but I always offer."

"And?"

"And...Dad wants Jacob to do it, not me." Ayden ran his hand over his hair but didn't look unduly stressed talking about the family issues. "He's the oldest. So, he's supposed to take over everything when Dad is either dead or too old."

"And he can't or doesn't want to?"

"He can and wants to, but he doesn't like to do the accounting and paperwork. Even though he gets upset that I offer, I help him with everything he struggles with. He can't even fix or tune up a tractor. All you need is the manual, for Christ's sake."

"Can he read?" Wade had no idea what was going on in Ayden's household.

"Sure he can. He went to school like the rest of us."

"Maybe he has dyslexia."

Ayden stared at Wade.

"Do you know what that is?" Wade asked.

"Yes. I never thought of that. If he does, he won't admit it."

"So...you don't look like any of your brothers..." Wade picked up a protein bar from the dashboard and peeled the wrapper. "You're smarter, taller, and better looking than they are."

"I suppose."

Wade offered Ayden the bar and he held Wade's hand and took a bite.

"Ever think you have a different father?"

Ayden choked on his mouthful and coughed in shock.

Wade tried to pat his back, but it wasn't possible with Ayden leaning against the driver's side door. "You okay?"

Ayden nodded and swallowed the bite then coughed a little more as he said, "What?"

"Just wondering if maybe your mom had an affair and you're not like them for a reason."

"Who would mom have an affair with?" Ayden appeared stunned, touching his chest.

"No clue. You tell me."

"She...she goes out on her own a few nights a week. I figured it was for church or playing cards with her lady friends. Ya know? I can't imagine mom having an affair."

THE FARMER'S SON

"Is she pretty?"

"She was. I mean, she's just a mom now. Mom-looking." Ayden tried to express himself with his hands, gesturing perhaps 'plump'?

"Well, you're twenty-two. What did she look like twenty-two years ago?" Wade ate a bite of the protein bar.

"Yeah. She was pretty." Ayden shook his head. "Holy shit. That makes so much sense I feel like a moron for not thinking of that. You think Dad knows?"

Wade shrugged. "Does he treat you worse than your brothers?"

"Yes."

"Then he may suspect." Wade offered Ayden another bite of the protein bar. He shook his head.

"Damn. Who's my real dad?"

"I may be wrong. Don't believe it without facts. I'm just saying—"

"No. No! It makes sense! I swear it does. I totally get why I'm treated like shit now. And it's not like they know I'm gay or anything."

"You sure?"

"They tease me, but have no proof."

Wade nodded, finishing the bar and putting the wrapper into the coat pocket he had placed the first one into. "Look, don't just believe it simply because I mentioned it."

"I wonder if I asked her point blank if she'd be honest."

"No clue. What kind of relationship do you have with her?"

"Eh. So-so. I suppose when I was little I was her baby boy. Now? Just another mouth to feed. She seems so unhappy all the time."

"Hmm. Sounds familiar." Wade raised his eyebrow in an obvious gesture to Ayden's state of being.

Ayden got it. "Yeah. I know."

"Do something about it. Don't just linger on in a place you're not wanted, not happy with. Aspire to do great things."

"I wish it was that easy."

"Oh, babe." Wade caressed his cheek. "Nothing you want in life is easy."

Ayden reacted by mirroring Wade's action, cupping Wade's face. "I already know that. I know."

Wade closed his eyes as Ayden leaned in for a kiss. When they parted Wade could see the sadness in Ayden. It made his heart break. To change the lousy topic, Wade asked, "How we doing on gas?"

"Fine. Like I said, I had a full tank."

"Up to you. We could shut her down and cuddle." Wade smirked.

"We could cuddle with the engine on." He grabbed Wade's shirt and dragged him closer so Wade was against him.

Wade rested his head on Ayden's shoulder and stared at the darkness, the rain still hitting the windshield and the interior dewy and running with condensation. "I'm so glad you found me. I'd be in that freezing car losing my mind."

"We found each other." Ayden put his arm around Wade and held him close.

Wade smiled and closed his eyes.

The Farmer's Son

Chapter 7

After a long moment of silence, where Ayden just held Wade, thinking of everything they had said, Ayden whispered, "You asleep?"

"No. I doubt I can get any sleep in a truck. I'm not a good sleeper in a bed."

Ayden checked the clock on the dash. "It's only eight. I usually don't get to bed until ten or eleven."

"Me? After midnight normally." Wade sat up again, wiping the dewy window and looking out. "Still raining. The road is going to be a mucky mess."

"Your leather shoes are going to get wrecked walking to the farmhouse."

"I know. I have tennis shoes in the trunk of my car, but I can't decide if I should to get them just as muddy as these are." Wade looked down at his feet.

"It's a long walk. But we really don't have a choice."

"How will your family react when I show up with you?"

Ayden shrugged. "They won't react. I'll tell them what happened. That I was out cutting trees and we both got stuck. I'll get some ribbing that I couldn't pull you out. That's about it."

"No one will come to any conclusions?"

"No." Ayden didn't care if they did. He was already imagining packing his clothing and running away. The sooner the better.

"Huh."

"What? Just because I helped a guy who got lost and his car stuck doesn't mean we did anything."

"Would they assume we were together all night?"

"Of course." Ayden tilted his head. "Don't get me wrong, they'll tease me and make allegations, I have no doubt. But none of them really believe I can be gay. It's just so against their belief system. If they truly did believe that, I would have been kicked out long ago."

Wade's expression became grim and he stared into Ayden's eyes. "Religious family?"

"Yes. Not extreme, but yes."

"What are your views on it?"

"I believe in something. I just don't know what."

Wade nodded, slouching in the seat and trying to stretch his long legs in the limited space. "Me too. I guess I believe in Mother Nature. Not the idea that there's some image of a man with a beard sitting on a cloud."

Ayden laughed at the thought. "I know. It sounds farfetched. I don't buy into that pearly gates crap either. But I wish I knew what happens when we die."

"Who doesn't?" Wade rested his hand on Ayden's leg. "Half of me thinks there is some other life, another chance to do things again, and the other part of me thinks we're just worm-meal."

"Ew. I like the reincarnation theory better."

"Me too. I would love to really know for a fact about past lives, shit like that."

"Yeah. Exactly. All that God stuff is hard to digest. I think the Bible was written at a time when we didn't have laws or cops. It was a way to stop people from fucking up." Ayden placed his hand on Wade's.

"Yes. That's where my thoughts are too. It was just a way to manage people, stop them from being crazy and hurting others."

THE FARMER'S SON

"Doesn't help. Whether it's the Bible or state laws. People are people."

"I know. Look at my brother." Wade shook his head. "We both came from the same parents. How did he end up so fucked up that he did dope and committed armed robbery?"

"Does he look like you?" Ayden teased, squeezing Wade's hand.

Wade glanced at him and laughed. "Yes. There is a strong resemblance. Same dad, unfortunately."

"I swear, I will ask Mom if it's true the minute I get back to the house."

"Will she be honest with you?"

"I don't know." Ayden reclined more deeply on the seat, resting on the headrest. "The more I think about it, the more I believe it. When you meet my family, you'll see. You'll see there is no similarity from me to my three brothers. How could I have not realized that myself?"

"You had no reason to believe it. Why would it even cross your mind?"

"Because. It's like I was left in a basket on the front porch, that's why." Ayden rubbed his forehead and felt as if he understood so much now.

"What if it is true?" Wade massaged Ayden's thigh. "What will you do?"

"Leave." Ayden lowered the heat blower, making it aim at the windshield to try and clear it. "Like you said. Why am I there? I need to get away from that place."

"Go. Go where?"

"I don't know. Just out of here. Away."

"What about your legacy? Your inheritance."

"It's not cash. It's just an income. Unless all my brothers decide to sell after both my parents die, there is no big money waiting for me in some will. And no one will sell. That orchard is all they know."

"Is the income decent?"

"Not split between all of us. I told you. It's low at the moment because we all live there for free and Mom cooks. It's about fifteen grand a year."

"Oh! Crap. That is low."

"I don't have expenses, so it's not impossible to live, but it's impossible to leave."

"And that will be forfeited if you go."

"Yes. It's mine because I work there. If I leave, then it's gone."

"Do you have enough in savings to help keep you going while you find a job?"

"It will have to be enough." Ayden scrubbed his face with both hands. Although he had not washed them, they were dry and no longer muddy. "God! I wish I could just do what I want."

"If you could, what would it be?"

"I want to draw superhero comics. But being a comic artist is like trying to become an actor. Impossible."

Wade turned towards him in the seat. "First of all, nothing is impossible." He gripped Ayden's hand. "If you're talented, and never give up, you will succeed."

Ayden never believed that. He believed success came with family wealth and connections. He sank lower, slouching down and stared at nothing.

"Are you good at the artwork? How well do you draw?"

"I've been drawing since I was old enough to hold a crayon."

"Have you ever submitted your stuff to anyone?"

"No. I don't know how to do that. And if I even tried to look up that shit on Dad's computer, he'd have a cow."

"So you have never gotten feedback on your work?"

The Farmer's Son

"I did in high school. I was voted most artistic in my yearbook. My art teacher was very impressed and told me all the time I had talent and should do something with it."

"Your high school art teacher." Wade frowned.

"Never mind." Ayden folded his arms over his chest and blew out a loud exhale in defeat.

"Look, I don't know a lot of people in the actual art world, but I certainly have the resources to look that kind of thing up for you."

Ayden glanced at him.

"Do you own a cell phone?"

"No."

"Jesus, Ayden!"

"What?" He threw up his hands. "Don't you get it? I work all fucking week, every fucking day! Sun up to sun down! I don't hang around the fucking malls and play video games!"

"Is it a family or a fucking cult?" Wade asked in anger.

"That's not fair." Ayden turned in the seat to face him. "It's not a cult. It's family obligations. Just like you going to a parole hearing. You don't want to, but you do."

Wade raked his fingers back through his hair in a gesture of frustration. "How can I help you? Huh? I can't even communicate with you once I head back. I can't email you contact information on how to submit your work."

Ayden bit his lower lip. He knew how Wade could help him, but would never ask. "I'll buy a phone."

"Don't you want one? Don't you miss the actual world outside this god-forsaken place?" Wade gestured to the dark woods.

"First of all, it's not god-forsaken. It's got beauty. Natural beauty. But how would a city guy even appreciate anything but concrete and glass?"

"Hang on. Now look who's being unfair."

"You're attacking me like I'm some moron who doesn't get there's a world out there!" Ayden waved his arm to indicating beyond the confines of the truck. "I know there is! Are you kidding me? I can't help the fact that I was born to parents who own an orchard, who need and depend on their sons to help them live and work."

"You are not a moron. I never said that. Don't put words into my mouth."

"I don't have a cell phone or a computer!" Ayden yelled, "So I must be some kind of cultish freak!"

"I did not say that!" Wade balled his fists. "A twenty-two year old young man should have everything any other kid his age has."

"Kid? Again you're calling me a kid?" Ayden blinked, even more insulted. "You really think I am just a little kid?"

"No! Fuck! Don't dwell on semantics! For cryin' out loud, Ayden."

"So? What are you? Fifty?" Ayden sneered, knowing there was no way Wade was.

Wade grabbed his muddy slacks from the dash and then his coat from underneath him, going for the door.

"Hang on." Ayden grabbed his arm. "Stop."

Ayden could hear Wade was breathing fire, see his posture in the dimmest of blue light. "I'm sorry."

"I'm not sure I am. You're right. I'm too old to have even touched you." He held his coat. "I'll wait in my car."

"No. You don't have enough gas and you'll freeze."

"I won't freeze." Wade opened the truck door.

"Wade! Get in here!" Ayden jerked his arm.

Wade spun around and the snarl on his face in the bright dome light surprised Ayden.

"Please. I'm sorry."

"Fifty? Fucking fifty?"

THE FARMER'S SON

"No. I only said that because you called me a kid. I know you're only like thirty-something." Ayden pouted. "Shut the door."

Wade slammed it, settling back in the seat, rather reluctantly.

Ayden could feel him fume. He tugged the slacks out of Wade's grip and pushed them back in their spot on the dashboard, then sighed loudly.

"You think I don't want to be like everyone else?" Ayden said quietly. "Have a smartphone, a laptop, be on all the networks and have hundreds of friends?" He kept hold of Wade's shirt sleeve. "You think I don't know what's going on out there outside this valley? How people get into each other at clubs? Live in big cities where men can be comfortable holding hands in public? You think I don't know?"

Wade's body language deflated and he rubbed his face wearily.

Ayden stared at his profile. "I do know, Wade. Every day when a degrading comment is thrown my way, when I wake up at four a.m. to cut down trees, or fix a fucking tractor. I know. Believe me. I know."

Wade looked at Ayden. "I'm sorry."

"I watch your LA world from afar, but you know nothing of mine."

"You're right. I don't. I have never even imagined being a farmer or living on an orchard. Never."

"I may only be twenty-two, but I am not stupid or naïve. I know everything that's going on. World politics, economics, shootings, love, hate, intolerance. I know it all."

"Oh, babe. Forgive me. I never meant any insult. I swear."

"Come here."

Wade shoved his coat back behind him on the seat and went for Ayden's embrace, holding him tight.

Ayden kissed his neck and closed his eyes. "We come from different worlds, but we're not so different, Wade. We see eye to eye on everything."

"You're right. It's my own insecurity. I know it."

"How on earth can a man like you be insecure?" Ayden leaned back so he could see Wade's eyes.

"I'm forty. That's why. It feels as if incredible men like you have no time for guys my age. That you either grow bored or cheat."

"Oh?" Ayden smiled. "Does that mean we're dating?"

"No...I didn't mean..." Wade lowered his head. "I'm just telling you how it is."

"I don't care how old you are. I only said that because you called me a kid. You know, as sick as you are of having people judge you because they think you're old? That's as sick as I am for people judging me because they think I'm young and an idiot."

"I get it."

Ayden hugged Wade as Wade leaned against him, his head on his shoulder, both staring out at the darkness as the defroster dried the moisture from inside the window. "I wish I was forty."

"No. You don't."

Ayden had his arm around Wade, resting his head on Wade's. "I'd be able to make good decisions. Feel more confident."

"You'd miss so much. Eighteen years of life, of youth."

"Did you miss it, Wade? Or did you enjoy it?"

Wade shifted on the seat, as if getting comfortable, his legs stretched out to the passenger's door by the floor. "I think I lived my life well. I enjoyed myself, got a good education, made great friends."

Ayden stared into the darkness, watching individual drops run down the windshield like tears. "So, you're not dating anyone now?"

"No. I stopped looking. It's tiring looking all the time."

"How long have you been on your own?" Ayden kissed Wade's hair, then stared out into space again.

"Um…I guess a year. The last guy I dated was Simon. He's moved in with a guy already. Well, he actually started seeing his new boyfriend within a week of us breaking up."

"Wow. That sucks."

"Eh. Not really. There was no spark. I wanted to fuck him and he wanted to fuck me, but neither of us wanted to bottom. And…the fire wasn't there."

"So…" Ayden struggled to think. "You both wanted to do the fucking, not get fucked."

"Yes."

"Huh."

"Yeah. Huh." Wade crossed his arms over his chest, almost in a defensive posture.

"So all the time you were together, you didn't actually have sex?"

"Not anal. No."

"Did you live together?"

"No. I haven't lived with anyone…formally. Ya know? I mean, some guys stayed a week, but nothing like a real partnership."

"I'm surprised." Ayden rubbed Wade's arm, feeling his solid build through his shirt. "I guess I would have thought someone would have stolen your heart at least once."

Wade let out a low laugh. "I think my heart had been stolen, but I wasn't able to steal one back. If you know what I mean."

"Right." Ayden nodded, pressing his face into Wade's hair. "Mutual affection. Hard thing to get. I see my brothers trying to date women. They go hunting at the taverns, looking for local women. They do go out on dates occasionally, but no one's actually has had a relationship. At least not one where they bring the woman home to meet us, or talk about it at the dinner table."

"Really? Not one of your brothers is dating anyone at all?"

"Not that I know of. No. I would figure someone would come over sooner or later. I mean, my parents and grandfather would welcome them."

"Grandfather?"

"Yes. He lives with us too."

"You have a heck of a houseful."

"I know. Luckily it's a big house with enough bathrooms for everyone." Ayden laughed and kissed Wade's hair again.

"Do you share your room?"

"No. We all have our own bedroom."

"Nice. That is a big house."

"Yeah." Ayden ran his hand down Wade's arm. "What's your place like?"

After a low exhale, Wade said, "Well, it's small, a two bed two bathroom condo in West Hollywood. You know—location, location, location."

"Ha. True. Do you like it?"

"I do. It's enough. I don't aspire to live in a mansion in Beverly Hills. Maybe I did ages ago, but not now. I think it's all about being happy with what you have."

"I tried that." Ayden caressed Wade's hair gently. "I tried to tell myself I was good with being a farmer's son, living without any type of time card, office cubicle kind of thing. And to be honest, an office may not suit me."

"I would imagine a cartoonist can work from home."

"I have no idea."

Wade made a move to sit up so they could see each other. "How could you not even look into it?"

"Well, like I said, Dad owns the computer, and if I sat there for hours trying to figure it out, he'd find out I was trying to leave the orchard. And...I simply doubt I'd have a chance in hell of actually making a living on my work."

"I'd love to see your drawings."

"When we get to the house tomorrow, I'll show it to you. I hide them. Most of them are really gay." Ayden laughed shyly.

"And you don't think someone will find it?"

"No. They don't do commando searches of my bedroom. It's not that bad. And they do know I draw. I mean, they've seen my non-gay stuff."

"But if you owned a computer..."

"They would snoop. Believe me. It would start out innocently, you know? Like Jacob would ask to use it for a night. I couldn't do anything on it."

"Right." Wade nodded. "I hate to admit, without the computer to look up publishers, to find submission guidelines, you are stuck."

"I know." Ayden ran his hand over his face and felt very tired suddenly. He yawned and used his windshield wipers to move the rain off, turned on his headlights for a second and looked outside of the warm truck. Since he was in a ditch, his headlights were angled upwards. Then he noticed bright green orbs. "Look." Ayden pointed.

Wade sat up and paid attention.

"Deer."

"Son of a gun."

Ayden leaned on the steering wheel as Wade did the same on the dashboard, shoulder to shoulder.

Three deer took notice of the headlights shining on them, then walked away. Ayden shut off the headlights and smiled.

"That was pretty cool." Wade rested against Ayden as they both settled back on the seat.

"Can't see that in downtown LA." Ayden grinned.

"Nope. Not walking down Sunset Boulevard."

Ayden yawned again.

"Come here, gorgeous. How about you sleep on me?" Wade dragged him to his side of the truck and used his coat to cover them both.

Ayden relaxed on Wade's chest, his ear against Wade's ribcage, hearing his heartbeat. He closed his eyes and said sleepily, "Spoiled, spoiled, spoiled."

"I think you can use a little spoiling." Wade petted Ayden's hair.

And you're the man for the job. Ayden smiled and held him tight.

The Farmer's Son

Chapter 8

Wade massaged Ayden's back and shoulders, brushed his fingers through his hair. He could hear Ayden's breathing change to the deep slumber of rest. It made him smile. He continued to caress him affectionately, thinking about everything they had learned about each other over the last few hours.

Oddly enough, Wade felt as if he knew more about Ayden in the short time they had spent together, than he had known about other men; men whom he thought he had shared his life with.

Twenty-two...

Wade saw that age difference as an insurmountable obstacle. Of course it was easy to fantasize being with Ayden in that way. Having Ayden stay in LA with him for a weekend...going to Hawaii for a vacation, or maybe taking him on a cruise...

What am I thinking?

Wade shook his head at his stupidity. If Ayden was allowed to explore the West Hollywood night life, drink at clubs, he too would be seduced by the lure of hairless taut bodies of young pretty boys. It was simply Ayden's inexperience that was drawing Ayden close. If Wade had been a straight married man ...well, Ayden would have walked back to the farmhouse alone to get help. They never would have even spoken more than a few words to each other.

It was the fact that Wade was gay...and hot for Ayden...and Ayden was a virgin...and gay...

Wade looked down at the young man while he slept. *Ya big brawny stud. Look at you. Anywhere else and you'd have men kneel before you. But you had to be a farmer's son.*

Wade shook his head at the irony. Fate. It was throwing him one heck of a curveball at the moment. He had ridiculous thoughts of asking Ayden, not for a weekend in LA, but for a lifetime in LA. Taking this babe out of the woods, literally, and mentoring him, getting him into college, art school, working side by side with him to get him a career in the field he loved, drawing superhero comics…going to crazy conventions where grown men dressed in capes and cowls.

Wade laughed to himself. But his smile soon faded. It was an impossible dream. If he took Ayden back with him to LA he knew what would happen.

Suddenly Ayden would realize just how many gorgeous men he could get simply by snapping his finger. Or, Wade would feel he cheated Ayden out of enjoying his looks, his youth, by trapping him, making Ayden dependent on him and locking him away.

As the rain became heavy again, battering the roof of the pickup, Wade thought about what Simon had said. How he wanted someone less independent, someone who needed him.

Doesn't everyone want someone who needs them?

Wade rested his head on the window of the passenger's door and stared into space, holding onto his sleeping prince. The reality was, once they walked back to this 'farmhouse' and got a tow truck to help them out? That would be it. If Ayden didn't even have a cell phone or internet access? How could they even say hi once in a while?

Nope. This one I'll have to chalk up to a little fantasy fling with the farmer's son.

Wade tried to be content with that, but he knew he'd feel very empty when he headed back to LA…alone.

The Farmer's Son

~

Ayden dreamed he was in the farmhouse and someone had left all the windows and doors open. In frustration he walked around the perimeter shutting gaping open windows, which had allowed in the heavy rain. Window after window had been left open and Ayden wondered why being responsible was always his job.

He opened his eyes with a blink, disoriented. Under him was a warm body. Leaning up to look, Ayden could see Wade had his eyes closed. A check of the clock on the dash and it was nearing one a.m. Not wanting to wake Wade, Ayden slowly laid his head back down on him and stared into the darkness of the floor of the truck. The engine was idling so low, he could barely feel the vibration or hear it. Rain still battered the exterior, so it blocked the sound of anything else. The only light was coming from the dashboard, that was it. Ayden sighed and closed his eyes, enjoying Wade sleeping with him, under him. He felt secure and safe in Wade's arms. Maybe he was like a little boy in some ways still, growing into a man—first with his body, then his brain would catch up…and he would become confident, wise, like his grandfather.

Lying on Wade this way, their bodies so close, having shared kisses and oral sex, Ayden dreaded the light of dawn and their walk back to the farmhouse. Not for the slop and long trek, but for the impending separation. Simply put, he'd miss Wade.

Yes, he did need a cell phone, he did need a laptop. How else would he communicate with Wade once he left?

As his thoughts made him fully awake, he felt Wade shift under him. He took another look to see Wade's eyes were open. "Did I wake you?" Ayden asked.

"No. I'm dozing a little, but not getting any real sleep."

Ayden moved slightly so they could see each other when they spoke. "I will get a phone. I don't want to lose you."

Wade smiled and touched Ayden's cheek with his fingertip, tracing a line down it. "You are one special guy, Ayden. I'm glad my navigator screwed up."

"Me too." Ayden inched closer and kissed Wade.

Wade enveloped him into his arms and they slid down on the bench seat so Ayden was on top of Wade, crotch to crotch, pinning him with his weight.

Ayden couldn't imagine having a partner like this. One he could get sex from whenever he desired. He enjoyed Wade's lips and tongue, the kisses soft and affectionate. Wade slipped both hands down the back of Ayden's jeans and under his briefs.

As his ass cheeks were cupped, Ayden's cock grew thick and he moaned against Wade's mouth. "I wish you could make love to me."

Wade let out a low mournful sound in exaggeration and Ayden felt Wade's cock throb against his own.

Ayden nestled into Wade's neck, sniffing his skin and tasting him off his own lips. As he did, Wade massaged Ayden's bottom, tracing the crack with his right fingertips. The tingles it sent over Ayden were powerful. He spread his legs and wished they were alone in a bedroom, with a rubber and lube.

A light brush passed over his rim and Ayden's cock thickened and he felt pre-cum make his briefs damp again. His self-stimulation was nothing compared to this.

"I want you in me." Ayden writhed on Wade. "So much."

Wade made another sound of longing and held Ayden tighter. "I want to be in you. You have no idea."

Ayden leaned up and unfastened his jeans, dragging them down his body to his thighs.

"I told you, I don't have any condoms." Wade met Ayden's gaze.

Feeling shy, Ayden pressed his mouth against Wade's ear and said, "Fingers..."

The Farmer's Son

Wade's cock pulsated strongly against Ayden's at the suggestion. Ayden leaned up and dragged Wade's pants down as well, so their bodies were naked from their hips to their thighs. Both men tried to see in the dimness. Ayden took a look around the sopping surroundings, then pushed the dome light so it lit them up.

After the shock of getting used to a brighter light, they both took a look at the sight of their hard cocks and dark pubic bushes pressed together.

"Oh fuck..." Wade closed his eyes and leaned his head back on the seat again.

Ayden shut the light off and went for Wade's right hand. He placed it against his own mouth and wet it with his saliva, then urged it to return to his ass.

Wade reached between them to Ayden's cock, getting a good grip on it, then made his way to Ayden's rim with his wet fingers.

Ayden closed his eyes, leaning up just enough to give Wade space between their bodies. As his cock was squeezed and pulled, Wade pushed his fingertip into Ayden's ass.

Chills rushed over Ayden so powerfully he choked as he grunted and his cock engorged, ready to climax.

Wade worked Ayden from both ends and Ayden couldn't believe how incredible it felt. "Shit! Shit!" Ayden arched his back. "Oh, God, that is unbelievable!" He gripped Wade's arm and came, spattering his cum all over Wade's cock and pubic hair.

~

Wade watched this fabulous man in climax. He stared up at his jaw line and massaged his finger over his prostate, feeling it pulsate with the throbbing of Ayden's cock. "You beautiful fucker. I could do this to you all night."

"Wade...God..." Ayden hung his head and his arms shook as he propped himself up. "Oh my God..."

Imagine my cock in you...I'd fuck you to heaven.

Wade released his contact on Ayden's ass and dick to allow him to recover.

"Fuck." Ayden shivered and appeared slightly overwhelmed by the intensity. Slowly he backed up, looking down at the creamy spatter on Wade's skin. He checked his pockets for something to use to clean him up.

Wade peeked down at himself. "Don't worry. Look, we're both a mess of cum and mud already."

Ayden rolled his window down and then up. He had found a paper towel or napkin and dampened it with the rain. Trying to be considerate, Ayden wiped the spatter from Wade and then Wade took the damp paper and tried to clean his hand, but it was an effort in futility without soap and water. As Wade was about to comment on them both reeking of sex, Ayden dropped down on Wade and engulfed his cock into his mouth.

Wade had lost his erection but had no objection to Ayden's sexual appetite. He was exhausted and didn't know if he could come, but that didn't mean he wasn't enjoying Ayden's hot mouth.

Ayden nestled in, holding Wade's hips and then smoothing his hands under Wade's shirt to his chest.

What a night. What an absolutely mind blowing night!

Wade couldn't recall this kind of crazy sex in any recent relationships. Maybe when he was in high school or college? *No. Nothing like this. This is unbelievable.*

Just when he thought he was too tired to come, Ayden was coaxing one out of him. Sucking hard, drawing to the tip, reaching both hands up Wade's chest to his nipples to pinch with delicious tweaks, Wade began to rock his hips into Ayden's mouth. "Oh, baby...what you do to me..." Wade took a look at

Ayden as he seemed to be in a state of bliss, finally having a man to enjoy. *I'm the luckiest fucker on the planet.*

Watching Ayden suck him, seeing his handsome face, his long dark lashes and shaggy brown hair, Wade grabbed Ayden's head and fucked him orally, dominating him and pushing himself over the edge as he did. Ayden moaned in pleasure and this time Wade knew Ayden was aware of exactly what to expect.

Ayden had allowed Wade to control the act of oral penetration and Wade's skin covered in chills right to his toes as he came. As the climax subsided Wade released Ayden's head, Ayden let Wade's cock to slide out of his mouth. They were both panting heavily and the windows had once again steamed up. Ayden rested his cheek on Wade's pelvis and his whole body seemed to deflate and weigh heavily on Wade.

"I want you."

Wade smiled. "Ayden, you have me. Holy shit. You've had me so much, I'm spent."

"No. I mean. I. Want. You."

Caressing Ayden's hair, Wade said softly, "You always want your first."

Ayden kissed Wade's soft cock and pressed his face into his groin.

Wade wanted him too. So much, he thought he must be overtired or just dizzy from no food and a crazy day. But for a split second, Wade imagined them living together in LA. Happily ever after.

His smile slowly faded as reality would eventually hit them, and of course, there really were no happy endings. Not in LA anyway. Not between a twenty-two year old farmer's son and a forty year old environmental planner. Was there?

~

Ayden finally found the energy to function and dragged his pants up his hips. They sat up for a moment, trying to fix their appearance, and Ayden looked over at Wade. "I know you think all my attachment to you is because you're my first."

"Yup." Wade gave him a sweet smile.

"But what's wrong with that? What's wrong with two people who really want something to—?"

"Ayden."

Ayden shut up, feeling slightly stupid.

"I've been around a while. I know how things go."

"So that's it?" Ayden stopped all his contact with Wade and sat behind the wheel of the truck properly.

"No. Heck no. Get a phone, get a computer, come see me every weekend. Are you kidding? I'm willing to give it a try. I just know how much you've been missing by living out here in the middle of…"

"How much I've been missing…" Ayden tried to interpret that comment.

"Yes. If I'm your first? The minute you hit Hollywood you'll feel like a kid in a candy store. I can't expect you to be satisfied with just me. Not until you've played around and seen what you can get."

Ayden stared at the dewy condensation. What he could get? What he wanted was a man like Wade. "What do you think I'd do if I went to LA?"

"You'd fuck like crazy. Are you kidding me?" Wade sat up with his back against the passenger's door again, so they could face each other as they spoke.

"Would I? Do you know me that well after tonight to think I'd become some voracious animal and fuck every man I meet?"

Wade's expression darkened. "No. I don't know you well enough. But I've been with younger men. They don't hang around long. I get attached, and I get hurt when they leave me for a younger model."

Ayden met Wade's eyes, and could see how hurt he must have been indeed. "I totally understand what you're saying to me. Don't get me wrong. I remember Jacob and Levi discussing not taking a virgin girl because the girl would become attached. I know that's likely."

Wade smiled and splayed out his hands in an obvious gesture. "Very likely. And I would feel as if I'm cheating you to make you commit to me when you have so little experience."

"And nothing I can say will convince you I'm not interested in 'fucking like crazy'?"

"No. Nothing would. Ayden! You have no idea how gorgeous you are. And the body on you?" Wade shook his head. "You'll strut down Santa Monica Boulevard and men would be all over you."

Ayden blinked. "They would?"

"Yes! Are you kidding me? If I took you to a club you'd have guys propositioning you in the men's room, begging to suck your cock."

"Shut up. They wouldn't really do that." Ayden's skin tingled.

Wade didn't answer, but appeared grim.

"It's that cool to be gay there? I mean, so liberal that guys have no reservations about asking you out?"

"In West Hollywood, yes." Wade interlaced his hands on his lap.

Ayden faced forward on the seat and thought about it. A world he craved, a lifestyle he desired so much he was in agony, and no judgment for his need for a boyfriend.

"Food for thought, eh, Ayden?"

"Yes. It is." Ayden rested his head on the seat behind him and stared at the running raindrops again, used the wipers to clear them, and turned up the defroster.

"Yeah. I figured as much." Wade shifted to sit forward as well, his legs falling to a comfortable straddle, his hands resting on his lap. "That's why it won't work."

"So, this is it, right? Just this moment in time and maybe a weekend in LA?"

After blowing out a loud exhale, Wade asked, "What do you want to hear? Huh? Reality or fantasy?"

Ayden turned to look at him. "Fantasy."

A smile formed on Wade's lips. "Okay." He thought a moment and said, "We fall in love after this night…so deeply, we can't stop thinking about each other. You manage to get to LA and live with me. You don't cheat. You aren't bored with me and you're content to make love to only me."

Ayden smiled but hid it as he stared out of the driver's side window.

"I put you through art school," Wade said softly, "After a huge effort you're published first online on gay websites, then you'll have your own comic book series, which of course will be an enormous success since gay superheroes are just coming out of the closet…so to speak…" Wade shifted on the seat, leaning his elbow on the passenger's door. "We live together for a year, maybe a little more, are madly in love, and get married."

Ayden's smile broadened. "I like that fantasy."

"Well, you draw fiction. So I expected you would."

"And that's impossible why?" Ayden looked at Wade's profile, his perfectly straight nose and strong jaw.

"Oh, babe…I just told you. You'd get propositioned at every turn and I can't expect you to say no." Wade slouched lower in the seat. "My luck, you'll use me to get out of your situation, and then once you are, off you'll go."

Ayden's smile quickly fell to a snarl. "What the fuck kind of asshole do you think I am?"

"I don't know. I don't think you're one now, but I didn't think a lot of the men I met were when we first started dating them. Then for some reason, I get stabbed in the chest after the honeymoon period is over."

"Maybe you get stabbed because you sabotage the fucking deal before it even happens!"

Wade opened his mouth to say something, then shut up, looking shocked.

"Jesus, Wade. Have you ever thought one of your relationships would actually last?"

Again Wade did not answer, staring out of the windshield.

"If I had that attitude, I wouldn't date at all. I mean, then every time I met a guy, I would feel as if I was setting myself up for disaster."

"It's not that."

"What is it then?"

Wade glanced at his hands and then turned to look at Ayden. "Our differences."

"Age."

"Yes. Age."

"Okay." Ayden threw up his hands. "I can't sit here and try to talk you into something you already have decided won't happen."

"There are no guarantees in life, babe. I would go nuts doubting myself and my capability to keep you loyal."

"There are no guarantees, you got that right. But there's a little fucking faith and trust."

"Whom do you trust?" Wade asked.

Ayden thought it was his mother...until... "My granddad."

"That's it?"

"Maybe my mom, if she tells me the truth when I ask her if I was the product of an affair."

"You'll have no way of knowing if what she says is true or not."

"That's what faith and trust are about, Wade. Taking people at their word and believing them."

"Good luck with that."

"Really?" Ayden blinked. "You're that cynical you trust no one?"

Wade rubbed his forehead then looked down at his hands in dismay, since both of them needed a shower and scrub-down from the mud and sexual contact. "I don't know."

"Damn. I would hope to hell when I met my man I could trust him."

"You may luck out."

"I thought I had."

"You're a virgin. How could you possibly think the first man you make love to will be 'the one'?" Wade used air-quotes.

"And how can you be so sure it's impossible? You do realize your attitude is just as crazy as mine."

"Right." Wade sounded completely sarcastic. "So now you've found true love, me, and will never cheat and will love me forever." He shook his head and made a noise of disbelief. "You do live in your comic hero world."

Ayden grew angry. "And now I know why your boyfriends left you."

~

Wade took the jab like a punch to the chest. Was he too cynical for his own good? Or was Ayden just too naïve to think there was even such a thing as true love?

"I'm sorry, Ayden." Wade stared at him and even in the dimmest of pale blue light he could see he hurt his feelings. "I guess in many ways I did sabotage my past relationships. No doubt. But how many couples truly make it?"

"I don't know. Half?"

THE FARMER'S SON

"Maybe." Wade asked Ayden softly, "What do you think your dad would do if he knew your mom had an affair and you were the product of that union?"

"I don't know. They've been together nearly thirty years. They never argue."

"Never?" Wade gasped and couldn't believe it.

"No. She and my dad know their roles in the household. I know it sounds archaic, but Mom is a very traditional woman and seems to be okay doing…mom stuff."

"And you've sat down with her to find out."

"No. I haven't."

"Then how do you know what that woman feels…deep in her heart?"

Ayden's shoe kicked the brake pedal, but Wade didn't think it was in anger. "She'd never leave him."

"That doesn't mean she didn't cheat on him."

"Jesus." Ayden covered his face.

Wade scooted closer to him on the seat. "Look, don't listen to me. You're not from an affair. Just because you don't look exactly like your brothers means nothing."

"No. It's more than that. I'm convinced you're right."

Wade put his arm around Ayden's shoulder to comfort him. "I had no business even saying it."

"I'm glad you did."

Wade tried to hold him tight, wanting to protect him…*from me.* Wade suddenly felt like he may have been the worst thing to enter Ayden's life. Even if Ayden wasn't perfectly content on the family farm, at least he was protected, secure…

Wade imagined he was the serpent, showing Ayden temptation and would lead to his ruin if he introduced him to Sin City.

Ayden rested his head on Wade's, letting out a low sigh.

"I got ya." Wade wished he could be 'the one'. The one to keep this man with him, he'd sell his soul for it. "Ayden?"

"Hmm?"

"You are by far the most amazing man I have ever met."

Ayden abruptly sat up and stared at him. Looking what? Astonished?

"You are." Wade was not lying.

"How...how could I...?"

"You're the complete package."

"I am?"

"You are. You're not only gorgeous and built like a fucking god, you're so damn nice." Wade wished he could believe in true love. Wished it very badly. "You're smart as heck...caring, giving, willing to risk your truck in a ditch to help a total stranger..."

Ayden's eyes grew glossy.

"And you're going to make some guy a very happy man."

"But not you?" Ayden bit his lip.

"You have made me happy. You have no idea." Wade used the back of his knuckle to caress Ayden's jaw.

Ayden turned away from him, as if trying to give Wade his back in frustration.

"Ayden..." Wade said in a scolding way. His arm was shrugged off and Ayden nearly pushed Wade to get him away from him.

Wade backed off hesitantly, staring at Ayden as he tried to vanish in plain sight.

"Now I wish this night would end." Ayden crossed his arms and leaned his forehead on the driver's door window.

The idea he'd hurt Ayden killed Wade, but better now than having some pipe dream of living together in LA blow up in their faces.

The Farmer's Son

Chapter 9

Ayden didn't want to keep welling up with emotion.

But he was so tired.

Tired physically, mentally, spiritually. Spent.

As the wee hours of the morning came, Ayden wondered what his family thought about him going missing. Maybe they did do a quick drive to where he had been cutting trees, just to see if he was lying injured. Of course when he wasn't lying face down on the dirt someplace, he imagined they'd shrug, say, 'oh well' and head back to the farmhouse.

They'd have had their home-baked dinner, maybe since it was Friday night his brothers would head to the local tavern to pick up women and drink beer...his granddad would be asleep on the sofa by seven, in bed by nine. His mom, cleaning and baking until maybe ten, his dad, on his computer or the phone, working on the accounts. But no one would panic that he had not returned.

Jacob had done it more than once, so did Jeremiah. They wandered in the next day, nothing was asked or explained.

Two days gone? Yes. Two days gone they'd grow worried. But no one on the orchard panicked. They'd seen it all. Horrific injuries from carelessness, their animals poached or killed by local dogs or predators...fires, floods, downed power lines...

Ayden glanced at Wade who was obviously trying to sleep, wedged against the passenger's door. *Don't want me. That's all it is. All those empty words, compliments...plain and simple. You do not want me.*

Ayden closed his eyes after he turned the heat up as he cooled off from their stillness in the damp truck cab. He envisioned that 'fantasy' in his mind again. Leaving with Wade when the tow truck got both of them out of the ditch, packing his drawings, his few clothing items, driving south to the big city.

With his thoughts came that longing again. He stared at Wade. The more he looked the more attractive Ayden thought Wade was. His unbelievable masculinity, his brown hair, conservatively cropped, and the darkest five o'clock shadow Ayden had ever seen on a man, coarse to the touch, to his lips. A body so beautiful, trim, sleek, and that hair on his chest, soft and alluring...his kiss, like honey.

Ayden used the back of his hand to wipe his eyes, knowing how filthy his fingers were. He was crying. He didn't want to cry. But he couldn't help it.

Unloved. Was there any crueler punishment on earth?

He held himself in a hug and faced the driver's door again, his forehead on the glass, sobbing for what he could never be, never have. *Trust? You won't even let me show you I can be trustworthy? Not even give me one chance?*

Ayden knew why Wade was thinking he would experiment if he had the opportunity. Because it stood to reason. His brothers would. If they were let loose in Las Vegas surrounded by hookers, strippers, whores? They'd fuck every one of them. Were his brothers virgins? He doubted it, but he knew the women they screwed locally would probably be nothing like the gals on the strip in a city known for its sex.

I am not them.

Ayden understood Wade's fear. How could he not? But Ayden was always willing to try. If Wade wasn't? Then there was no fantasy, only failure.

The Farmer's Son

~

Wade heard a sound. The rain had stopped but the trees were still dropping water on them, and wind blew outside, competing with the blower of the heater inside the truck. But that wasn't the noise he was hearing. He opened his eyes and looked across the small space they were confined in.

Ayden was curled against the door, his back facing him, appearing to have his arms crossed tightly over his chest. And...he was crying.

Oh God no.

Wade reached for him immediately. Ayden's first reaction was to shrink away and hide. There were so many things Wade has done and said to stir bad feelings, Wade felt like a nasty heel and wished he never said anything controversial, but...it was who he was. Open. Honest. Outspoken. Maybe too outspoken.

"Sweetness." Wade caressed Ayden's hair. "I'm sorry. What did I say? Please."

"Nothing." Ayden appeared embarrassed and wiped his face with his sleeve.

"We're exhausted and hungry. That's not helping." Wade scooted closer to try and spoon Ayden, snaking his arms around his chest and holding him tight. He pressed his mouth against Ayden's soft hair and neck and inhaled him. "Forgive me."

Ayden finally seemed to surrender and unwound his tight posture. His head fell back on Wade's shoulder and another mournful sob was let go.

"What did I say? Which careless horrible thing came out of my mouth to upset you?" Wade died inside. He'd said too much.

It was as if Ayden couldn't answer verbally, so he just shook his head.

"Come here. Baby..." Wade forced Ayden to turn towards him. Ayden did, almost as if he couldn't fight any longer. They embraced and Wade pressed his cheek against Ayden's feeling the dampness of his tears. "I'm sorry. It's me. I've been let down too much."

"Me too." Ayden wiped his eyes on Wade's shirt and calmed down. "Me too," he echoed softly.

Wade closed his eyes and rubbed Ayden's back, feeling his size and power. "I want you. Make no mistake."

"How much?"

"A whole lot." Wade chuckled but was not happy about his feelings or their effect on Ayden. "If I could, I'd keep you to myself."

"You can."

Wade shivered and knew that was not only unfair to Ayden, it was the impossible dream. "The risk of us failing is so damn high."

"Especially if we don't try."

Wade moved back to see Ayden's eyes. "Is this all because of your need to get the hell away from the family? The work?"

"No." Ayden shook his head and his eyes seemed about to overflow. "I want you."

"How…" Wade tried to think before he said more hurtful things. "How do you even know me?"

"Like you told me. You're the complete package. You're gorgeous and built like a fucking god, you're nice." Ayden's voice choked up. "You're smart, caring, successful…" Ayden sobbed the last line, "And you're going to make some guy a very happy man."

Wade watched the two rivers of tears run down Ayden's cheeks. "Oh, Ayden." Wade grabbed him in a bear hug and held on tight. He hid his face in Ayden's hair and bit back his own feelings. "How can this be? Huh? How?"

"I don't know." Ayden inhaled a few times deeply.

Wade cupped Ayden's face in his hands and took a huge leap of faith. "I want you too."

The Farmer's Son

"Do you?"

"Oh yes."

"Can we try? Can we at least fucking try?"

Wade repressed a cringe of terror, knowing his heart was going to be trampled, badly, when Ayden found a young man his own age. "Sure. What the hell. I can't get any more cynical than I am, can I?"

"No!" Ayden said, laughing as tears rolled down his face.

Wade held him tight and closed his eyes as he did, struggling not to dread the future, because in a few hours, daylight would begin to creep up on them. And the future would be now.

~

Ayden tried not to be too embarrassed for growing emotional. But since that moment when he'd seen Wade's car stuck in the ditch, so much had happened to him. He was trying to absorb it all. Ever since he was a small boy he had wanted men, and what had felt like eternity had ended—and Ayden now had touched one, intimately. Not only had he enjoyed the man-love immensely, he was growing so fond of Wade he felt like he had a mad crush on him, which Ayden hoped could grow into mutual love, despite all of Wade's doubts.

He sniffled, wishing he had a tissue and dabbed at his nose with his sleeve again.

"You okay?"

"Yeah. I'm good now." Ayden smiled at Wade. "Maybe it is crazy, but if you just vanish on me and I never even…"

"I know." Wade touched Ayden's chin lightly. "I'll try."

"How…" Ayden cleared his throat and felt much more himself now with Wade's comfort. "How will we do it?"

"I assume you'll just head back with me. Is that what you want?"

"Oh, God yes." Ayden's tension dissipated instantly.

"So, how will you break this to your family? I mean, 'Hi folks, I'm in love with this old guy and leaving?'"

"You're not old!" Ayden shook his head. "Jesus Christ. My granddad is eighty. That's old, okay?"

"How old is your dad?"

"Fifty-five."

Wade nodded, looking relieved.

"I am not going to say anything about you and I being a couple. Maybe I'll say you're going to help me find a publisher or something."

"Okay. Where will you say you're living?" Wade brushed Ayden's hair back from his eyes.

"Where am I living?" Ayden tensed up, expecting something harsh.

"With me. Right? Isn't this what this is about?"

A fire lit in Ayden, one so powerful he had never felt it before. It was as if Wade was holding out a burning torch to his darkness. "Yes. Is that okay?"

"Of course. I assume you can't afford a place. And even if you could, what's the point? I mean, you're in this for good, aren't you?"

"I am if you are."

Wade said, "Just don't burn your bridges with your family. You need an escape route if we fail." Wade held up his hand before Ayden could reply. "I'm just saying."

"I know. And yes. I'll try not to piss anyone off. But…Dad will be mad."

"I expect he would be."

"There's no other way to do it unless I lie completely. And I really don't want to do that. I can just tell them how we chatted all night and you said you would help me try to get a drawing career going if I came to LA."

"And you're going to tell them you're shacking up with me?"

THE FARMER'S SON

"I can say it's temporary until I'm on my feet."

"Then it is a lie."

"A white lie, until we know..." Ayden touched Wade's thigh. "Until *you* *k*now, you can trust me."

Wade smiled shyly. "So you trust me. Trust that I'll never go out on you? Really?"

"Will you?"

"No."

Ayden shrugged. "Why shouldn't I believe you?"

"Because men lie."

"Are you lying to me?"

"No." Wade laughed. "But that could be a lie too."

Ayden chuckled and shook his head. "No. You're not lying. I already trust you."

"I don't know whether you're naïve or crazy."

"Both. But, Wade...I feel like I do know you." He smoothed his hand up Wade's thigh to his crotch. "Your scent, your taste..."

"Oh dear lord you're going to get us going again?" Wade laughed. "I haven't come this many times in one night since college."

"I can't help it. You really turn me on."

"The feeling is mutual."

Ayden leaned closer and wanted a kiss. He got one. Closing his eyes, pressing gently against Wade's lips, Ayden moaned and began scooting nearer, overlapping their thighs. With every contact, Ayden grew more confident and familiar with Wade. He ran his hand along the inseam of Wade's jeans to his bulge and began massaging it, going for his balls and rubbing between Wade's legs hungrily.

Wade responded by digging his hand into Ayden's hair and deepening the kiss. That sand-papery new growth on Wade's jaw made Ayden's skin tingle and his cock thick. The amount Ayden wanted to sit on this man's length was powerful. In the tight space, he straddled Wade's legs, facing him, and began rubbing hot friction crotch to crotch.

Ayden held the seat behind Wade and felt where Wade's stiff cock was under his jeans. He positioned his bottom against it and dry humped him, closing his eyes and letting his head fall back as he imagined actually being fucked.

~

Wade stared at Ayden's expression—his parted lips and closed eyes, looking as if he were in heaven. Wade held Ayden's waist and thrust up against him, wanting to fuck this man very much.

"So good," Ayden said hoarsely, struggling in the impossible space to get friction against his own bottom using Wade's groin. "You…in me…I can't wait. God, I can't wait."

Jesus! Wade felt his own cock throbbing and couldn't believe how hot this young man got him. He never even thought to bring a condom or lubrication. Why would he? To attend his brother's parole hearing and go home?

A brief craving to ride Ayden bareback raced through his mind. Wade was negative, and, well…Ayden was a virgin.

But no. No way was Wade going to do it. Not without lubrication, a bed, and preparing Ayden properly.

Ayden reached down and opened his own jeans, exposing his beautiful cock.

Wade stared at it and his mouth watered at the sight. Ayden held himself, and as he ground his ass against Wade, he fisted himself, cupping the head.

A solo performance. Oh, motherfucker. I am in heaven.

Wade began gasping for air even though all he was doing was witnessing Ayden getting off, yet again. He smoothed his hands up Ayden's chest under his shirt and cupped Ayden's pectoral muscles, using his palms to rough up Ayden's hard nipples.

THE FARMER'S SON

"Fuck me! Wade, fuck me!"

Chills covered Wade's skin. As he watched Ayden's expression, as well as his act of jerking off, he knew Ayden was imagining Wade doing just that. The young man came, choking on the intensity and caught his cum in his palm. Seeing the grimace of pure lusty pleasure on Ayden's face, Wade envisioned having this stud in his bed, fucking him every which way he could.

Wade's cock throbbed in reaction to his fantasy, but he didn't want to coax another one out. He was already spent.

As he recuperated, Ayden rested his head on Wade's shoulder, catching his breath. Wade let him, closing his eyes, knowing dawn would be coming. They had been together since five p.m. He couldn't recall ever having an evening like this...*ever*. The bonding the two of them were doing, both mentally and physically, was intense.

Ayden finally sat upright and looked down at his palm, which was full of spunk.

"Now what?" Wade chuckled.

Ayden climbed off Wade's lap and used his clean hand to open the driver's door. It had stopped raining, so Wade did the same. He stood near the side of the truck and relieved himself, hearing the absolute silence around them, all but the very low idle of the pickup truck.

He fastened his jeans and ran his fingers over the wet tree limbs to wash his hands, at least a little, shaking off the drops and then using his jeans to dry them. Once he climbed in the truck, shutting the door, Ayden appeared to have done the same, drying his hands on his jacket.

The dome light shut off as both doors were closed and each man slumped in exhaustion in the seat. It was nearing three a.m.

"I have never been so satisfied." Ayden turned to look at him. "We can fuck a lot once we live together, right?"

"Yes." Wade laughed. "It doesn't stop like when a straight couple gets married."

"Ha. Yeah. That's the rumor." Ayden looked shy suddenly, as if asking about their life together after tonight was taboo.

"I've always had a pretty high libido. Don't worry. I'll keep up with your twenty-two year old hormones."

"Shut up." Ayden laughed and gave Wade a playful whack on the chest.

Wade chuckled and stared down at his own hands and clothing. "I am seriously in need of a shower and change of clothes. I feel as if I've been camping in the rough with a porn star."

Ayden cracked up and doubled over with hilarity.

Wade loved seeing him happy and filled with laughter. Ayden had a wonderful laugh and looked even more fabulous smiling, his dimples showing, his shining smile.

They calmed down from the humor and each let out a sigh simultaneously. "I can't recall the last all-nighter I had to pull." Wade yawned.

"Yeah. Me neither. I go to bed early since we all wake up well before dawn."

"What time is dawn, usually?"

"This time of year, around six-thirty...seven."

"And...you get up at?"

"Four-thirty, five."

"Really? Why?"

"There's just a ton to do. Mom has breakfast ready for us and we eat and get going."

"Will you miss living here?" Wade gestured down the road. "At the farmhouse?"

"I'll miss Mom's cooking." Ayden stared at him. "Can you cook?"

"I can. Nothing too fancy. But yes."

The Farmer's Son

Ayden nodded, running his hand over his hair and resting back again on the seat, closing his eyes.

Wade was nervous for him. Nervous for them both. He imagined some backwards hick family, suspicious of everything the minute they walked in together; assuming the worst when Ayden made some grand announcement that he was leaving, living with a stranger from LA. It had disaster written all over it.

"Ayden."

"Yeah?" he answered without opening his eyes.

"Does your family own guns?"

Ayden peeked at him. "Why?"

Wade didn't reply.

"Think they're going to shoot us?" Ayden asked.

"Do you think they will?"

"No."

Wade relaxed on the seat and went for Ayden's hand, holding it. The closer it came to dawn, the more nervous he was getting. Until he had his car pulled from the ditch and was headed back to LA, Wade knew he'd be a nervous wreck.

Chapter 10

Ayden opened his eyes.

Sunlight was filtering into the truck. He checked the dashboard clock—it was seven-forty-five. They had finally fallen asleep. He looked over at Wade. His eyes were closed and he had wedged himself against the door, his coat over his lap like a blanket. Ayden stared at him in the morning glow.

Wow.

Wade's jaw was nearly black with his dark beard growth, his hair was thick and full and gray appeared just at his temples. Through his shirt Ayden could see his powerful arms and chest, and his legs from his knees down to his shoes, which were mud covered.

He flipped down the visor to inspect his own reflection. Wiping at the mud smeared on his cheek, Ayden tried to tame his wild hair but could not, popping the baseball cap on it…then he noticed redness around his mouth. Kissing that coarse whisker growth had made his skin raw. He touched it lightly then looked down at his hands. Even though he had tried to 'wash' them with the wet leaves and rain, they were still filthy.

His jeans were caked with dried dirt and he didn't even want to see what his briefs looked like after coming in them.

"Wade…" he said, touching his arm.

Instantly Wade opened his eyes.

"We should walk back now."

THE FARMER'S SON

"What time is it?"

"Almost eight."

"Jesus." Wade looked down at himself, then lowered the visor seeing his reflection. "Christ. I look like hell."

"No. You look unbelievable."

Wade spun around to meet Ayden's gaze.

"Blue. Your eyes are blue." Ayden smiled. "Like mine."

"Yeah. Like yours." Wade's smile appeared and he laughed. "You are even more spectacular in morning light, babe."

At the compliment, Ayden's cheeks went hot and he began putting his coat on and zipping it. "You ready for a muddy trek?"

"As I'll ever be." Wade slipped his wool coat on and wrapped his scarf around his neck.

Ayden shut off the truck and hopped out, standing near a tree to relieve himself quickly.

Wade brought his dress slacks to the trunk of his car and tossed them in, using his key fob to lock it up, as if he were in the city and someone would steal it from out of the ditch.

Ayden wiped his hands on the wet truck and shook them off, trying to wash them, even though it was a useless attempt.

They stood for a moment looking at the position of their vehicles. "How did we manage to do that?" Ayden adjusted the brim of his cap and put his gloves on.

"Me. I'm the one who got us into this mess." He shook his head at his car. "One U-turn too many." He tugged at the wire still attached to his axel and released it, appearing frustrated.

"My truck usually gets me out of every type of jam. I can't believe it fell into that ditch with you."

"They fell in love." Wade grinned wickedly.

Ayden walked right up to him, looking into his light eyes with pleasure now that they could see each other perfectly. "Yeah. Two machines from opposite worlds, imagine that."

Wade cupped Ayden's jaw affectionately, but it was such a masculine gesture, Ayden melted at the touch.

"You gorgeous fucker!" Wade laughed as if he was just now enjoying Ayden's beauty.

"Took the words out of my mouth, Wade."

Wade kissed him and then said, "Let's get ourselves out of here and back to my home where I can have you my way."

Ayden hugged him and they began their walk along the rutty mud-filled lane. Wade reached for Ayden's hand as they did. Ayden took off one glove and they held hands, side by side, smiling.

~

Wade couldn't believe how pretty Ayden was in the light of day. Not that it would have made too much of a difference since he had gotten to know Ayden on a deep level, but... His excitement at a possible relationship with this man began to make him giddy.

Each of them avoiding deep mud puddles, Wade enjoyed the walk in the country, not getting out of the city much. The air was cool, and still slightly misty, but not the dense fog of the night before.

As Ayden had said, it was a few miles of nothing but trees and rocks with drainage ditches on either side of the gravel lane. Wade took out his phone to see if he got a signal, but still seemed to be devoid of any communication in the valley area. He wanted to let Cole know he had not forgotten him, and of course, to find out how the hearing went.

"Nothing?" Ayden asked.

"No."

"It should get better once we hit the actual orchard."

Wade nodded and put his phone back into his pocket. As they continued on their way, walking in silence, Ayden released the clasp on Wade's hand. Wade knew why and didn't comment.

The Farmer's Son

After over an hour of walking, Wade spotted trees cut down, disks of wood left where Ayden had used the chainsaw to cut them. He looked out in the distance and there were trees, all in neat rows, for acres around them. "This is it?"

"Yes. This is where the actual almond orchard begins."

"You have such a big piece of property. Motherfucker." Wade shook his head.

"A hundred and forty acres."

"What?" Wade gaped at him. "Are you kidding me?"

"No. That's how much we own, but it's not all orchard."

"Holy shit." Wade suddenly knew the extent of the sacrifice that Ayden would risk if he left. "Please think carefully before you make any decisions."

"I have. I know, Wade. I know." Ayden looked around at the rows of trees, standing like battalions of soldiers. "But how much is happiness worth?"

"Fuck. I have no idea." Wade grew more anxious knowing exactly how much Ayden had to lose over this decision.

At the end of a very long gravel road Wade could see dwellings, vehicles, and outbuildings. He didn't know about Ayden, but he was growing anxious. Out in the distance Wade could hear the distinct noise of chainsaws.

Wade held Ayden back. Ayden stopped and turned to look at him. "Do we look as though we've been messing around?"

Ayden shrugged. "I doubt it."

Wade touched the reddened skin of Ayden's upper lip. "My beard growth...you're red."

"I know. But the wind and dry air can do that. Please calm down." Ayden touched Wade's shoulder. "Let me do the talking if you're unsure of what to say."

Since he was, to the extreme, he nodded.

The scent of burning wood on the breeze, Wade looked up at the roof and could see smoke coming from the chimney.

Taking off his gloves, Ayden entered the enormous one level farmhouse. Wade looked down at his muddy shoes in dismay and stood just inside the door on a mat that covered the wood flooring.

"Ma?" Ayden called, tugging off his work boots and headed deeper into the house.

Wade looked around the cavernous living room. On one wall was a stone fireplace, reaching to the cathedral ceiling, loaded with burning logs. It was located on the right side of the space, surrounded by a beige sectional sofa and coffee table. Traditional paintings of landscapes and barns were on the walls. It was not LA chic, but certainly not poorhouse dwellings. Another wall was full of electronics, including a flat screen TV. Quite the opposite of what he expected. This family did very well selling almonds. Very well indeed.

Wade felt his phone vibrate and heard it chime indicating his phone reception had returned. He took it out of his pocket and immediately called the jail to get a message to his brother.

~

Ayden located his mother in the laundry room, taking wet clothing from the washer to place in the dryer. She looked up at him and asked, "Where have you been?"

"I was out cutting trees at the north side of the property when I noticed headlights far off down that back road." He looked down at his filthy hands and then at her as she continued to load the dryer. "A guy had turned onto that old logging road and slipped into the ditch."

She nodded, not giving him much attention.

"I tried to pull him out but my truck slid right in with it. We walked here when the daylight hit."

She tilted her head at the mud on Ayden's pants. "I can see. Gimme those jeans. Let me wash them."

"I need a shower. I'm filthy from crawling under his car."

THE FARMER'S SON

"Is he here?"

"Yeah. He's waiting in the living room. His name's Wade."

"Okay. Well, why don't you both get cleaned up and I'll make you something to eat."

"Thanks, Mom. I'll call Stu for his tow truck."

She nodded and continued in her task.

"Is…is Dad here?"

"No. He went with Tony to town."

Good. Ayden nodded and returned to the living room. When he spotted Wade, he was on his phone, still standing at the door.

"…yes, I understand." Wade nodded and met Ayden's gaze. "I just wanted Cole to know I did try. Can you tell him I'm sorry I missed the hearing?"

Ayden removed his coat and ball cap and looked down at how dirty he was. He put his hands on his hips as Wade wrapped up his call.

"Thank you. I do appreciate it. No, I won't have time to visit Cole today. But tell him if he wants to call me this week, he can. Right. Bye." Wade slipped his phone into his pocket. "No parole."

"You didn't think he'd get it." Ayden thumbed over his shoulder. "Mom's the only one here at the moment, and she's doing laundry. Why don't you give me all your stuff so she can wash it?"

Wade smiled. "And walk around naked?"

"No. I'll loan you my clothing. Come on. We both need a shower and food."

"Is she cool?"

"Sure. I have to call Stu. He's a local guy with a tow truck." Ayden noticed Wade look up quickly. He turned around to see his mother. "Mom, this is Wade."

119

Wade extended his hand but didn't approach her. "So nice of you to help me out." He looked down at his muddy shoes. "I don't want to track dirt all over your house."

"Nice to meet you." Ayden's mom reached for Wade's hand in greeting. "Ayden, go get Wade something to wear. I'll wash his clothing for him."

"Thank you, Mrs…"

"Helen." She smiled sweetly.

"Helen." Wade removed his shoes and took off his wool coat.

"Look at the state of the two of you." She shook her head. "I can't imagine the night you had." She left the room.

Ayden gave Wade a secret smile. "Bet she can't."

"Behave." Wade grinned and followed Ayden in his stocking feet.

Ayden headed to his bedroom and removed two clean pairs of jeans and briefs from his dresser drawer, then two flannel shirts from his closet. As he did his mother entered their room and placed a basket on the floor. "Put your things here. I'll get you boys some breakfast. Is there anything you don't like to eat, Wade?"

"No, ma'am. I'm easy."

She smiled sweetly at him and closed the door.

Ayden began to strip. "See?"

"Yeah, but that's your mom, not your homophobic brothers." Wade removed his clothing and dropped it into the basket.

"Bathroom is right there." Ayden pointed.

"Great. I need a shower and shave before I go crazy."

Ayden watched Wade, who wore just his briefs, enter the bathroom, and close the door. Ayden placed all his dirty clothing into the basket, then locked his bedroom door.

~

Wade stood naked outside the shower stall, his hand under the running water. He stepped into the hot water and moaned in relief. He felt like a grimy mess after the mud and sex. As he scrubbed up, he jerked his head up to see the bathroom door opening. "Ayden?"

Ayden pulled open the glass shower door with a click and peeked in. "Oh man. Look at you."

"Uh, you sure this is cool?" Wade was terrified this visit would turn into some horror movie where three good ole boys would lynch the city gay guy…and his lover.

"Dad and my grandfather went into town and my brothers usually aren't back here 'til eleven or so to eat lunch." Ayden gave Wade's body a good once over. "Sweet."

"Still. I respect your household, and your mom."

"I know. We won't do anything. I just had to see you."

Wade poured shampoo into his palm, washing his hair, facing Ayden. Ayden pulled on his stiff cock as he stared.

Wade said, "You're not so bad yourself, farm boy."

"I want to jack off watching you shower."

Wade laughed and it echoed in the small shower stall. "Okay. Uh, do you have a razor I can borrow?"

"I do."

Wade watched Ayden through the misty glass stall. He rinsed his hair and soaped up his pits, groin, and bottom. Ayden poked his head back in. "On the sink is a new razor and shaving gel."

"Thanks, babe." Wade washed himself off and glanced at Ayden who was still fingering his erection.

"Do you have a towel I can use?" Wade laughed at how distracted Ayden was by him showering.

"Oh." Ayden vanished and reappeared. "Here ya go."

"Do you want to just step in?" Wade indicated the running water.

"Yup." Ayden moved aside and Wade squeezed passed him, getting a kiss as he did. While he dried his hair, Wade looked back at Ayden as he wetted down, using soap on his hand and working his cock.

"Don't move." Ayden stared at Wade.

Wade wiped off his legs and back quickly, then stood still, watching Ayden. Seeing Ayden's gaze go to his groin, then up to his eyes, Wade felt like a model, handsome in Ayden's eyes. It made him feel proud to be the object of this man's desire.

"Yes. Smile. You look unbelievable." Ayden fisted his cock more quickly and then aimed his body at the shower wall and came.

Wade chuckled, shaking his head. "You're going to be fun to live with, big fella."

"God, I'm dreaming."

Wade closed the shower door to let Ayden finish, then wrapped the towel around his hips and shaved over the sink.

As he finished up, Ayden did as well and the water shut off.

Wade wiped his face of shaving foam and grew nervous about them cleaning up together, even with just 'Mom' in the house.

He left the bathroom and put Ayden's clothing on. Although Ayden was slightly taller than he was, the clothing fit well enough to be comfortable. Wade buttoned the buttons of the flannel shirt, seeing himself in the mirror of a dresser. "Farm boy," he said to himself, sitting down on the bed to put on a pair of socks.

"Huh?" Ayden asked from the bathroom.

"Nothing."

After he too had shaved, Ayden exited the bathroom naked and began dressing. Wade watched, loving how muscular Ayden was, and his height…well, the young man was perfection. Once they were clothed, Ayden said, "Let me show you something before we eat."

"Okay."

Ayden gestured for Wade to get up off the bed, then reached under the mattress.

Wade imagined he hid his naked men magazines there when he was handed something else, a drawing pad. "Your comics!" Wade grew excited and they sat side by side to look.

Ayden leaned on his shoulder, and asked, "Ready?" holding the cover closed for suspense.

"Yes!"

Ayden flipped back the pad cover and handed Wade the drawings.

Wade was floored. In blue pen, obviously original art, without pencil sketches underneath, were panels with dialogue bubbles, of two men. He began reading the storyline and was truly in awe at the talent of Ayden's art.

"Neo Magnay?" Wade asked.

"An anagram for One Gay Man."

"Excellent!" Wade laughed and looked for the other character's name. "Boo?"

"Booverly. Lover Boy."

Wade could not believe it, nor had he expected anything quite like it. "You don't need art school. You need an agent."

"Yeah? You like it?"

Wade flipped the pages of the pad and couldn't get over the number of completed stories and comic strips. "Holy shit. You are unreal."

"Ayden!" his mother called through the door.

"Mom's got our food ready. Come on. I need you with me to tell her."

"Shit. You sure?" Wade handed him the pad and Ayden hid it.

"Yes." He unlocked the bedroom door and carried out their dirty clothing in a basket.

Wade ran his hand over his damp hair nervously and hoped they could get out before the 'men-folk' returned.

~

Ayden put the basket into the laundry room and loaded the washer with everything they had piled into it. He started the machine and walked to the kitchen, feeling Wade's apprehension as he did.

Ayden gestured to the large oblong table where his mother had set two full plates of hash-browns, eggs, toast, bacon, as well as a pot of coffee on a hotplate.

"I can't imagine being stuck out in the rain last night." Helen poured the coffee into mugs. "How do you take your coffee, Wade?"

"Just milk. Thank you, Mrs…uh, Helen. You shouldn't have gone through all the trouble."

Ayden smiled as he ate a crispy slice of bacon. "She likes to cook. Don't you, Mom?"

"Did you call Stu?" She set a carafe of milk on the table near Wade.

"Nope. I need to do that now." Ayden stood and his mother passed him the cordless phone and a handwritten phone number on a pad. He dialed as he watched Wade eat.

"Where were you headed when you got lost, Wade?" she asked.

Wade gestured for her to sit and she joined him at the table, making Ayden smile. "I was going to see my brother…"

"Hello?" Stu said on the other end of the phone connection.

"Stu!" Ayden turned away from his mother and Wade's conversation. "Hey, buddy, last night I tried to help a guy pull his Beamer out of a ditch and now we're both stuck."

"Ya dummy. Why didn't you call me?"

"I thought I could do it, but that road behind the orchard is slick as snot." He noticed his mother laughing during her conversation with Wade and it stunned him. He'd not seen her laugh in a long time, but something Wade had said made her giggle.

"Anyway," Ayden continued, "How soon can ya come and yank us both out?"

"An hour? I'll be at the farmhouse to pick you up so you can show me where you got stuck."

"Cool. Thanks, I owe ya."

"Yup. See ya."

Ayden hung up, set the phone down and joined his mom and Wade, eating his meal.

"Wade said you tried to pull his car out and ended up in the same ditch." She smiled.

"I did. I had no idea what I was doing. I had some fence wire and tried to haul him out…well…" Ayden shrugged, eating his bread dipped in the runny yolk. "Mom?"

"Yes?"

"I…" He looked at Wade for courage and said, "Wade said he can help me out a while. In LA."

"Help you out?" She tilted her head curiously.

Wade appeared grim and didn't make eye contact.

"You know I like to draw."

"Oh, Ayden, not those silly cartoons. Your father needs you here."

"I'm not happy here. Mom, come on. I can't stand doing the work my brothers do."

She stood from the table, as if ending the conversation.

"Mom. Come on. Sit down. I'm going to go whether I have your blessing or not."

She left the room.

Wade shook his head. "I saw that coming a mile away."

"Fuck." Ayden finished his food quickly and said, "Wait here."

"Where else am I going to go?"

Ayden put his plate in the sink and searched for his mother.

He found her in the laundry room, folding dried clothing. "Mom."

"Ayden, I don't want to discuss it."

"Well, then you'll just lose me."

"Why? Why are you going off with a stranger? You know nothing about him. What if he's a con-man? He said he was coming down here to see his brother in prison. What does that tell you about him?"

"It tells me he loves his brother. Mom, stop folding and look at me." Ayden touched her hand and she met his eyes. He inhaled deeply and asked, "Is Dad my father?"

"What? What on earth are you talking about? Of course he is."

"No. I mean…" In anxiety, Ayden dragged his fingers through his hair, taking it out of his face. "I mean, did you have an affair twenty-two years ago with another guy?"

She went as white as the sheet she was trying to fold. "Who…who mentioned this to you?"

"Then it's true?" Ayden felt sick.

"Did you hear it from one of your brothers?"

"Do they know?"

She turned her back on him and her fingers trembled as she tried to fold the sheet.

"Mom! Who's my real dad?"

"I can't. I can't, Ayden." She dropped the sheet into a basket and covered her face.

Ayden put his hands on her shoulders from behind. "I think I always knew something was up. I'm nothing like my brothers. And no one treats me like I am. Somehow I knew there must have been a reason."

"Is…is that why you want to leave?"

"No. I just am so unhappy stuck here. Can't you see how miserable I am?"

"Your father will be furious."

"What did he do when he found out I wasn't his?" Ayden felt numb. He wondered if this would eventually kill him, but it hadn't hit him yet.

"I can't talk about this." She shook out of his grasp and left the laundry room.

Ayden lowered his head and walked to his room to pack.

CHAPTER 11

Wade finished the breakfast and sipped his coffee, waiting for Ayden to return. He topped up his mug and stirred in milk, looking at the neat country kitchen with its wooden cabinets and brass fixtures. The dining area was permeated with the scent of bacon. He heard the front door and stopped short of his sip of coffee, staring at the entrance to the kitchen in apprehension.

Male voices, deep and masculine, were chatting as they drew near.

A man appeared, short in stature, at least in his late to mid-fifties, scruffy, wearing a green baseball cap with a yellow tractor logo on it and a denim jacket. The man halted in his tracks at seeing Wade at the kitchen table. Behind this worn out looking man was an elderly gentleman with eyeglasses, a bald head, sagging skin and heavy baggy outer clothing.

Wade stood up immediately. "Hello. I'm Wade Reed."

The elderly man responded to the greeting, reaching out his hand which was cold to the touch from the chilly morning. "How do you do, Wade? I'm Tony, and this is my son, Josiah."

Wade nodded and released Tony's hand. "My car got stuck in a ditch last night. Ayden was kind enough to try and help me."

"Where's Ayden?" Josiah asked, appearing annoyed.

"I think he's talking with his mother." Wade looked down at his empty plate and felt as if he were freeloading or something even worse, judging by the strange look Ayden's father was giving him.

Tony took off his coat and hung it on the back of a chair. "Sit. Did you get enough food?"

"Yes. Thank you, sir." Wade took his dish to the sink and stuffed his hands into the pockets of the jeans nervously.

Josiah vanished down the hall.

Tony glanced briefly at his son and then sat at the table. "Which road did you manage to get stuck on?"

Wade approached the chair he had sat in previously, holding the back. "It's a few miles behind the orchard." Wade pointed to the direction.

"How on earth did you manage to find that old logging road? No one's used that for decades." Tony smiled kindly, again gesturing for Wade to sit.

Wade did. "Can I pour you a cup of coffee?"

"Sure." Tony looked into the cup Ayden had used and offered it to Wade. Wade poured it for him.

"My satellite navigation system screwed up. It kept telling me to turn. It was so foggy out, I just listened to the crazy thing." Wade set the coffee pot down and tried to relax. He couldn't hear any shouting, so hoped Ayden's father wasn't losing his temper.

"Where were you headed?" Tony stirred sugar and milk into the cup.

"Corcoran prison. My brother had a parole hearing. Needless to say, I missed it."

"And you came from where?"

"LA." Wade sipped his cup. "I feel terrible to have intruded on all of you."

"Nonsense. It's always nice to get visitors. We don't get very many."

"Thank you." Wade was glad Ayden had at least one kind family member.

~

Ayden shoved as much clothing as he could into a suitcase and a duffle bag. He packed his shaving kit and toiletries and when he exited the bathroom his father was standing in his bedroom. "Dad."

Josiah looked down at the open bags, then up at Ayden. "Where do you think you're going?"

Struggling against the intimidation, Ayden crouched down to put his toiletries into the suitcase. "LA."

"I don't think so."

"I am." Ayden opened his nightstand drawer and removed more personal items from it, having already packed his drawing pads into the duffle bag.

"I said…I don't think so."

Ayden turned to look at him. Seeing him as not his father, but as a guy who raised him, disliked him, and never truly loved him. "You're not going to stop me."

Josiah took a menacing step closer.

When Ayden stood, he towered over this man. Although his dad was short, he was not weak, but the heart attack had taken its toll.

"Who is that man?" Josiah asked, sneering.

"He got stuck on the back road." Ayden zipped up the duffle bag.

"And? You think you're going someplace with him? LA?"

"Yup." Ayden picked up both pieces of luggage and laid them on his bed, then pulled his hair out of his eyes and confronted his dad. "If you knew me. Knew anything about me, you'd see how miserable I am."

"Miserable?" Josiah's teeth showed in his snarl. "You don't know the meaning of the word."

"Don't I?" Ayden laughed sadly, his hands on his hips. "When were you going to tell me you're not my real dad?"

The look on Josiah's face betrayed his shock.

Ayden said, "Yeah. I know. Twenty-two years of living a lie."

"Who told you? Did Jacob? Is that why you're leaving?"

"No." Ayden looked around his room for anything he simply could not live without.

"I asked you how you found out? Who told you?"

Ayden faced him. "Why? Does everyone in this house know *but* me?" Ayden looked behind his father. His mother was standing there, appearing defeated.

Josiah spun around and accused her, "You told him?"

"No."

Ayden stepped closer, to defend his mother, but he'd never seen his dad raise a hand to her.

"I put your clothing in the dryer, Ayden," she said, walking off.

"Thanks." He stared at his father again.

Josiah said, "You leave here, you'll get nothing from us."

"You think I don't know that?"

"Did that city man say he was going to do something for you?"

"What do you care?"

"Bet he's a fag and is after something from you."

Ayden snarled and picked up his suitcases, headed to the hall. "Get out of my way."

Josiah puffed up. "I never treated you any differently than any of my boys!"

"Your boys?" Ayden scoffed. "I know they're yours. Believe me, every day you ignore me, tell me I can't do anything, I know." Ayden shook his head tiredly. "Dad. Let me go. Okay? I tried. I tried to do this farm thing. I can't."

Josiah pointed his finger into Ayden's face. "You leave, you don't even think of coming back."

"Fine." Ayden walked passed him and brought his bags to the door. He could hear his grandfather telling Wade a story… Granddad liked to do that. Tell stories.

~

Wade stopped listening to the old man when Ayden's dad appeared at the threshold of the kitchen, looking hostile. Tony stopped talking and turned around in his chair to see his son.

"What did you promise him?" Josiah clenched his fists. "What lies did you tell my boy to lure him away from his family?"

Wade stood up immediately to defend himself if he needed to. "I told him I would help him. And I'm not a liar."

"Help him what?" Josiah yelled so loudly, Wade stepped back in reflex. Appearing shocked, Tony reached out his hand as if to calm things down.

Ayden entered the room behind his father. "Dad! Don't start something you won't be able to stop."

"Who are you?" Josiah approached Wade, snarling. "Who are you and what have you said to Ayden to make him leave his family?"

"He made his own choices. Not me." Wade tried to stand his ground but was never a fighter.

"He never made those choices before. Suddenly you show up and he's leaving. Why?"

"Because I hate it here! Because I want to be an artist." Ayden tried to intervene, and when his dad actually straight-armed Ayden to keep him back, Wade nearly attacked the man.

Tony stood, unsteady on his feet, and asked, "Why are we shouting? What is going on?"

Josiah pointed at Wade. "He's taking our boy away, that's what's happening!"

"Away?" Tony looked confused.

THE FARMER'S SON

"Granddad," Ayden touched his grandfather, "I'm going to LA."

A knock at the door startled Wade.

Ayden said, "That's Stu." He called down the hall, "Mom, doesn't matter if the clothes are dry. We're leaving now." Ayden spun around to answer the door.

Wade and Josiah locked into a staring match. Josiah closed the gap between them, the anger like a cloud around him. "I know what you want my boy for."

"No. I'm afraid you don't. This is about what Ayden wants."

"His brothers will kick you right back to LA for what you're doing."

Wade could hear Ayden telling Stu to wait at the door, then spotted Ayden look into the kitchen but continue on, obviously to get their clothing.

"Your son is unhappy working here. That has nothing to do with me." Wade tried to withstand the glare and hoped to hell Ayden's brothers were miles away.

"It has everything to do with you. You're going to take him with you, right? And what will you do with him in LA, you pervert?"

"Pervert?" Tony echoed, appearing shocked.

Wade flinched. "Insulting me won't change Ayden's mind. He wants to pursue a career in art. Not almonds."

"Don't you touch my son," Josiah sneered, his finger getting closer to contacting Wade's face in warning.

Ayden had an armload of clothing as he walked by the room. "Wade! We're going!"

Wade made a move to get past Josiah but was blocked.

Tony asked, "Can someone tell me what's going on?"

Josiah spat in disgust, "This man is stealing my youngest son!"

"Stealing?" Tony gave Wade a suspicious look.

"He's twenty-two and I am not 'stealing' anyone."

"Dad!" Ayden shouted, "Move! Wade, let's go!"

Wade tried to walk around Josiah, but he could guess what was coming. Josiah shoved Wade backwards, so he hit the doorframe of the kitchen. Before Wade could even react, Ayden was on his father so quickly, everyone was stunned.

Ayden had his father's shirt by the scruff of the neck and looked so mean and violent Wade didn't recognize him.

"You wanna do that to me, Dad? Huh? You wanna push me like that?" Ayden was breathing fire.

Helen said, "Ayden, don't."

Wade just noticed her hovering close.

Ayden shoved his father away in disgust and picked up his suitcases. "Wade, come on."

Stu appeared stunned as he stood by, witnessing the chaos.

Wade grabbed his coat and slipped his muddy shoes on. "You got everything?" he asked Ayden quietly.

"Yeah." Ayden left the house and threw his bags into the back of the tow truck's front seat. He signaled for Wade to get in first, and then climbed in and shut the door.

As Stu got behind the wheel of his rig, Wade watched Josiah get into a truck and take off in the opposite direction from where he had gotten stuck.

"Go, Stu. He's headed to get my brothers." Ayden pointed to the lane.

Stu shook his head. "What did you get me in the middle of, Ayden?"

"Nothing. Just pull us out of the damn ditch." Ayden exhaled loudly and looked tense.

Wade felt sick to his stomach and wondered what the hell he had just done to this family. A pervert? Wade rubbed his face in agony and had no idea why it had gotten this far.

~

THE FARMER'S SON

"Just down this lane, Stu. About two miles or so."

The tow truck rocked on the rutty lane.

"So, you're leaving for LA? Now?" Stu asked, his hands grimy and dry, his skin marked from acne as a youth, a mustache and beard trying to cover it up.

"Yeah. Had enough."

"Man, was your dad mad. I've never seen him so pissed off."

Ayden caught Stu glance at Wade.

Wade was staring out of the window, silent.

"He'll get over it. He doesn't let me do anything anyway. He wants Jacob to do everything because he thinks I'm stupid."

"He's the oldest." Stu shrugged. "There's your truck."

"Yeah. Wade's car is right behind it."

"Okay. Easy enough." Stu pulled up beside Ayden's truck and climbed out.

Ayden asked Wade, "You okay?"

"No. I feel like complete shit about what happened at your house."

"Change your mind?" Ayden felt cold in his gut.

Wade didn't answer, hopping out of the tow truck.

Ayden followed, taking his bags and putting them into his truck.

While Stu used his winch to pull Ayden's truck out of the ditch, hauling it slowly to the level lane, Ayden thought he heard something behind him. He spun around and could see out in the distance three pickup trucks headed their way. "Shit."

Wade spun around and looked as well.

The winding of the winch now covered over the distant noise, but Ayden could see them making their way steadily.

Once he had hauled the truck out, Stu unhooked it and backed up towards Wade's BMW.

"That was easy." Ayden laughed and shook his head. "Uh, can ya hurry it up, Stu?"

"Just gotta know what you're doin', Ayd." Stu tugged on the wire that was hanging under Wade's bumper. "What the hell is this?"

"My lousy attempt at yanking him out." Ayden looked at the advancing trucks. "Stu, hurry the fuck up."

"Why? Let me take the wire off first." Stu lay on his back under the car.

Wade said, "Yes, please."

Ayden stood beside Wade as Stu removed the wire fencing and tied the winch to his car. "You change your mind. Wade, you have to tell me now." Ayden and Wade both were keeping their eyes on the family members on the move.

"Are *you* sure? Because we're about to get into a confrontation." Wade stared into his eyes.

"Hundred percent. You?"

"Ninety nine?" Wade didn't smile. "I feel like shit for fucking up your family." Wade pointed to the road. "And I have a feeling things are about to get ugly."

"You?" Ayden blinked. "You didn't fuck anything up." Ayden shifted nervously. "How much longer, Stu?"

The tow truck engine whined as Wade's car was dragged out of the ditch slowly. "Give me a minute. What's your damn rush?"

Ayden pointed to the advancing trucks.

"Oh." Stu tried not to be distracted.

"Christ, look at the slop on that thing." Wade shook his head and glanced back down the lane. "What are they going to do to me, Ayden?"

"Nothing. Just be mouthy. I'm still leaving with you." Ayden was not worried about his brothers, he was worried about Wade changing his mind.

Stu unhooked the winch and took off his gloves. "You're free, boys."

The Farmer's Son

Wade took out his wallet and said, "Nothing is free. How much?"

"Naw. I did it for Ayden." Stu held up his hand.

"I insist."

Ayden watched Wade hand Stu cash. He had no idea how much but was glad Wade did. Stu needed the money.

"Thanks. Good luck to ya, Ayden." Stu waved.

"Look, Dad's coming this way with my brothers, block him, will ya?" Ayden took his truck keys out of his pocket.

"You have got to be kidding me."

"Stu, go!" Ayden nudged him.

"I don't want to be in the middle of this, Ayd!" Stu climbed into the tow truck and began driving towards the advancing pickups.

"I'll follow you." Ayden climbed behind the wheel.

Wade nodded, looking very unhappy.

As the BMW made its way back to the main road, slowly, in and out of the water-filled potholes, Ayden scowled, angry his family had turned an exciting event, into a nightmare.

Please, Wade. Please, don't change your mind.

Looking in his rear view mirror, Ayden could see Stu's truck had made the one lane road impassible for his brothers.

As Wade drove at a mere ten miles an hour, trying not to damage his car, Ayden noticed Jacob, Levi and Jeremiah exiting their trucks and jogging around Stu's pickup towards them. He beeped his horn to alert Wade and had no idea what would happen if a confrontation began. But it would be ugly.

Ayden followed the muddy car and kept looking in the rear view mirror as the 'posse' closed in for a battle.

~

Wade drove carefully so his car didn't scrape bottom on the pits and holes. How he ever managed to enter this lane in the fog and pouring rain last night was beyond him.

A honk of a horn made Wade look behind him. "I'm driving as fast as I can!" Wade said, only to himself since Ayden was not with him. Then, seeing in his side mirrors the sight of men running towards them down the lane, Wade was stunned.

"Are you kidding me?" Wade gazed into his side mirrors and noticed three men in denim, baseball caps, and flannel were closing in on Ayden since they were moving so slowly. Wade hit the gas and his backend fishtailed on the slick mud. He couldn't 'burn rubber' out of the road or he'd be in the same boat he was last night. Stuck. But he did increase the speed, dreading what would happen if they were confronted by a bunch of rednecks who were out for blood.

"I am not living *his* nightmare. No fucking way!" Wade finally spotted the turn off for the main road.

Still wearing Ayden's clothing, feeling out of it from lack of sleep and the guilt of taking a son from his family, now intensified by the threat of retaliation, Wade finally emerged from the back-road-to-nowhere and turned left, remembering the direction he had come from very well. He checked to see Ayden right behind him, and since they could move quickly now on tarmac, the sight of what felt to Wade like a mob of villagers after Frankenstein vanished. Wade shook his head in amazement.

"You'd better be twenty-one." Wade suddenly had his doubts and if Ayden was a minor, he was going to be in hot water.

Within a few miles he saw a sign for State Route 144 and knew he was on the right track to hit Highway 99 south.

In his rear view mirror was the image of an enormous Ford pickup truck. Would Ayden's father report it stolen? Who knew? If Wade had to guess he'd say it was registered to the family farm, not Ayden.

As he accelerated up to the speed limit, Wade could hear the mud and debris spinning off the tires of his car and hoped he didn't send a rock onto Ayden's windshield. He reached into his coat pocket and felt the two wrappers from the protein bars in it. Ignoring them, he dipped into the opposite pocket and took out his phone, glancing at it. No reception again. He placed it on the console and rubbed his forehead wondering why on earth he thought inviting this 'twenty-two'—*if you are indeed legal aged*—year old to live with him was a good idea.

You'd better not be a fucking minor!

Though Ayden's dad had made Wade feel as if Ayden was underage, what was Wade supposed to do? Ask for proof?

What did he expect? A warm bear hug from the guy who was losing the only son he had with a head on his shoulders? A loving thank-you from parents who watched their youngest son leave home for the first time with a man old enough to be…to be…his…

Wade groaned and turned on the CD, loudly, listening to his music so he didn't think, but every time he looked into the rear view mirror he knew. And he was terrified he had made an awful decision with a young man who just might be a minor.

~

After an hour Ayden followed Wade off an exit, seeing he was headed to a gas station. Since Wade was low on fuel last night, Ayden had expected he would stop sooner rather than later. After a few miles on Interstate 5, Wade pulled off at the first exit with a gas station sign.

Ayden parked behind him, climbing out and filling his tank as well. Once he had the nozzle in his truck and pumping, he walked over to Wade who leaned back on the car as he filled it.

"Hey."

"Hey." Wade glanced at him, then stared at the pump gauges.

The coldness made Ayden anxious. "You okay? Or want me to turn back?"

"I'm okay. Are you okay?"

Ayden craved touching Wade but there were too many people around. "Yes."

"Ayden."

"Yeah?"

"You're really twenty-two, right?"

"Huh?" Ayden tilted his head. "Yes. You want to see my fucking ID?" Ayden wondered just how old Wade thought he was. Pulling his wallet out as a gesture only, Ayden was stunned when Wade actually reached for his driver's license to look.

"Wade! How old do you think I am?"

"Just glad you're not fucking sixteen." Wade gave him the ID back, but was not smiling or joking.

"Jesus Christ!" Ayden put the driver's license back in his wallet in annoyance. "Sixteen…" He shook his head.

"I'm going to drive through that carwash." Wade pointed to one behind the gas station.

"Okay. Whatever." A metallic click made Ayden spin around. The nozzle had shut off as the tank filled. He returned to his truck and finished topping it off, taking the receipt and closing the cap.

Wade also tucked the nozzle back on the pump and closed his gas cap. He drove behind the gas station and pulled up to a keypad for the carwash. Ayden drove the truck behind him and watched as Wade's car moved into the hot spray and spinning brushes. He pulled up to the machine and used his debit card to buy a carwash as well. *Clean start. LA-fresh, washed and ready to go…sixteen?*

Ayden stared at Wade's car as the machine's spinning brushes made its passes over it, soaping it, rinsing it, and then blowing it dry. As he watched the water and suds Ayden thought of Wade in the shower that morning, and grew stiff in his jeans. Taking his turn in the carwash, Ayden had a nasty thought that when he pulled out, Wade's car will have vanished. He grew anxious but tried to shake off the doubt.

Trust. He had to have that or he'd lose his mind.

After what felt like an eternity, Ayden drove his truck out of the bay and spotted that black BMW gleaming in the sun as it waited.

He blew out a loud sigh of relief and they resumed their drive south to the City of Night.

~

By the time Wade pulled into the underground parking at his condo, he was so tired he was punchy. He used a remote control on his visor to open his private garage which was reserved for the most expensive units in the building. When he climbed out of his car, the pickup truck was idling behind his rear bumper. Wade headed to the passenger's door and Ayden lowered the window. "Use guest spot number five-oh-eight."

Ayden looked in the direction Wade indicated. "Okay."

While Ayden parked, Wade popped his trunk and removed his luggage and the pair of muddy dress slacks from the trunk. Shutting it, using the remote on his keychain to lower the garage door, Wade waited by the lobby entrance as Ayden removed two bags from the truck and approached him, appearing as worn out as Wade felt.

Before they entered the lobby, Wade asked, "Who's the truck registered to?"

"Solomon Almond Farm."

Wade had figured. He unlocked the security door and stood at the elevator, pushing the call button.

"Wade."

Entering the elevator, tapping the number five floor button, Wade asked, "Hmm?"

"You're already regretting this. I know. Can I just catch some sleep and leave in the morning?"

"You can do whatever you want." Wade made sure all their bags were inside the small space so the doors closed properly.

They rode up in silence, and Wade didn't know what he wanted anymore. He hated complicating his life, and had done this to himself too many times…with pretty young men.

Will I ever learn?

The Farmer's Son

Chapter 12

Ayden carried the duffle bag on his shoulder, the suitcase in his hand as they walked down the long carpeted hall. Since he was used to the farmhouse and orchard, the sense of claustrophobia had hit as they drew closer to LA on the interstate. Even on a Saturday there was heavy traffic and crazy drivers cutting off slower cars and riding up his ass.

Wade stopped at a unit door, number five-oh-eight, reaching into his pocket for the key. Ayden could see the toll the lack of sleep and long drive had on Wade. Once they were inside, Wade toed off his shoes, and carried his own bag down a hall.

Removing his shoes as well, Ayden followed, looking at the high ceilings and admiring the contemporary minimalist décor. The interior space was expansive, for a condominium, and a round white dining table was bathed in sunlight shining through sliding doors, which led out to a balcony. The kitchen had stainless steel appliances and track lighting hanging over an island. In the living room was a black leather sofa and side chairs, facing a wall of electronics and a large built-in flat screen television.

Ayden continued following Wade to a massive master bedroom suite with a king-sized bed, loaded with throw pillows. Wade had placed his suitcase on a chair and removed clothing and his toiletries from it. "I'm beat. I'm going to nap. Anything you need, Ayden?" he said, hanging up clothing he'd never got to wear.

"No." Ayden removed the clothing his mother had cleaned for Wade and set the folded pile on Wade's bed. "Do you hate me?"

Wade turned to look at him. "No. Of course not."

"Then why are you treating me like you do?"

"Ayden." Wade's eyes appeared red from his exhaustion. "I'm the pervert who has stolen you away from his family."

The shock Ayden felt at that statement was strong. He closed the gap between them and held Wade by his upper arms. "Please tell me that's a joke."

Wade looked away.

"Is that why you wanted to see proof of my age? Because you thought I was a minor?"

"I don't know what to think after that ordeal at your house." Wade moved out of Ayden's grip and began unbuttoning the flannel shirt. "I'm so tired I can't think straight."

Ayden watched Wade strip. "You want me to sleep on the couch?"

"No. Am I the only one who is exhausted?" Wade stripped down to his briefs...Ayden's briefs.

"Nope." Ayden began undressing. "If we got three hours of sleep last night I'd be surprised."

"I'm dead on my feet." Wade vanished into the bathroom.

As he removed it, Ayden folded the clothing and placed it on the top of his duffle bag, retrieving his toiletry kit, then his drawing pad. He placed the pad on a dresser and inspected the bedroom. It was twice the size of his room at home, which surprised him since this was a condo, not a house. Another balcony was behind opened drapes, overlooking tall skyscrapers. Ayden walked closer to the view and stared out. They were on the top floor of the building and he could see the flowing traffic below though he didn't know what street they were on. As he drove behind Wade to his home, Ayden had dazed off, not paying attention to the location or street names, too worn out to care. All he knew was he was in the big city.

He hadn't been out of the Great Central Valley much, and a major metropolis was not in his comfort zone.

And with the incident with his father creating so much doubt in Wade, Ayden figured he'd be leaving tomorrow to drive back. He had to think of a way to ask his dad to forgive him. It brought the bile up in his throat in anger. He didn't want to go back. No way.

Wade emerged from the bathroom. "It's all yours." He began tossing the throw pillows into a corner and then crawled under the covers. "I left something out on the sink. If you're still interested in sex, use it."

Slightly confused, Ayden entered the bathroom, looked at himself in the mirror and frowned unhappily. Then he spotted a disposable enema and picked it up to read the box.

~

As he tried to rest, Wade glanced at the balcony's sliding doors and got back out of bed, closing the heavy curtains to try and keep the room dim enough to actually sleep. It was nearing noon and even if he had a two hour nap he could function much better than he was now.

As he shut the curtains he spotted the drawing pad on his dresser. Peering back at the closed bathroom door, Wade approached the pad and opened the cover to inspect Ayden's comic art.

The two superheroes were in business suits, inside a library with wall of books and a ladder to reach the top level. All very Bruce Wayne and Dick Grayson.

Neo Magnay said to Booverly, 'I heard there was a beating at the local high-school...a gang of bullies.' Booverly replied, 'I hate bullies.'

Wade smiled and kept reading.

'I think it's time you and I go back to school, Boo...and see if we can teach some bad boys a lesson.' Boo replied, 'I love it when you get mean.' 'I only get mean when young men and women are teased...for love.'

The door opened behind him. Wade looked over his shoulder and he and Ayden connected gazes. It was then Ayden realized what Wade was doing. He smiled shyly.

Wade brought the pad with him to the bed, and turned on the lamp so he could see in the dimness. Wade got under the blankets, propping himself up on his pillows on the headboard. He patted the spot beside him playfully.

Ayden walked around the bed and climbed under the blanket with him. Without a verbal comment, Wade scooted closer to Ayden and they leaned shoulder to shoulder as Wade kept reading, wanting to finish the first comic story before he napped.

The next cartoon panels had the two superheroes in their crime fighting outfits, masks on their faces, police-like utility belts around their hips, muscles *and* crotches bulging, with no detail left to the imagination as to just how well endowed these two gay heroes were. They exited a car that was low slung, sleek and sexy—a futuristic rocket-esque type vehicle that was a combination of Italian Ferrari-phallus and NASA creativity.

Wade stifled his smirk at the group of 'thugs' appeared to be caricatures of Ayden's brothers—he had no doubt they were. They were surrounding a frail young man who was on the ground in a defensive posture.

Neo said, 'Someone have an issue with this young man?'
One of the thugs said, 'Screw you, faggot!'

The Farmer's Son

Boo bristled and Neo held back his arm. 'Let me take care of this, baby.'

Neo removed a 'ray'-gun from his belt and ZAP! all the thugs were suddenly drag queens with exaggerated curves and high wigs.

Wade cracked up with laughter and dabbed his eyes, looking over at Ayden. "You're fucking hilarious."

"It's just a joke. Ya know?"

"I know. But it's so damn funny." Wade wanted to read all of them, but was too tired. He folded the pad closed and placed it on the nightstand, shutting the light. As he rolled to face Ayden he cuddled near, feeling Ayden's warmth. Ayden shifted lower, eye level with Wade and propped himself up on the pillows. They stared at each other.

Lost in the tranquility of Ayden's blue eyes, Wade felt better about him being there. Drowsy, maybe slightly infatuated, Wade withdrew his arm from the sheet and combed his fingers through Ayden's soft hair. Ayden closed his eyes and Wade imagined him purring like a cat at the stroking. Scooting closer, sealing their bodies undercover, Wade pressed his lips against Ayden's. A low moan came from Ayden in pleasure. He felt Ayden's hips shift and the press of his hard cock.

Wade parted from their gentle kiss. Brushing Ayden's hair from his forehead, Wade asked, "Can I catch a nap and then…"

"Anything." Ayden rested his head on Wade's chest. Wade looped his arm around Ayden and held him close, closing his eyes.

How good does it feel to have you in my bed? In my arms?
Too good.

Wade kissed Ayden's hair and fell asleep.

~

Ayden dreamed he was in a different house this time, not his family home. The carpet was green as grass and the second floor had white walls and a railing balcony that looked like a picket fence. He stood at the rail looking out of a window which was so large it went from the floor to ceiling. Through the glass was a view of an expanse of land, so vast Ayden couldn't see a tree or home for miles. He turned to look over his shoulder and a door was in the corner of the strange narrow balcony configuration. He walked towards it, compelled to go, and when he opened the door, a tight staircase was revealed. Climbing the steps, Ayden immediately felt a ghostlike presence and was gripped with fear. He made it to the top of the staircase to an attic, as enormous as a gymnasium from a school, and filled with treasure. The moment he reached towards a box filled with jewels, something terrifying materialized.

Ayden sat up in bed with a start and looked around the room. His heart was pounding as he caught his breath.

"What's wrong?"

Ayden turned to see Wade lying in bed with him, appearing concerned.

"A dream, one I've had before. Just weird." Ayden settled back down.

"You mean a nightmare, judging by the way you bolted upright."

In order to see Wade so they could talk, Ayden rolled to his side and propped up his head on the pillow. "I'm in this odd house...green carpet, like grass with stark white walls."

Wade shifted to mirror Ayden's position on the bed, paying attention.

"I know something is in the attic, but I go anyway. And every time I do, I enter this huge space filled with wonderful things, but there's always something terrifying there."

"What do you think it means?" Wade reached to brush the hair out of Ayden's eyes.

"I don't know. Maybe I know there's a good future for me, but not without some scary decisions."

Wade nodded. "Maybe. I'm not very good at remembering my dreams. And when I do, they're so disjointed, I can't make heads or tails out of them."

"What time is it?" Ayden looked around the room for a clock.

Wade leaned up on his elbow to see the nightstand. "Five."

"P.M.?"

"Yes."

Ayden dropped to his back and stared at the ceiling.

Wade scooted closer, overlapping their legs.

"You want me here, Wade, right?" Ayden asked.

"I do. But I want us to be smart about it."

"How will we do that?" Ayden narrowed his gaze on Wade. "If you think you're going to get approval from my parents, think again."

"No. I know that won't happen. But I also don't want you to lose everything in the process."

"Then I'll ask again. Do you want me here?"

"Yes."

Ayden had to believe him. He had to take Wade at his word. What else did he have?

"Do you need more rest or...?"

"I'm good. If I sleep too much now, I doubt I'll sleep tonight." Ayden put his hands behind his head and gazed at a black and white print of what appeared to be the New York skyline on Wade's wall. He recognized the Empire State Building.

"Are you hungry? How about I take you out someplace?"

Ayden caught Wade's arm as he rolled over to get out of bed. At the touch, Wade turned around to face him.

"Don't go anywhere. I did what you needed me to do." Ayden felt shy. "The thing you left on the sink."

Wade gave him a sly smile and shifted to his side again, staring at Ayden. "What do you want?"

"You. Why do you think I came here?" Ayden began nudging the sheet down Wade's torso.

Wade watched as his body was revealed. "Yeah. I know why you came here."

Ayden suddenly felt silly. "No. Wade, that's not the only reason."

A hand cupping Ayden's jaw in affection stopped Ayden from continuing to justify why he had indeed come to LA. "I know." Wade slid his fingers behind Ayden's head into his hair and drew him to his mouth.

Ayden opened his lips for that kiss. As he was about to climb on top of Wade to feel his body against his own, Wade made the move first, pinning Ayden to the bed. Dominance. Ayden remembered what Wade had said that night in the truck. As they kissed Ayden spread his legs and bent his knees, giving Wade an invitation. *You let me into your life? I let you into my body.*

~

Wade made his way between Ayden's legs, reaching down to right both their cocks. With an elbow on either side of Ayden, Wade enjoyed the hot kissing. The night in the truck washed over to him like a delicious fantasy. And now? After that crazy experience, Ayden was indeed, in his bed, in LA, spreading for him.

For now, Wade put his worry and doubt aside, wanting to enjoy this carnal act. One he was looking forward to. Taking a virgin. Had he ever? No. At least no man had admitted they had been.

A whimper from Ayden in longing made Wade's skin tingle. He parted from Ayden's lips and kissed his neck, his earlobe, chewing his way downwards.

The Farmer's Son

Ayden hissed out a breath of air, running his hands down Wade's back and pushing his hips up, grinding to get friction.

Wade made his way to Ayden's nipple, teething on one as he peeked up at this gorgeous young man. Ayden had closed his eyes and the contact between their crotches grew sticky. Lapping at Ayden's nipple, enjoying it against his lips, Wade moved to the second one to get it as hard and stimulated as the first.

Other than moans and huffs of air indicating his delight, Ayden allowed Wade to do as he wished. The act of submission couldn't have aroused Wade anymore than it did.

Once he had enjoyed Ayden's nipples, he pinched them as he licked and nuzzled his way down Ayden's six-pack abs. The natural beauty of Ayden got to Wade and as he grew closer to Ayden's treasure trail and cock, Wade joined him in a low lusty moan of anticipation.

He pressed his face against Ayden's crotch, inhaling his scent and then knelt between his thighs and pushed Ayden's knees against his chest, taking a look at his ass and balls. Perfection.

Wade went for Ayden's balls first, sucking one into his mouth at a time, running his finger over Ayden's rim and massaging his inner thighs.

"Wade…Oh, God…"

I'll make love to you like a prince and spoil you for any other man.

Wade used long wet laps of his tongue under Ayden's balls and began chewing his way to his rim, bending Ayden in half to get at him.

~

Ayden blinked and stared at the ceiling as his body was devoured—better than any of his fantasies. He tried to see what Wade was doing, propping up his head, but Ayden's eyes kept closing at the intensity. Even without touching his cock, Wade had managed to get Ayden on the edge of a climax. The urge to grip his own length and jerk it was strong, but Ayden didn't. Instead he had the bedding in a death grip, thrilled with the opportunity to be with such an experienced lover.

And about the age gap? This was why he loved it. This amazing sex from a man who knew. Knew things. Knew things Ayden could never even imagine.

As a tongue wet his rim, Ayden had to pinch the head of his cock not to come. He withstood the surge of pleasure to his groin and released himself to grip the bedding again. After Wade had immersed himself in oral sex—oral on Ayden's balls and ass, not his cock…something Ayden was now going to want… constantly—Wade sat up and wiped his face with his forearm.

Ayden couldn't contain his breathing as his chest rose and fell quickly. He watched as Wade reached across him to the nightstand, staying still, not knowing what Wade needed him to do other than being passive and allowing him to play the top dog.

Wade removed a strip of condoms and a bottle of clear gel.

Ayden grew even more excited at the possibility of real anal sex, so much so that he began to writhe on the bed.

With his teeth Wade tore one condom off the strip and set it beside him. Then he poured lubrication onto his fingertips.

As Ayden's mouth watered and his cock bobbed and dripped pre-cum, he waited in anticipation. With his left hand Wade pushed Ayden's right knee backwards, and touched Ayden's rim with his slippery right.

Ayden gasped and splayed out in a wide straddle.

Slick fingertips pushed inside him. Ayden closed his eyes at the rush of pleasure mixed with fist-time-virgin nerves. Yes, he had tried to penetrate himself, but never could do it successfully. He was afraid, having no experience. And what was he supposed to use? He'd never order a dildo. But Ayden wasn't afraid anymore.

THE FARMER'S SON

Wade's soothing in and out motion relaxed Ayden completely, yet stimulated him to the extreme at the same time. Ayden's cock was erect, standing straight up from his body, and blushing red as his excitement began to get out of his control.

Wade pushed deeper and slightly faster, running his fingers over a sweet spot inside Ayden that gave him so much pleasure his cock began to run with cum. Ayden didn't know if he was having a true climax, but he was certainly on cloud nine.

As if completely aware of Ayden's state and measuring every movement, Wade penetrated into Ayden's ass with more than a single finger, and this time, Wade grabbed Ayden's cock and sucked it at the same time as he pushed at least three fingers up to his second knuckle into Ayden.

Ayden arched his back and threw his head into the pillow behind him in reflex, craving to scream the sensation was so intense. This time there was no mistake about his climax, since his cock throbbed. Wade sat up, allowing Ayden's cum to spray his chest. Ayden's groin went into a power-rush of chills, and his skin broke out into goose bumps. He opened his lips to grunt or cry out, but nothing but air escaped him as he tried to comprehend the pleasure his body was giving him in the hands of an expert. Ayden gripped the bedding in a vise hold and bucked off the mattress as he came.

The internal friction was making Ayden's head swoon and he started gasping for air. Finally able to vocalize his pleasure, Ayden coughed out, "Fuck! Fuck!"

Before the final waves of pleasure subsided in Ayden, Wade rolled on the condom and pushed deep inside him. He held onto Ayden's legs and thrust in, closing his eyes and biting his lower lip in his bliss.

Trying to recover from what was almost too much pleasure to conceive of, Ayden held on tight as Wade fucked him, rode him hard and fast. Ayden struggled to decide if what he was feeling was pain or pleasure, since the aftershocks were still rocking him.

Before he had time to come to a conclusion, Wade grunted and thrust so deeply their bodies were one. Inside him, Ayden felt strong pulsating throbs of Wade's cock and he blinked his eyes in amazement at the sensation of physical bonding. Seeing Wade's euphoria at the act combined with Ayden's own unbelievable pleasure, Ayden was in love. Yes. In love with his first lover. It had happened to him. So was it the stuff of myths? Or reality?

Wade pulled out and sat on his heels, breathing hard and glistening with sweat.

Ayden looked between his own spread legs at the full condom and Wade's trim physique. Like he had been released from an electrical charge, Ayden's tense muscles relaxed and he drooped into the bedding and touched his cock gently. "Oh my fucking God."

Wade opened his eyes and a wicked smile formed on his lips.

"Wade…" Ayden shook his head in denial. "You have to be kidding me."

Laughing softly, Wade climbed off the bed and walked to the bathroom.

"Wade!" Ayden called out, chuckling. "You have to be kidding me!" he echoed, trying to get out of the bed but unable to move. Ayden touched his beating heart through his ribs and stared at the ceiling. "Holy shit. I am hooked."

The Farmer's Son

Chapter 13

Wade kept chuckling as he stepped into the shower to clean up. Most virgins were taken by men close to their own age and with similar experience. No doubt the contact could be painful and awkward if not done right. And that included straight relationships. He knew how to prepare Ayden, and…how to please him.

Wade looked up when Ayden stood at the gap in the sliding door of the shower, leaning against the wall watching him.

"Yes?" Wade soaped up his crotch and grinned at the handsome young man.

"I'm in love."

Wade laughed, flattered. "Happens to the best of us." With a tilt of his head Wade invited Ayden into the shower with him.

Ayden accepted eagerly, stepping into the tub and wetting down.

Wade backed up to watch the water cascading over Ayden's hairless young body as if he were in a gay porn video. *Do I want you here? Yes. Do I want to fuck you like that all the time? Yes.*

Will you be loyal?

Wade's smile fell and he knew there was no definitive answer to that question. But time would certainly tell.

Wiping the water off his face, Ayden's smile was enchanting, like a young man who has found paradise. It brought Wade's back instantly. He moved closer, pressing their wet bodies together. "How about I wine and dine my new lover in LA style."

"Oh, yes, please." Ayden appeared modest and sweet.

Wade went for his kiss under the warm spray and backed up to allow Ayden to finish washing.

Although he appeared very shy, Ayden gave Wade a sultry glare as he washed his own cock and balls, making Wade want him all the more.

~

Ayden dressed in a pair of black slacks and a button-down, long-sleeved cotton shirt—his church clothing. Items he rarely wore since he didn't go every Sunday like his mother, granddad, and brothers did.

But he was glad he had something to wear other than blue jeans and flannel.

As they both got ready, Ayden watched Wade discreetly, seeing how comfortable the man was in business attire. LA chic meant flair and style. Ayden didn't envy him, he admired him. He knew if he stayed with Wade, he'd learn. It wasn't as if Ayden wanted to be pretentious, deny he was a farmer's son, or lie about his roots. But he could appreciate the class. Was there anything wrong with aspiring to better oneself? Ayden didn't believe so. Would he fit in? It wouldn't be for lack of trying. He wasn't a country hick like his brothers. A good time for Ayden didn't consist of canned beer and acting obnoxious in a local tavern.

If he thought about it, a 'good time' for Ayden, was locked in his bedroom drawing. He didn't have any friends to hang out with, to share what he really thought. Fear had been a big factor in his life and maybe it still was.

Wade stood directly in front of Ayden, opening one of the top buttons of Ayden's shirt and adjusting the collar. Ayden dropped his arms to his sides and allowed Wade to tend him. He got a

The Farmer's Son

nice kiss after and watched as Wade loaded his pockets with his phone and keys. Ayden ran his hand through his hair, trying to tame it, pulling it back through his fingers, away from his face.

"Do you have any preference for food?" Wade asked, walking to the front door of the unit.

"No. I'll try anything."

Wade opened a closet and removed a leather jacket, putting it on. As he did, Ayden looked at his, where he'd left it, tossed over the sofa in the living room; old, frayed, and denim. Not to mention, dirty from oil and hard work.

Feeling self-conscious about it, Ayden looked down at his clean, dress clothing. Before he reached for the denim jacket, Wade handed him one from the closet and said, "Try this."

"Huh?" Ayden brightened up and took the supple brown leather jacket and slipped it on. The silk lining was soft as butter, as was the hide. "Beautiful." Ayden ran his hand over the texture.

"Made in Italy. I never wear it. I don't know why." Wade touched the shoulders and sleeves. "Fits you nicely."

"Thanks."

"You're welcome. Ready?"

"I am." Ayden grinned happily, ready to explore a new world.

~

Taking the elevator to the parking garage, Wade had a smile on his face. Yeah, he did. Maybe Simon was right and he needed a guy who needed him. Even if that need may be slightly co-dependent. Wade liked it. It made him feel secure.

He gestured for Ayden to go first when the elevator stopped at the lobby floor, and stared at Ayden in the leather jacket and his black slacks. With a stunner like this on his arm, Wade felt like a million bucks.

As Ayden stopped at the lobby door, leading out to the parking area, Wade cupped Ayden's ass and leaned against his back, kissing his neck.

"You're going to get me hard." Ayden held the doorknob and reached back for Wade sensuously.

"My apologies." Wade smiled and opened the door with Ayden. He put his arm around Ayden's waist as he used his remote to open the garage door.

"I can't believe we can be ourselves here." Ayden held Wade close.

"Here and there. Most areas I hang out in are accepting of the lifestyle." Wade released him to walk to the driver's side of the BMW, using the key fob to unlock the doors.

Ayden lowered into the leather interior and touched the console and seat as if he was enamored with everything tactile around him.

"No big monster pickup truck, is it?" Wade started it up and waited as Ayden belted himself in before backing out.

"No, it's not. But I do love a good car." Ayden investigated the dials and textures as they left the garage.

The urge to give Ayden everything he desired was strong in Wade. But he also didn't want to be played like an old fool. How many times had he seen that happen? Boy toys in LA? Old fucks getting conned into buying them everything from luxury loft apartments to high end watches and sports cars.

Uh uh. Not going to happen to me.

Wade drove out of the complex's garage and his phone rang. He used the hands-free mode and said, "Hello?"

"How did it go with Cole?"

"Hi, Simon." Wade looked over at Ayden and mouthed, '*Do you mind?*'

Ayden shook his head no.

"I never got to the parole hearing." Wade headed to Santa Monica.

"Why not?"

"My satellite navigator screwed up, and I got lost in the Tule fog."

"You have to be kidding me."

"No. I thought that fog was just a myth. I was wrong."

Ayden chuckled and Wade rested his hand on Ayden's thigh affectionately.

"So what did you do? Turn back?"

"Nope. I got stuck in the mud and a gorgeous farm boy found me." Wade winked at Ayden and it made Ayden blush.

"You are so full of shit, Wade."

"Really?" Wade said to Ayden, "Say hi to Simon."

"Hi, Simon!" Ayden said, leaning closer to Wade.

"Shut up!" Simon laughed. "Are you telling me some young stud came to your rescue and you brought him back to LA? Are you out of your mind?"

Wade glimpsed at Ayden's profile before he entered the Interstate ramp on his way to the coast. "Probably."

"Is he gay?"

"Yes. Lucky me, huh?" Wade ran his hand along Ayden's inseam.

"How old?"

"Twenty-two."

"Oh, fuck you!" Simon laughed. "It's not fair! Will I be jealous?"

"You will be when you meet him." Wade flew down the speed lane. Saturday night traffic was not too bad at the moment.

"Where are you guys? Can we meet?"

"Not tonight. Tonight he's mine. I'll be in touch with you."

"Is he living with you?"

"Yes." Wade didn't know why it felt good to say that. Was he gloating? Maybe a little? Showing off to Simon who had left him for a younger man. Gloating that Wade had found an even younger one?

"Wade, you have lost your mind."

"I'm not sure about that. Look, I'll call you when Ayden and I have a free night."

"You'd better!"

"Bye." Wade disconnected the call and looked at Ayden. "He's insanely jealous."

"You sound happy about that."

"I am. He left me for a guy in his twenties." Wade held Ayden's hand. "And, well, I told you we weren't compatible in bed. Two tops don't make a good combination."

"I remember."

As they left the highway and drove on local streets, Wade approached the promenade, looked for parking.

Ayden pointed to a car pulling out from a spot on the street. "That guy's leaving."

"Good job." Wade stopped behind it and parallel parked into the open space. Since it was January, it was chilly and already dark at six. They met on the sidewalk and Wade brushed Ayden's hair back from his eyes affectionately as the wind blew it in. "There's quite a bit to choose from here. Let's walk around and see what you're in the mood for."

"I can smell the sea." Ayden sniffed.

"It's right there." Wade pointed west beyond the buildings.

"Can we go there first? I don't get too many chances to see the ocean. And I love it."

Wade hooked Ayden's arm and held him close, strolling towards the waterfront and pier.

"Life can be good, can't it, Wade?" Ayden smiled contentedly.

"Yes. I guess it can be. It's had its moments for me. How about you?"

"Moments." Ayden nodded.

Wade escorted Ayden to a walkway which ran the length of the beach, overlooking the pier. They stopped to take in the night time ocean view. Ayden leaned on the rail with his forearms and his hair blew in the strong breeze.

Wade did the same beside him, his body pressing against Ayden's shoulder as he tried to see the world through his innocent eyes.

"Look at that Ferris wheel." Ayden laughed.

"Kind of tacky, huh?" Wade watched the electronic colored lights flash and spin on it.

"I'd love to write that into my comic strip."

"Now that would be great." Wade inhaled the cool air deeply and sighed. "There's a wonderful seafood place right there." He pointed.

"Anything. Really."

"You're easy." Wade tried to tuck Ayden's hair behind his ear, but it was just an excuse to touch him.

"I try to be."

Stay with me. It was a phrase going through Wade's mind now…now that they had made love. Now that Ayden was really here with him. He wanted Ayden to be his partner. But he'd been through this before. The 'honeymoon' stage of a relationship. When did it change to bitter anger and boredom? What was the timeline?

"Come on." Wade tapped Ayden's arm and they walked down the street which was crowded with pedestrians since it led to the amusement area and eateries.

Wade led the way up a set of stairs to the entrance and opened the door for Ayden. The interior was dim, loud, and packed with diners. He walked up to the hostess. "Two for dinner."

"I can seat you in just a minute. Do you want to wait in the bar?"

"Yes. That sounds great." After he gave the woman his name, Wade reached out his hand to Ayden.

They wove their way through the tables to the bar. Wade opened his jacket in the warmth of the room and noticed Ayden getting a few admiring glances. He reached out for him and tugged him close, possessive as hell. "What would you like?"

"Beer is good." Ayden took off the jacket and folded it over his left arm.

"Beer is good," Wade smiled as he repeated the reply, loving the simplicity of this man. He got the bartender's attention. "How about the winter ale on tap for my friend, and I'll have a scotch and soda."

As Wade removed his wallet to retrieve his credit card he noticed Ayden scanning the surroundings. Another young man was in the direction of Ayden's gaze. It appeared they may be staring at each other. Trying not to judge Ayden for his curiosity, since the young man had not been out much, or at least *claimed* to not have been, Wade fought his own insecurities and didn't comment.

When a glass of frosty ale was set down, Ayden snapped into focus and picked it up. Once Wade had been served his drink, and the tab had been paid, Ayden held his glass up for a toast. "To my man."

Wade lit up at the praise, raising his glass. "To my man." They tapped them and sipped the drinks.

"Mm!" Ayden nodded, licking the foam off his top lip. "Good beer."

I want to spoil you. Please never ruin this for me. "I'm glad."

"Wade?" the hostess called into the crowd.

THE FARMER'S SON

"That's us." Wade waited for Ayden to lead the way, giving the young man who had been staring at Ayden a warning glare.

Fucking twenty-year-olds, they're everywhere. Wade tried to adjust his attitude when they were seated at a table with the view of the Ferris wheel and ocean.

"This is awesome." Ayden put his coat on the back of the chair and sat down, appearing to be thrilled.

"Thank you," Wade said as he was handed a menu.

"Your server will be with you shortly. Enjoy your meal."

After she left Wade sipped his drink and looked at Ayden as he read the menu. "Do you get out to eat much?"

"Sometimes. Mom cooks really well, and since there are so many of us, it's cheaper for her to cook than for dad to take out seven of us." Ayden looked up from the menu. "What are you getting?"

"Probably the fish and chips."

"Sounds great." After he closed the menu, Ayden drank the beer down like water.

"Was that guy cruising you?"

"Huh?" Ayden wiped his mouth on the cloth napkin and then put it on his lap.

"That guy." Wade tilted his head to the bar.

"What does cruising mean?"

"Checking you out. Flirting."

"Who? Which guy?" Ayden looked concerned.

"You..." Wade shut up and wondered if Ayden was even clued in to that type of behavior.

"What? Did someone do something? Who?" Ayden turned towards the bar area, seemingly totally baffled.

"Never mind."

The waitress approached and smiled at them. "Have you two decided?"

"Yes." Wade pointed to the menu, "We'll both have the fish and chips. Ayden, would you like another beer?"

"Yes. Please."

"Another winter ale for my...man." Wade grinned wickedly at Ayden to see his reaction. The blush to Ayden's cheeks was priceless.

"You got it." She smiled and took the menus.

"My man. Ha." Ayden looked down at his lap and fussed with the napkin nervously.

"Bet you can't say that at the farmhouse."

"Not unless you're a woman." Ayden leaned closer to Wade. "I love LA."

"Yeah. I think you do." Wade reached out, bringing Ayden's hand to his lips and kissed it lightly.

~

Ayden was smitten. All he could see was Wade. And the fact that Wade could kiss his hand in public? Call him 'his man'? Ayden felt as if he had fallen into his own comic strip.

When the waitress brought his beer, Ayden withdrew his arm shyly and sat on his fingers. "Thank you."

"My pleasure. I'll check on your order."

"No rush," Wade said, leaning on his elbow and giving Ayden the most delicious smile.

Feeling bashful, Ayden looked out of the window again. The colorful lights on the spokes of the Ferris wheel were distracting, but he could see the white caps of the ocean waves far behind it if he tried.

Below their window perch, a crowd of people came and went to the amusements and restaurants, strolling Ocean Avenue, even walked on the sand in the darkness.

A pang of nerves hit as Ayden thought about the rest of the family; how they would have already eaten their evening meal, been discussing...him. Or maybe now his name was forbidden to be mentioned. Like the word 'gay' or 'homosexual' was. In the morning everyone would rouse to do their work, trim trees, saw down the old ones...maintain the... *Who would maintain the machines? Jacob certainly couldn't. Maybe Granddad could help him out?*

"Penny for your thoughts?"

Ayden perked up and stared at Wade. "Just thinking." He picked up his fresh beer and drank it.

"Of?"

The waitress brought two baskets of fish and chips, setting them down. "Anything else I can get for you?"

"I'm good. Ayden?"

"Good." Ayden nodded shyly.

She took the empty beer glass and left.

"Just thinking?" Wade didn't let Ayden off the hook as he dipped a french fry into tartar sauce.

"About what may be going on back home. You know. The routine."

"Miss it already?"

"No." Ayden picked up a piece of fish, dipped it and bit off the batter, seeing steam rise out. He set it back down and sipped the beer to cool off the bite. Once he had swallowed he said, "I can't just live off you. I want to work."

"I know. Tomorrow we'll look at how to submit your work to publishers, agents...the works."

"So, you don't actually know anyone in those fields? Personally?" Ayden ate a french fry.

Wade seemed to think about it. "No one comes to mind off hand. I'll call some friends I have in town. You never know."

"So, you said you're an environmental planner?"

"Yes."

"I assume that's nine to five?"

"You assume correctly. What will you do while I work? Any ideas?"

"I want to look for a job. Like I said. I can do anything until I get something I want. You know?"

Wade nodded, eating. "But I don't want you flipping burgers."

"Why not?"

"Because my man does not flip burgers."

Ayden stopped eating to see Wade wasn't joking, and actually looked slightly hostile. "Okay. What does your man do?"

"We'll discuss it. Don't worry too much. I can support us fine."

"Live…live off you?" Ayden wasn't so sure he liked that idea.

"For now. Until you find your career. Babe, it's what I figured we'd do."

"What will I do while you're at work?"

"Draw. Build up your portfolio."

"I can do something. It doesn't have to be—"

"Ayden."

Ayden looked up from his meal.

"Let me do this. Okay?"

"You won't hate me for it?"

"Hate—" Wade put his fork down and wiped his hands, leaning over the table closer to Ayden. "Hate you for it?"

"For not pulling my weight?"

"No. Of course not. Let me help you. I want to."

Ayden stared into Wade's eyes, into the blue ring of color surrounding a black hole. Trust. There it was again. "Okay."

"Good." Wade picked up a fry, and held it up to hand feed Ayden.

The Farmer's Son

Ayden leaned closer and ate it, smiling. "How did I get this lucky?"

"I'm asking myself the same thing." Wade winked at him and picked up his glass to sip.

After they finished eating, and Ayden had a third beer, Wade paid the check and asked, "Ready to go?"

"I need to stop at the bathroom." Ayden took the jacket from the back of the chair.

"Okay. I'll go too. My hands feel really greasy."

They stood and headed to the rear of the restaurant. Wade held open the door for Ayden and he spotted urinals against the far wall. After putting the jacket on, Ayden stood at one, unzipping his pants as Wade washed his hands at the sink behind him.

A young man entered and stood at the urinal beside Ayden, separated by a metal divider. Ayden drank a lot of beer and was trying to hurry, feeling the gaze of the man. He peeked at him and noticed the young man was trying to see his cock. Ayden said, "Hey! What the hell?"

The young man immediately pretended he didn't look.

"What?" Wade asked.

"Nothing." Ayden finished, flushed the urinal, and stood at the sink beside Wade. "He looked at my dick. Is that what you mean by cruising? When a guy looks at you like he would a girl if you were straight?"

"Yes." Wade turned to look at the man in question.

"I understand now." Ayden dried his hands and reached for Wade's. "Come on." He could feel Wade's resistance, like he wanted to say something to the young man, but Ayden didn't need the conflict. He'd had enough at home.

He tugged on Wade and they made their way to the exit, walking outside through a line that had formed of patrons waiting for a seat. Ayden continued walking until he was at the far side of the pier, where a metal railing kept people from falling off the high wooden structure.

"Did he stare at your dick?" Wade asked.

"Yes. Man, if a guy did that in my hometown, he'd be knocked sideways."

"And Neo and Boo would save him."

Ayden glanced at Wade, who was smiling mischievously. "Yeah. Pretty much. But I can see how easy it is here to get a guy. That's why you're so uptight."

"Yup."

Ayden leaned both his arms on the metal railing and stared into the dark ocean. "I would never fuck this up. Do you have any idea how much I appreciate what you're doing for me?"

"Never's a long time." Wade put his arm around Ayden and held him close as they both stared into the distance.

"Living on the orchard, seeing some bad things happen to the workers, I never take anything for granted." Ayden heard Wade say something under his breath. "What?"

"You're right. I'm beginning to believe you're the mature one out of the two of us."

Ayden smiled and turned so they were face to face. "Can we kiss?"

"We can."

Ayden held Wade's jacket lapels and drew him close, kissing him. They parted to smile at each other. "I won't go out on you, Wade. I trusted you to help me. And that's a leap of faith on my part. Now you have to trust me."

"I do. I mean, I will. Until I find out otherwise."

Ayden poked Wade in the chest playfully, shaking his head. There was nothing to say. He couldn't convince a man like Wade with words. Only actions. "Take me home. I want to be naked in your bed."

THE FARMER'S SON

"Don't you say all the right things?" Wade put his arm around Ayden and walked up the sloping pier, back to where they had parked the car.

Chapter 14

Wade sat behind the wheel of the BMW and started it up. Before he got his seatbelt on, he was pinned against the driver's door by a horny young man. Ayden attached his mouth to Wade's and dug between Wade's legs to his balls, giving them a good grope.

At the surprise attack, Wade blinked and looked beyond Ayden out to the busy street. "Okay, babe," Wade said against Ayden's lips. "On our way home."

"You really turn me on." Ayden ran his hand under Wade's jacket to his chest, chewing Wade's neck and earlobe.

This is why I love young men. Wade moaned and enjoyed the tease before he stopped Ayden. Wade whispered, "Ya want it, Ayden?"

"Yes." Ayden began sinking down onto Wade's lap.

"Not here." Wade's cock swelled and, *yes!* he wanted a blowjob right here. Under the streetlights with pedestrians walking by. *How hot is that?*

Ayden chewed on Wade's cock through his slacks and then sat up, looking dazed.

Holy crap. Wade had never been the kind of man to do naughty things in risqué places, but allowing the world to see this fabulous young stud was his? Tempting. Very tempting.

He inhaled a deep breath to calm down and put his seatbelt on.

"Can I suck you as you drive? Huh? Never did that. Can I?"

The Farmer's Son

Wade looked over at Ayden, his pleading expression, his parted full lips.

"My cartoon characters do all sorts of kinky stuff. I want to. Can I?" Ayden pushed his fingers against where Wade had grown hard.

How was he to answer that? Wade had no idea. Did he want it? Sure. But was it worth getting pulled over? Or worse, getting into an accident? Texting while driving? How about blowing while driving!

He pulled out of the parking spot along the busy promenade and tried to pretend he was not going out of his mind.

He headed to the highway, and glanced at Ayden who was touching himself through his pants. Ayden turned to look at him. They caught eyes.

Wade gasped as Ayden lunged for him, opening his belt buckle, button, and the zipper of his trousers.

"Oh, Christ!" Wade held onto the steering wheel with both hands as his cock was engulfed into a hot mouth. In acute paranoia Wade looked around for highway patrol officers. Although he had never been stopped before, there was certainly always a first time. He stayed in the right lane, not driving one mile over the speed limit, pissing off the hot-headed California drivers who wanted to fly at ninety in a sixty-five mile an hour zone.

Ayden was going crazy on him, sucking with loud slurping noises, pressing his face against Wade's clothing and holding his stiff cock in his mouth, drawing circles on and around it with his tongue.

"Holy fucking Christ!" Wade was stunned. He was just an average guy, really. Worked nine to five...didn't earn millions but wasn't broke...sort of happy. "Holy fucking Christ!" he shouted again in awe, peeking down at Ayden's head of shaggy brown hair. "Ayden...you're going to make me crash. Jesus!"

"Mmm!" Ayden sucked hard and strong.

"Fuck!" Wade peered at the passing cars in terror, having no idea who could see in and who couldn't. An eighteen wheeler sure could. "Ayd...Ayden!"

"Huh?" Ayden raised his head enough to answer, but was between Wade's chest and the steering wheel.

"I appreciate you wanting to fulfill your fantasies—"

"Thanks." He dove down and sucked all of Wade's cock into his mouth.

"*Auugh*! Motherfucker!" Wade swerved and thankfully was approaching his exit. He drove down the local streets, peeking into his rearview and side mirrors, knowing—just knowing—a black and white patrol car with overhead flashing blue and red lights was going to show up.

~

Ayden imagined he was Boo with his Neo superhero partner. They could do anything they wanted, at any time. He'd drawn them fucking—in their hero costumes, of course—on the tops of tall buildings, on dark street corners under lamps, after beating up thugs in the alley... Neo and Boo did 'it' everywhere!

The car came to a halt, and it wasn't until the engine stopped that Ayden looked up. "Oh."

"Yeah. Oh." Wade caught his breath, his hands gripping the wheel.

"The garage is boring."

"Holy shit." Wade looked down at his wet cock. "Are you for real?"

"Loved it." Ayden grinned wickedly at Wade, licking the head of his cock. "Glad you didn't come. Wanna fuck me?"

Wade moaned and his head dropped back against the seat rest. "You are unreal."

"Mm!" Ayden sucked Wade's cock once more and then hopped out of the car in excitement. "Coming?"

THE FARMER'S SON

"Yeah! Almost! Because of you!" Wade tucked his cock into his pants.

Ayden smiled in delight and danced out of the garage and into the open parking area as Wade followed. Spinning, his arms over his head, feeling free and alive for the first time in his life, Ayden closed his eyes and reached for the stars, which was in fact the ceiling of the cement parking area.

"Come here, ya nut." Wade grabbed Ayden by the sleeve and nudged him towards the lobby door.

Simultaneously, Ayden cupped and rubbed both Wade's cock and ass as Wade tried to get his key into the steel lock. With the distraction, Wade was struggling. Ayden didn't let up on the tease.

Once they were in the elevator, Ayden opened Wade's pants again, got to his knees and drew Wade's cock into his mouth.

"I've created a sex monster!" Wade gripped the elevator walls for balance.

Yes. You have. Ayden dropped Wade's pants to his shoes and held Wade's ass tightly as he sucked.

"Ayden! I have neighbors in this building!" Wade reached for his clothing.

Ayden allowed Wade to drag his pants up his legs, feeling delirious and high from being able to play with a man like Wade.

Holding his pants up as he walked, Wade made it to his unit door and opened the lock, looking both ways down the corridor. Ayden waited just long enough for Wade to get inside, then shut the door and lunged at Wade, tackling him to the floor.

"God!" Wade reacted to catch himself and not slam against the hardwood floor. He gaped at Ayden as Ayden stripped Wade of all his lower attire. The key in his hand, his jacket still on, Wade said, "You're insane!"

Ayden pushed Wade's knees apart and sucked his cock again, moaning and squirming on the floor.

"*Ohhh*," Wade moaned, "And I fucking love it."

Getting Wade's cock good and hard, Ayden sat up and began stripping off his own clothing, throwing it aside. "Screw me!"

Wade rubbed his face and asked, "Am I dreaming? Who are you?"

"I'm a superhero!" Ayden shimmied out of his pants and briefs and gave Wade's cock another slurp. He stood up, hands on his hips, naked, and said, "I think it's time for Neo to fuck his sidekick."

Wade gazed up at him in disbelief.

Reaching his hand down, Ayden hauled Wade up to his feet, smacking Wade's bare butt to herd him to the bedroom.

"I'm moving! Holy Christ, Ayden…hang on!" Wade batted Ayden's hand down and began removing his jacket and shirt.

Ayden went of the condoms and lubrication, making sure they were within reach, leapt on the bed with a bounce, face up, and held his knees. "Do what you do to me."

Wade froze mid-way from taking off his shirt and stared at Ayden. "I am dreaming."

"Should we do it like this again? Or…?" Ayden rolled to his hands and knees and wriggled his bottom at Wade. "Like this?" He dropped to his side and bent one leg. "Like this?"

Wade moaned and stood naked at the foot of the bed.

"Can we do them all?" Ayden grinned and pulled on his stiff cock.

~

Wade had never been with a guy whose child-like enthusiasm was so endearing—and genuine—he wanted to eat him up. He tore open a condom, rolled it on, and reached for the lube. "What way ya want it, Boo?"

"Yes!" Ayden reached for Wade. "You are so cool!"

Wade crawled over the bed from the foot up, and gave Ayden's balls a lick before he put lubrication onto his fingers.

"Love you in me. Love it!" Ayden held back his right leg, opening his body up.

"Are you drunk?"

"Nope. High on you."

"Am I going to have to buy a cape and cowl for our role playing?"

"Would you?" Ayden's eyes lit up devilishly.

Wade chuckled and tugged on his sheathed cock to keep hard. "Be quiet and let me fuck you."

"Mm." Ayden relaxed against the pillows, watching.

Wade ran his slick fingers over Ayden's rim, massaging him to make it easier for Ayden to let go. He slowly penetrated him with the tip of his finger. "Sore?"

"Uh uh." Ayden shook his head no.

Wanting Ayden to stay that way, he applied more lubrication. As he entered Ayden, using tiny circular rubs against his prostate, Wade made a sweep of Ayden's body from his stiff cock to his expression of pleasure.

"That is so amazing." Ayden's body went completely limp, all but his dick. It was what Wade was waiting for. He inched closer and pointed his cock towards Ayden's ass, getting the head of his dick in him. "How's my baby doing?"

"So good." Ayden slid downwards, making Wade's contact deeper.

Adding a little more lube to his palm, Wade clasped Ayden's length tightly and with his thrusts he worked his cock.

"Wade...you are such a great lover." Ayden's eyebrows knotted together and his hands ran up his own chest and nipples.

Not wanting them to come too quickly, Wade used slow, deep, thrusts, keeping an eye on their act, and Ayden's reactions. After a moment, he nudged Ayden to face the bed, fucking him from behind, holding Ayden's hips. He got the deepest penetration this way, but still did not want them to come.

Ayden groaned and tucked the pillow under his chin.

Wade tugged on Ayden's balls affectionately, watching as he took this fabulous young man, and enjoying every moment. He pulled out, rolled Ayden to his back, and raised Ayden's legs to rest on his shoulders. Now that they could see each other, Wade pushed as deeply as he could, and grabbed Ayden's cock, ready for them to rock and roll.

Ayden seemed to know, because he gripped the bedding tightly and his sensual glare intensified.

Wade admired this handsome man as he took him, pulling his cock out to the tip and thrusting back in, matching the movement with his hand on Ayden's cock.

With Ayden's vocalizations getting louder and his breathing accelerating, Wade began thrusting quickly, trying to heat Ayden up inside, while he kept pace with his hands outside.

"Wade! Fuck!" Ayden bit his lower lip and threw his head back into the pillow as cum spattered his chest.

The sight of Ayden in climax pushed Wade over the edge. He milked Ayden's cock and came, shivering as his body washed with chills and his groin burned with pleasure. He hung his head and recuperated, pulling out and needing sleep.

"Wade."

"Huh?" Wade tried to wake from the lethargy of a good climax.

"I love you."

Wade smiled slyly. "Yeah, it's easy to say that after good sex. Been there, done that." He climbed off the bed and removed the condom.

"I mean it."

"I know you do, sweetie." Wade headed to the bathroom to wash up. He tossed the condom and noticed Ayden in the mirror's reflection. Ayden hugged him from behind, getting him coated with his spunk.

The Farmer's Son

"I do." Ayden chewed on Wade's shoulder, meeting his eyes in the mirror. "Do you love me?"

After just a split second to think about it, Wade looked into those innocent young eyes and said, "Yes." *Sure. Why not?*

Just as Ayden was about to spin Wade around to kiss, the sound of a ringtone made Wade halt and listen. "Can I just see who that is?"

"Sure." Ayden released him.

Wade grabbed a towel and wiped the gel and semen off his body as he returned to the bedroom to see who was calling. The ID read 'Corcoran Prison'. He immediately answered it.

"Where were you!"

"Cole. I'm sorry. I tried to get there, but I got turned around in the stupid fog." Wade heard the shower running and sat on the bed, the towel on his lap.

"Are you still near the prison?"

"No. I came home. My car slid into a ditch. It was really fucked up." Guilt hit Wade hard.

"Then you didn't even think to come and see me? At all?"

"Cole." Wade shook his head. "I slept in my car. I just wanted to get back to LA."

"Yeah. Life must be really hard for you, Wade."

Wade could hear the sarcasm. "I'm sorry. But I'm not the one who committed armed robbery."

"Fuck you! I was twenty-two!"

Wade flinched at the number, looking towards the bathroom as he did. "My being there would not have made a difference."

"You don't know that!"

"Cole. Calm down." He heard his brother take a deep breath.

"I hate it here, Wade. No one calls, no one comes to see me. I feel so fucking left out."

"I'm sorry. I should have come by. I just…" Wade looked towards the bathroom again. "I'm sorry."

"When are you going to visit?"

"I don't know." Wade rubbed his face and he heard the water in the shower stop.

"How about next weekend? Come on, Wade. All I have is you."

"Can I let you know?" Wade looked up as Ayden stood at the doorway, a towel around his hips.

"Sure, Wade…sure."

"Cole." Wade heard the line disconnect. "Cole?" He looked at the phone and put it down, exhaling loudly.

"Everything okay?"

"That was my brother. He's upset with me since I never showed up at the hearing…or visited him."

Ayden approached, sitting beside Wade on the bed. "Families…huh."

"I know. Right? Like it's my fault he's in jail?" Wade rubbed his face. "I've never even gotten a speeding ticket. How hard is it to stay the fuck out of trouble?" Wade stood and headed to take his turn in the shower. He looked at his reflection in the bathroom mirror. *I'm not the moron who ended up in jail. You are.*

~

Ayden looked at the fancy cell phone on Wade's nightstand. The sound of the shower running in the bathroom followed the door closing. Ayden picked up the phone and inspected it. As he touched the screen, icons appeared. "Cool." He had seen advertisements for these smartphones as well as the latest computers, on TV and wasn't completely ignorant of their use. Did he want one? He didn't know what he would do with it if he had one.

He thought about calling home, asking for his granddad, but knew that would cause nothing but trouble. Standing, placing the phone down, Ayden held the towel and walked back to the bathroom, opening the door. Steam filled the room and he could see Wade showering through the frosted sliding doors. Ayden hung the towel up and watched him. "You okay?"

As if waking from a daydream, or deep thought, Wade perked up and looked out of the shower door.

"Sorry. Did you want privacy?" Ayden pointed behind him.

"No." The water shut off and Wade reached for a towel, rubbing it over his head. "Is it my fault he's in jail?"

"No." Ayden crossed his arms and leaned against the wall, watching Wade. "It's his fault."

"I should have gone to see him. I should have."

"Now, *that*...is my fault." Ayden pouted.

"No. I'm not blaming anyone but me." Wade dried his back and then under his arms, showing dark tufts of hair that turned Ayden on.

"If you didn't have me tagging along, you may have gone to see him."

"Stop. I can't deal with it." Wade tossed the towel over the shower door and left the room.

Ayden shook his head sadly and wondered why families were so screwed up. When he entered the bedroom Wade had dressed in a pair of pajama bottoms and walked out of the room.

Ayden slipped on clean briefs and followed him.

He found Wade standing at a cabinet, pouring himself a shot of booze. It was dim in the room, which was lit only by a nightlight near the kitchen counter. Ayden had no idea on the time, but if he had to guess, he'd say nine or ten. "Wade." He put his hands on Wade's shoulders from behind.

"I'm fine. He pulls the guilt card on me a lot. No one else even speaks to him."

"Then he should be thankful for you."

Wade looked over his shoulder at him, his eyes appeared glossy, as if he were either upset or very tried.

"Come to bed. I can give you a massage."

"You know how to massage people?" Wade sipped more of the amber liquid.

Ayden shrugged. "Is it complicated? I just thought it was like this." He rubbed Wade's back.

"Oh." Wade smiled and finished the drink, bringing the glass to the sink. "I'm good. Thanks."

Ayden watched him walk out of the room and didn't know how much of Wade's mood was because of him, or if it was all Cole. And he had a feeling he never would know.

Seeing Wade shut off lights, check the front door, and then walk down the hall to the bedroom, Ayden followed until Wade entered the bathroom. He heard Wade brushing his teeth and looked over at the bed, seeing it disheveled from their lovemaking.

Wade finished getting ready for sleep and gestured for Ayden that the bathroom was all his. Ayden had placed his toiletry bag on the sink vanity, and as he brushed his teeth he looked at his reflection. *Life's not easy. Whether you're a city boy or a country boy...it just isn't.*

~

Wade pointed the remote control at a small flat screen TV he had on a bookshelf in his bedroom. In bed, the pillows propping him up, he surfed the channels in vain to find something that did not insult his intelligence. Muting the sound, he used the device to see which movies were available to view and again, was disappointed at the selection. He had champagne tastes in a soda pop world.

Ayden shut the bathroom light and stood by the bed. Seeing Ayden in just his boxer briefs, looking adorable, Wade patted the bed beside him in invitation.

"Are you still upset about Cole?" Ayden climbed under the blankets and snuggled.

"Nope. Over it. I can't hold onto that shit. It'll give me a stroke."

Ayden rested his head on Wade's shoulder. "What are you watching?"

"Nothing." He handed Ayden the remote, curious of what he would choose. "You want a shot?"

"I hate TV."

"Another thing we have in common." Wade handed Ayden the remote and lowered down to rest his head on Ayden's lap, enjoying having a big brawny man in bed with him.

"Nice." Ayden's cock throbbed against Wade's cheek and he caressed Wade's hair.

"Down boy. I've had enough for the night."

"Aww..." Ayden teased.

Getting cozy on Ayden's lap, Wade watched him scroll through the selection, obviously seeing the same crappy television shows as he did—reality bullshit, repeats ten years old, talking heads spouting political excrement...

"There's nothing on." Ayden put the remote down.

"Shut it."

"We could just watch some tolerable old rerun."

"Sure." Wade closed his eyes and tried to decompress. He lied. The phone call with Cole still haunted him.

He heard the familiar character voices of 'Seinfeld' and smiled to himself. "That the best you can do?"

"I can change it."

"No. It's okay." Wade rolled over so he was looking up at Ayden. "I'm surprised you'd watch that."

"It's funny." Ayden shrugged. "The news is depressing and the new shows are stupid."

Wade stared at Ayden. "Maybe we are alike."

"Maybe." Ayden leaned down and kissed him, then stroked Wade's face tenderly. "I can't believe how coarse your beard growth is."

"I know." Wade rubbed his cheek. "It's like sandpaper."

"Mine's not nearly as dark as yours."

"It's all my macho testosterone." Wade chuckled.

Ayden's expression became serious. "You are really masculine."

"Thanks." Wade reached up to tug on Ayden's hair.

In a deep voice Ayden said, "A man's man."

It made Wade laugh. They stared at each other, Ayden using his fingertip to trace Wade's features, down his nose, up his cheekbones…

Wade couldn't recall a moment like this with anyone else. "You're so beautiful."

Ayden's eyebrows raised expressively.

"Yes." Wade didn't want Ayden to deny it.

Ayden pointed the remote at the TV and it quieted. He placed it on the nightstand and lowered down the bed, and they kissed. Wade dug his hand into Ayden's soft hair, closing his eyes and allowing Ayden to lead them in a session of sensual necking. It sure beat the TV.

The Farmer's Son

Chapter 15

Sunday morning the light filtered into the bedroom through the drawn curtains. Ayden wasn't used to sleeping in, and had woken up a few times during the night, but managed to fall back to sleep again.

When he rolled to his back his morning hard-on tented the blanket. Glancing over at Wade as he slept, Ayden touched himself, liking sharing a bed with a man. Liking sharing it with a man like Wade in particular.

Not wanting to wake him, Ayden slowly climbed out of bed, knowing he wouldn't be able to relieve himself until his raging erection softened. So, he picked up his pad, located his favorite drawing pen, and returned to bed. Sitting up, he flipped to a fresh page in his drawing pad, with lines already added for the comic's strip panel, three rows to a page, three boxes to each row.

Ayden began drawing one of his two main characters, thinking of him and Wade in their crime-fighting outfits. Ayden drew Neo Magnay while looking at Wade's features—his wonderful high cheekbones and square jaw, in profile. A mask protected Neo's identity, and Neo was seated behind the wheel of his super-hot-mobile. The pen scratching on the high quality sketchpad was the only noise Ayden could hear. He drew Neo's stern expression, his muscular thighs and his big bulging crotch.

In a balloon he wrote his dialogue. '*Another thug taught a lesson.*' He drew the gadgets of the dashboard—the laser shooters, the stun guns, buttons for flying nets and tranquilizer darts. In the next box he drew Boo. Himself. He was looking at Neo as Neo drove. '*Yes. Another win for same-sex couples everywhere...I'm horny.*' Ayden sketched Boo, his teeth showing in a sensual snarl, his hard cock visible through his tight costume.

In the background of the drawing, outside of the interior of the super-mobile, Ayden made the car look as if it was driving fast, maybe flying down a super-highway, darkening the sky with his blue pen.

In the third box he drew Boo exposing Neo's huge cock from his clothing. '*Now?*' Neo asked, looking down in panic. '*I'm driving!*'

At the sensual cartoons, Ayden's cock throbbed. He bit his lower lip as he drew Neo's perfect cut dick in detail—an enormous rod with a mushroom-shaped head and dripping slit, his balls visible outside his costume.

Ayden shaded it in, the blue ink staining the heel of his palm, like it usually did when he drew too quickly. Giving the ink a minute to dry, he teethed on the back of the pen and ogled his own drawing, getting off. The next box in the cartoon he sketched Boo's head on Neo's lap, '*mmm!*' in the dialogue balloon above Boo's act. Ayden drew the car interior, being consistent, adding all the buttons and dials. The next panel he drew Neo's reaction, a look of shock on his face and in big letters indicating actions, instead of '*BAM!*' "*POW!*" he wrote, '*SLURP!*' '*SUCK!*'

Ayden grew crazy. He put the pen in his mouth, crosswise and stared at the comic as he pulled on his cock. He could come. Just remembering sucking Wade in the car, he could so easily come.

Capping the pen, putting the pad and pen on the nightstand, Ayden lowered the blankets to see Wade's naked torso and knelt beside him, jerking off as he stared at his rounded chest and the hair covering his sternum.

Wade's eyes slowly opened. When he noticed a cock about to blow its load on him, he looked up at Ayden in surprise.

"I gotta come." Ayden jerked his cock, riding the edge.

"Come!" Wade rolled to his back and reached out as if to catch what was about to hit.

Ayden came all over Wade's chest, spattering Wade's hand and splashing white cream against Wade's neck and shoulder.

"Sorry." Ayden panted, milking his cock. "Christ."

Wade blinked and looked down at himself in amazement. "I would have helped you. Why didn't you wake me up?"

"I was too far gone." Ayden stumbled out of the bed. "Christ, you get me so hot!" He closed himself into the bathroom.

~

Wade peered down at the mess and wiped at it in vain. He sat up and shook his head in amazement. Climbing out of bed, trying not to get cum on anything, he noticed the sketch pad and before he headed to the second bathroom he walked around the bed and looked down at it. Seeing what Ayden had drawn—and drawn so damn well!—Wade cracked up with laughter. "Oh, babe. You are one amazing cartoonist. I have got to get someone to see these. They are too much!" He leaned closer to have a good look at the lines. No pencil rough sketch. It astonished him. Then he realized something. Neo looked like him. A lot like him. Laughing and loving the compliment, Wade headed to the spare bathroom to wash up and when he looked at himself in the mirror he couldn't stop smiling. "That boy is gold." He washed his sticky skin and kept cracking up.

By the time Wade returned to the bedroom, Ayden was naked in bed, on his belly, legs spread. He peeked at Wade and smiled wickedly.

Wade stopped short and admired the sight. "I can get used to this."

"Get used to it." Ayden smiled dreamily and reached out his hand.

Wade sat next to him on the bed, riding his palm from Ayden's hair to his bottom.

"Want in?" Ayden wriggled.

"I'm good. Probably later." Wade tilted his head to the sketch pad. "I cannot get over how good you draw."

"I got a little carried away. I don't know if art that sexual will be sellable."

"Oh yeah, it is. We just have to find out where." Wade propped his head up on his palm and cupped Ayden's ass, his perfect tight ass. "Do you work out?"

"Huh? Work out? You mean like in a gym?"

"Yes."

"Hell no. You know how hard working on the orchard is?"

"Was?"

"Oh." Ayden rubbed his face against the pillow. "Hmm."

"Hmm." Wade scooted closer and caressed Ayden's broad back and shoulders, then down to his cute bottom again.

"Do you work out?" Ayden asked.

"Yup. I don't cut down trees for a living."

"I guess neither do I. Anymore."

Wade touched the soft hair on the backs of Ayden's thighs. Ayden parted his legs as if inviting him to play.

"Nope. You don't either." Wade inched closer, eye level with Ayden's bottom, admiring it. "You'll have to go to the gym like the rest of us pencil pushers." He stroked between Ayden's legs. "Or you'll lose this fantastic physique."

"I have a nice body?"

"You know you do." Wade climbed over Ayden spread leg, wedging between Ayden's thighs so he could kiss his butt as he fondled it.

"No, I don't know I do. Other than looking in the mirror and imagining I'm another guy."

Wade thought about it while he nibbled Ayden's bottom. "Have you jerked off to your own image?"

Ayden didn't answer, hiding his face in the pillow.

"It's okay, baby. You were the only man you had to admire." Wade licked Ayden's low back making his way down, smelling his shower gel and clean skin.

"I'm so embarrassed I did that."

"Don't be. You're a young man with a high libido and no way to get sex. Other than your hot artwork. Man, you can draw a cock like I've never seen before." Wade burrowed into Ayden's crack and moaned.

Ayden laughed. "Tickles." He spread his knees wider. "Have you seen many cartoon dicks?"

"A few online. After we have breakfast we'll do some research." Wade lapped his tongue over Ayden's rim.

"Am I your breakfast?"

"Maybe." Wade parted Ayden's cheeks and loved everything about this man's body. He wetted his rim with more saliva and massaged his thumb over it.

"That just puts me over the moon." Ayden moaned and tried to get to his knees.

Wade looked at his pajama bottoms. His cock was tenting the fabric. "Yeah. It's having the same effect on me."

"Got lube?"

Wade cracked up with laughter. "You're insatiable."

"I'm horny as hell. Been saving it for years for you."

"I'm beginning to believe that." Wade slipped off his bottoms and reached for the lubrication.

"So, you don't like to actually get fucked?"

"Not really. I like a prostate rub, don't get me wrong." Wade tipped the lubrication onto his fingers. "But I just prefer topping. Why? You aching to fuck me?"

"Not aching. No. If you don't want it, I'm okay with that."

"I'll think about it."

"No need. I said I like the arrangement."

Wade did too. He coated Ayden's balls in slippery gel and ran them through his fingers, working his way along the root of Ayden's hard cock to his rim.

"Damn!" Ayden bucked his hips. "I will never get out of this bed!"

"Like a boy with a new toy." Wade used his thumb to rub Ayden's rim in circular motion.

"Do all guys know about that inside spot?"

"Don't know. I suppose the smart ones do." Wade pushed his thumb inside Ayden and Ayden moaned and arched his back.

"I'm going to get cum all over your bed."

"I need to change the sheets anyway." Wade continued to toy with Ayden's hanging balls as he made his way inside him.

"Wade, I swear!"

"I know, Ayden. I know. It's a drug." Wade ran his fingers lightly along the length of Ayden's stiff cock, but knew he didn't have to jerk it to make him come. As the act heated up, Wade considered putting on a condom. He hadn't had this much great sex since college.

Working his fingers into Ayden, Wade felt him relax and heard Ayden moan into the pillow. *Fuck it.* Wade reached for the strip of condoms and heard Ayden chuckle. "Shut up." He swatted Ayden's bottom with a playful *crack*!

"Yowza!" Ayden glanced over his shoulder. "I heard about spanking."

The Farmer's Son

"Don't even!" Wade pointed at him in warning as he rolled a condom on.

"Why not? I'm willing to try it all."

"I'll bet you are, superhero." Wade knelt behind Ayden and used the head of his cock to run up and down Ayden's crack, dipping inside him and pulling out again to play.

"One more swat. Come on."

Wade laughed. "Fine." He spanked Ayden with a good slap on his bottom and pushed inside him more deeply. "Well?"

"Still thinking about it."

"Think about this." Wade rocked inside Ayden's body, getting great friction and penetration. "This one's for me."

"Unfair."

"I'll get you after." Wade held Ayden by his hips and watched the act of penetration, getting off on it. "Feel good?"

"Mm."

"Then moan like a whore."

Ayden cracked up with laughter and complied. "Oh, yes! Fuck me! Yes!"

Knowing it was for fun, Wade chuckled, then tuned into the sex, ramping up the tempo and depth.

"Yes! Wade! Like that! Oh, yes! God, yes!"

Ayden was giving a convincing performance. Wade was on the edge in no time.

"Yes! Wade! Fuck me! Fuck me hard!"

Before he could control it, Wade came, closing his eyes and pushing in deeper, feeling his cock throb in the tight heat. He heard a mischievous snicker and smiled, shaking his head.

~

Once Wade pulled out, Ayden rolled to his back to see Wade removing the condom. He looked down at himself, at his own hard cock and gave it a tug.

"Hang on." Wade left the room and Ayden heard the sink in the bathroom running.

"Want more." Ayden spread his legs and closed his eyes.

"Spoiled brat."

"I know." Ayden smiled.

Wade returned and stood by his nightstand, opening the drawer. Before Ayden could ask why, Wade removed a dildo. Ayden's eyes widened and he didn't know what to say.

"Ever use one?" Wade coated it with lubrication.

"No. You kidding? Can you imagine the grief I'd get when someone found it?"

"Open up." Wade leaned on the bed beside Ayden and tapped his thigh.

"You sound like my dentist." Ayden spread his legs, toying with his own cock.

"You're about to get drilled."

The cool gel made Ayden jump, but he soon relaxed. As Wade worked the phallus into him gently, he sucked on Ayden's cock.

Ayden released his own hold and splayed out on the bed. "You know so much..."

"Too much." Wade turned on the dildo and Ayden felt a vibration and warmth, right where he wanted to feel it.

"Oh my." Ayden closed his eyes.

Wade held Ayden's dick by the base and pushed the dildo in and out gently as he sucked Ayden's cock as deep as he could.

With the hum of the dildo inside his bottom, Ayden felt the urge to climax hit quickly. "Wade, unreal."

Wade fisted Ayden's cock into his mouth, pushing the dildo in and out in time with his sucks. Before Ayden could announce he was there, he went into a tailspin. He came and thrust his hips up in reflex, feeling pure pleasure from his ass to the tip of his cock, and then reverberations all over his body.

THE FARMER'S SON

Ayden parted his lips to savor the climax. "Love you...love you..." he huffed.

He heard Wade laugh. "Come on. We need to function. I head back to work tomorrow, and I want you to have homework to do...i.e. submissions!"

"Emissions."

Wade started laughing as he walked into the bathroom.

Ayden opened his eyes and grinned dreamily at the ceiling. "I'm in heaven."

~

After eating a nice breakfast that Wade had prepared of eggs, toast, and home fried potatoes, Ayden sat beside Wade at his computer, which was situated in a spare bedroom.

With a notepad and pen in his hand, Ayden waited for instructions. He had no clue how to get his cartoons published, but wasn't intimidated. He had learned how to maintain farm equipment by reading the manuals. How hard could anything be if you had a 'How to' guide?

Wade tapped keys and appeared dead serious. "Hm."

"Yes?"

"Well, it doesn't look easy. Writing comic books isn't an open field. I mean, maybe for straight comic characters...but..."

Ayden studied the computer screen. "Tell me what you are looking for."

"Publishers." Wade put in different words into a search engine.

"Like Marvel?"

"Yes."

"No way, Wade. They wouldn't even look at my work. I mean, they're the big guys."

"Somehow they must have a way in." Wade picked up his phone and tapped buttons, putting it to his ear.

"Can I try?" Ayden pointed to the keyboard.

Wade stood up and gestured for him to sit down. As Ayden hunted for something else, entering 'erotic gay comics' into the search, he gulped in awe at the images that appeared. "Whoa!"

"Hey, Simon?" Wade said into his phone as he leaned down to see what Ayden had found. "That ain't gonna help," he said to Ayden and took a step away. "Do you have a minute?" he asked into the phone.

Ayden looked over his shoulder and then investigated the naughty drawings. "Wow." He loved this kind of kinky art and licked his lips at the exaggerated sizes of the cocks as they protruded from cartoon men's bodies.

"Look, do you know anyone in the publishing biz?" Wade touched Ayden's shoulder.

Ayden tried not to get embarrassed since he was supposed to be searching for work, not getting off on ogling pictures. But it wasn't as if he had a computer to do this type of thing with previously. So, he typed in 'nude gay men', and waited to see what came up.

"Ayden is a very talented cartoonist, but he draws gay sexy superheroes. I'm at a loss as to where to get him help to publish."

Ayden peeked back at Wade. Wade saw what he was doing and shook his head as if Ayden was a naughty boy. He was one. And seeing gay porn? Images of men fucking and sucking? Ayden knew if he owned his own computer he'd be busy all day…getting, uh…inspired.

"I have no clue, Simon. But I swear, if you could see Ayden's drawings…they're…"

Ayden's cheeks blushed at the content of the site he was watching. He took another look over his shoulder and noticed Wade giving him an exaggerated gape of shock.

Ayden closed down the kinky site, cleared his throat and went back to hunting down the publishing pages.

The Farmer's Son

As if in reaction to Ayden's diversion, Wade whacked him on the shoulder. "Kidding. Just don't go to a chat site. Then I will be pissed."

"Huh?" Ayden asked, "Chat site?"

Wade went back to the call. "Look, just ask around. We both know what it's like. It's who you know."

Chat site? Ayden didn't want to chat. He had Wade to have sex with and love. Who would he chat with?

"Why are you so hyped to meet him?" Wade asked Simon, but Ayden could hear the smile in his voice.

"I'll let you know what our schedule is like. Maybe next weekend, if…"

Ayden met Wade's gaze.

"If I don't go visit Cole." Wade's smile faded. As Wade left the room to talk privately, Ayden heard him say, "He gave me a real guilt trip, Simon…"

Ayden sighed sadly and returned his attention back to hunting for a way in. *Where there's a will, there's a way.*

~

Wade stood in the hall and said, "I should have seen him, Simon. I was just thrown for a loop after meeting Ayden."

"I'll bet. What's he look like? Come on, Wade."

Wade smiled. "Tall, built like a truck, and blue eyes."

"Tats?"

"Nope."

"Damn."

"You'll make Michael jealous. Let me go. I have to figure this out or Ayden's going to be bored all week while I'm at work."

"Uh oh…idle hands…you know what they say."

"Shut up. Bye." Wade looked down at his phone and noticed a missed call. He sighed in annoyance. He hit dial and walked to the kitchen, shutting off the coffee pot and dumping the remainder into the sink.

"Wade."

"Hi, Mom."

"What happened at the parole hearing?"

"If you and dad went to the prison, you'd know." He dumped the filter and grounds.

"Don't be smart."

"He didn't get it. He's really upset no one will see him. Would it really be too much for you and dad to just visit him? Come on, Mom. He's been punished for sixteen years in that hole."

"He deserves it."

Wade wiped his hand on a dishtowel and leaned on the counter. "I may go next weekend. Come with me."

"Oh, I don't know."

"Mom. Cole is still a member of the family."

"No. He's a criminal. He's a terrible man."

"He was twenty-two." Wade looked in the direction of Ayden.

"You didn't do drugs! You didn't use a weapon to rob people!"

"Right. Whatever. Then why do you care if he got parole?"

"Because if he did, he'd come here. Your father and I don't want him here."

"Oh." Wade ran his hand over his hair in exhaustion. "Well, nice to know he's got the support of the family."

"You take him in! You're single."

"I've got a boyfriend living with me. So, no. I'm not."

"Since when? Did you and Simon get back together?"

"Nope. Look, I am busy right now."

"You're always busy."

The Farmer's Son

"Now you know how Cole feels. Bye." He hung up and stood still, trying to decompress after the conversation. He was as bad as his parents. But Cole was not the victim here, he was the suspect.

~

When Wade returned Ayden had located a website for comic book art. He waved Wade closer. "Check this out."

Wade leaned on the chair behind him to read the screen.

"Any gay friendly?" Wade asked.

"Um. They don't say...exactly."

"Well, go ahead and try. What have you got to lose?"

Ayden nodded and then watched Wade carefully. "You okay?"

"Yeah. Look, I need to go food shopping, hit the gym, you know."

"Okay. I don't want to interfere."

"You can either stay here or come."

"You mind if I tag along?"

"Nope." Wade gave him a smile.

Ayden felt relieved. "How do I save this?" He pointed to the screen.

Wade used the mouse, leaning against Ayden from behind, and printed off the information. Ayden closed his eyes and leaned back against him, wanting him. Probably way too much.

"Don't ever go to jail," Wade whispered into his ear.

Ayden smiled. "Don't worry. I won't."

Chapter 16

Wade enjoyed the companionship.

Ayden's innocence was pure fun. Even food shopping was an experience. As Wade tugged their cart along the aisles, picking items off the shelves, Ayden played like a kid in a toy store, juggling oranges, going out for a long pass and catching boxes of cereal, and appearing to love being…free?

Free to be normal? Free to not wake at four a.m. and be saddled with work he did not want to do, with a family that did not like him?

Wade could only wonder, and again, thought of Cole. But Cole was in jail…perhaps Ayden was confined against his will in his own way.

After they returned home to stock the kitchen with fresh supplies, Wade changed into his workout clothing. "Time to get you a membership."

"Yeah?" Ayden yanked his shirt over his head, making his shaggy hair a delicious mess.

If Wade were honest with himself, he wanted to show this beauty off. He'd been a regular at the fitness center in West Hollywood for years, and most of the pretty young things there wanted other 'pretty young things'. There were some younger men with a taste for older guys, but usually they were shallow and looking to be 'kept' financially while they cheated with other men their age.

The Farmer's Son

Wade glanced at Ayden as he tugged a pair of sweatpants up his long, muscular legs. Ayden didn't want to be kept. Quite the opposite. Yet now it was Wade who wanted to 'keep' him.

Taking Ayden to the gym was also a test. A test to see how Ayden would react to men his own age, ogling, leering, and most likely propositioning him.

So far, Wade was impressed with Ayden's attention. The farmer's son did not have a roving eye. But he'd been in LA all of one day.

When Ayden slipped a worn out faded gray T-shirt over his head, sleeves cut off and torn at the chest, Wade stopped short.

"No good?" Ayden touched the material. "Too ratty?"

The silk screening of a sports logo had nearly worn off the front, and the material was so thin and tight, Wade could see all of Ayden's sculpted muscles through it. He finished putting on his tank top and walked across the bedroom towards Ayden. "Love it."

"Love it? This old piece of shit?" Ayden laughed and brushed the hair out of his eyes.

"It's sexy as hell." Wade glanced down at Ayden's crotch in the dark blue sweats. "You're sexy as hell."

Ayden's eyes widened and his arm muscles flexed, as if he were trying to digest the compliment. Before Wade could get out another word, Ayden tackled him to the freshly made bed and rolled around with him on it.

Wade smiled in delight and said, "Be more fun after. When we're pumped."

"I'm pumped." Ayden grabbed his own crotch.

"You've got a never-ending supply of spunk. I know."

"Aw," Ayden pouted at being denied.

"You horny, baby?" Wade kissed his forehead.

In proof, Ayden flipped out his hard dick.

Wade stared at it. "I take that as a yes."

"I can just jack off on you." Ayden knelt up, already tugging on his cock.

"I got ya." Wade wrestled him back to the bed and scooted down to suck on his man. He closed his eyes and held the base tight, wanting this to be quick since it was growing late and he knew the gym would be swamped on a Sunday.

"Yes...oh yes." Ayden gripped Wade's head and held tight as Wade dug into Ayden's sweatpants and rubbed friction under his balls. Even quicker than he anticipated he tasted Ayden's cum. He blinked and slowed down his suction, milking him and cupping Ayden's balls. He leaned up on his elbows and looked at Ayden as he lay still, catching his breath. "To be twenty-two again."

"I've been going crazy since the grocery store."

"The grocery store got you hot?" Wade sat up and tucked Ayden's cock back into his clothing.

"Knowing I had the best fucker in the place did."

"Over the top, cookie." Wade laughed and hopped out of bed, headed to the bathroom to check his appearance.

"No. Not if I love you, it's not!" Ayden called from the bed.

Wade smiled at his reflection and couldn't recall seeing himself this happy. Ayden appeared in the reflection and held Wade from behind. "Love me?"

"Do I." Wade did. "A lot."

~

On their way to the gym, cruising the sunny streets of LA, Ayden relaxed in the passenger's side of the BMW.

He had packed a small nylon bag with his change of clothing and a towel inside it. It was at the floor by his feet. Wade drove them down Sunset Boulevard, and Ayden was getting a sense that he was living in a fantasy, and this kind of life could not be reality. Since he was five he had been trained to help on the family orchard, and although he did enjoy some of the work, he

The Farmer's Son

hated to admit, if it wasn't for feeling like an outsider, he may not have wanted to leave.

Now he knew why. He wondered if the question of who his real father really was, would ever been answered. And if he did find out? What then?

When they passed the gym, Ayden could see windows on the second level of the building with men running on treadmills along the interior glass. After a search for street parking, Wade found a spot a few blocks away and stopped Ayden from getting out immediately.

Ayden stared at him curiously.

"This is West Hollywood. So, don't be surprised at the assertiveness."

"What assertiveness?"

"The way some men will behave."

"Like how?" Ayden didn't want any trouble. "I'm your man."

"Come here." Wade cupped the back of Ayden's head and pulled him to his lips, smiling at him. "Let's go."

Ayden picked up the gym bag and walked with Wade down the street. The air was cool and a strong breeze blew from the west. The palm trees waved and spun their fronds high above the buildings, and the area was overflowing with pedestrians. Ayden wasn't used to so much humanity—every shape, size, color, and not a flannel shirt or denim blue jacket as far as his eye could see.

He followed Wade up the staircase and could hear loud music and see men working out through the glass panes. As he drew closer to the entrance, level with the gym, Ayden caught eyes through the windows and could already understand exactly what Wade had said was true. These men were not shy or covert in their admiration.

Wade dropped his gym bag on the floor near a desk and greeted the man standing behind it. "Joe, this is my partner, Ayden. I want to sign him up."

"Okay, Wade." The man produced a clipboard and pen. "Can you fill this out, Ayden?"

Ayden put his gym bag on the floor between his feet and picked up the pen, writing his information in boxes. He leaned on Wade and whispered, "What's your address?"

Purring, Wade pressed his mouth to Ayden's ear and told him, sending chills rushing up Ayden's spine it was so sexy. As he heard the information, he wrote it.

Joe said, "You new around here? I've not seen you before."

"From the Valley." Ayden continued to work on his form.

"Silicon Valley?"

"No. Great Central," Wade replied for him.

"Yeah? Never been there. What's there?" Joe asked.

"Almonds." Ayden smiled and peeked at Wade. He kept ticking boxes, most about his health, potential issues that would make him topple over and die, of course without the gym being held responsible. As he did, he heard Wade and Joe discussing him.

"When did you guys meet?"

"Recently."

"He's adorable, Wade."

"Yeah. He is."

Ayden blushed and didn't look up from his form, signing it.

"What membership does he want?" Joe looked at the information Ayden had supplied.

"Same as mine. Just do the deductions with mine."

"Mm. Twenty-two?" Joe batted his eyelashes flirtatiously but Ayden didn't think he was handsome. "Daddy's little boy?"

"Huh?" Ayden took offense and puffed up.

The Farmer's Son

"Never mind." Wade tugged Ayden to come along. "We'll stop by on the way out for his membership card."

"Okay, Wade."

Ayden snarled at Joe and followed Wade into a locker area, which was loaded with men changing and chatting, showers running in the background, echoing on the white tile.

Wade tugged open a locker and tossed in his bag, wallet, keys, and cell phone. "Don't take that the wrong way, Ayden. That's what I was talking about."

"I don't even know my real father."

"He meant me." Wade shut the locker and took the tiny key out of the lock.

"Huh? You?" Ayden opened the locker under Wade's and stuffed his bag in. "You're not—" Ayden got it. "That's gross."

"It's just slang for our age difference. I don't give a shit, so don't you."

"You're way younger than my dad!" Ayden thought about it. He had no idea how old his real dad was. He dropped down to sit on a bench that was in the middle of the row of lockers and rubbed his face in frustration.

Wade shut Ayden's locker and handed him the tiny key, then sat beside him. "We don't care. Right?"

"Right." Ayden felt distracted and wanted to confront his mother again.

"Ayd?" Wade touched his cheek.

It woke Ayden out of his thoughts. He stood and tucked the tiny key into the pocket of his sweats. "I'm ready. I'll do your workout since I don't have one."

"You got it, champ." Wade grabbed Ayden behind the neck and shook him playfully.

As they walked out of the locker a man yelled, "Wade! Who's the movie star?" and whistled.

"Good taste, Reed!" another man shouted.

"Does he have a twin?"

Ayden felt his cheeks go red. Although Wade had tried to warn him, Ayden had no idea gay men would be this comfortable around each other, that they had no inhibitions about what they said, or to whom.

Wade touched the small of Ayden's back to guide him out of the room, seeing Wade only smile in return at the teasing.

"I warm up first on the treadmill. But seeing they're packed, how about the row machines?"

"Good." Ayden rubbed his arms self-consciously, feeling as if everyone was staring at him. "The guys in this place know you well, huh, Wade?"

"Yup. Been coming nearly every day for four years." Wade sat on a row machine and gestured for Ayden to sit on the one beside him.

Ayden sat down on the plastic molded seat and mimicked Wade's movements as he placed his feet onto pedals with straps.

"Ayden."

"Huh?" He turned to look at Wade.

"You okay?"

"Sure." Ayden didn't know.

"You want to leave?"

"No. I'm good." He gave the area a scan and noticed several men eying him, a few boldly talking about him. Focusing on the workout, Ayden muttered to Wade out of the side of his mouth, "Ya get used to the ogling, right?"

"Yup, 'Boo'. You do." Wade picked up the handle and began pulling, 'rowing' on the machine.

Ayden matched his stride and stared at the gauges on the machine, ignoring the leering men around him.

~

Wade didn't know whether to be impressed or suspicious. Ayden didn't so much as meet the gaze of another man throughout their workout, giving him his undivided attention, and only nodding briefly at other men who approached Wade for an introduction.

It was obvious Ayden was overwhelmed. Coming from a home where 'gayness' was frowned upon and landing at the end of a rainbow in West Hollywood, land of the free-sex and home of the gay. Wade wondered if, once Ayden was used to being the object of desire, if he would shrug indifferently, or begin to stray.

Trust. Wade had to have it or he'd lose his mind. So far, Ayden had been perfect. He had no reason to complain or doubt him.

After a grueling workout, they headed to the locker room, both dripping in sweat from nearly an hour of rowing, lifting weights, and running on the treadmill.

Wade opened his locker and took off his workout clothing. As he did, he noticed Ayden peek.

"Down boy." Wade chuckled.

"Um. I've never been naked in a locker room like this. I mean, with gay guys. In high school, yeah."

"And?" Wade took his bag out and removed clean clothing and a towel.

"Um."

"Stay in your briefs. Take them off in the shower stall." He noticed Ayden glance around in paranoia. Wade took a look and spotted a couple of men waiting for the show. Wade shook his head at them. "Come on, guys. A little tact?"

"Oh! Isn't she on the rag." The man turned up his nose and left with his friend.

Wade checked back with Ayden. "Keep your briefs on. It's okay."

"I feel like a baby." Ayden took off his soaked shirt.

"You're not. You're just not used to it." Wade kissed Ayden's shoulder, tasted salt and licked it with the tip of his tongue playfully.

It made Ayden smile, and that was all Wade wanted. "You beautiful man."

"Stop." Ayden's cheeks grew crimson with his smile, and he dropped his sweatpants down his legs.

"Knew I'd find you here."

Wade spun around at the sound of Simon's voice. "You're unbelievable." Wade suspected his ex was dying to see his new beau, but he didn't think he'd stalk him. He spotted Michael beside Simon, not looking pleased his boyfriend hunted his ex-lover down.

Wade tried to make light of the situation. "Ayden, this is Simon and Michael."

"Hi." Ayden, even though he was still wearing his briefs, Ayden held the towel in front of his crotch.

"Hubba hubba! Wade Reed! I am so damn jealous!" Simon gave Ayden a good once over.

Knowing Ayden was already struggling, Wade nudged him. "Go shower."

Ayden nodded and held the nylon bag in his arms with the towel and left the three of them.

Simon watched Ayden walk away and shook his head. "Oh. My. God."

Wade said, "You're making your boyfriend jealous."

Michael folded his arms over his chest and rolled his eyes in annoyance. "I'm used to it."

"He's delicious!" Simon moved closer to Wade to speak softly. "Let's all go out to dinner."

"I just went food shopping. And we only have tonight on our own before I head back to work in the morning." Wade wrapped the towel around his hips.

THE FARMER'S SON

"Aww, you are so cute." Simon puckered his lips mockingly. "Afraid he'll be tempted?"

"Nope. He's not you." Wade walked passed them to shower, smirking as he did.

~

Ayden hung the little nylon bag up on a hook and stepped into a shower stall. Another hook inside the tiny space was where he placed his towel. He took off his briefs and draped them over the rod, then turned on the water and noticed two dispensers on the wall, one read 'shower gel', the other, 'shampoo'. The water was warm immediately and Ayden wetted down, trying to feel comfortable around gay men. This was what he wanted. Why he started drawing his comic heroes. So gay men could be themselves.

He'd get used to it. He just had to let go of his shyness. He soaped his chest and stared at his arms and legs. Compared to the other guys working out, he was a big man. Not muscle-bound like some of the tattooed heavy-hitters, but big. Taller than most. Since he was not used to actually lifting weights and doing rowing or treadmill machines, his body felt fatigued but good. He was happy to work out with Wade, very happy, and knew he'd miss the physical routine at the orchard very much if he became lazy.

Ayden also thought about having an ex-boyfriend who wanted to see the new man so much, he actually hunted for him.

Was Ayden jealous? Maybe. Not that Wade would ever cheat on him. No. Ayden was jealous of the fact that Simon was so comfortable in LA, and with the culture.

I'll get there.

I have Wade. Ayden smiled and rinsed, shutting the water and taking his towel off the hook to dry himself. Once he had, he reached for the bag hanging outside his stall, and dressed behind the curtain. His wet towel and sweaty briefs in the bag, Ayden pulled back the curtain and headed to where he had left Wade.

Wade was using the towel to dry his hair, naked, while Simon and Michael stood and spoke to him. Ayden bristled slightly, wanting Wade's body to be his, not public.

Wade spotted him and smiled, then seeing something in Ayden's expression, he cocked his head. "Okay. Who propositioned you?"

Simon and Michael spun around to look at him.

"No one." Ayden dropped his bag near Wade and pressed his mouth to Wade's ear. "I don't like anyone else seeing you naked."

"Ahh. Okay." Wade grinned happily and reached to get dressed.

"What did he say?" Simon leaned on a locker, arms crossed, pouting.

Ayden sat down on the bench, using the towel to dry off his feet, and then put on his socks and shoes.

"Nothing. So, no. We don't want to go to dinner. Stop asking." Wade tucked his shirt into his jeans and tossed his towel on the bench.

Ayden peered up at Simon, then Michael, seeing them both staring at him. He was glad Wade didn't want to go out to dinner with them. He and Wade had just met. The last thing Ayden wanted to do was go out with men who knew Wade better than he did.

"Ayden," Simon said, poking him. "I hear you're an amazing artist."

Ayden rolled his towel up again and stuffed it into the bag. "Not amazing." Modest of his talent, Ayden looked down at his tennis shoes.

"I'd like to see your work," Simon said, "then I can say I knew you before you were famous."

The Farmer's Son

Ayden looked up at Simon. He was smirking. The guy was only around five foot seven with closely cropped brown hair, clean shaven, and dark brown eyes. Simon did not appeal to Ayden at all. Neither did his boyfriend, Michael, who had his head shaven and a black goatee, and was also quite small in stature. Both men were well-dressed, however, in tailored clothing and wore gold rings and earrings. Should he be envious of that? He wasn't.

Ayden stood and picked up his gym bag. "We good to go?"

"We are." Wade closed the locker after stuffing his wallet, phone, and keys into his pockets. He too crammed his towel and gym clothing into his bag to take home.

"Nice meeting you, Ayden." Simon held out his hand.

Trying to be polite, Ayden shook it and said, "You too." He nodded to Michael, who did not offer his hand, and followed Wade out of the gym.

They stopped at the desk and Ayden was given two membership cards, one was credit-card sized, the other a tiny plastic tab to attach to his keys. Both had a barcode.

"Just scan it right there every time you come in." Joe pointed to a scanner.

"Okay." Ayden put both cards into his wallet and he and Wade left the gym, trotting down the stairs as men walked up, passing them.

Once they were on street level, Wade put his arm around Ayden's waist. "Sorry about Simon."

"It's not your fault. But I can tell he still wants you."

"I don't want him." Wade tugged Ayden closer as they shared the sidewalk, allowing pedestrians to walk by, coming from the opposite direction.

Ayden wondered on how love could fail and trust could be shattered. Was it that hard to maintain a relationship? If he and

Wade continued to treat each other this well, why would Ayden want anyone else?

Once they were seated in the BMW, Ayden asked, "Did he ever say why he cheated?"

"I never asked." Wade started the car and pulled out of the parking space.

Ayden dropped the gym bag at his feet. "I wonder why people move on? I mean, what happens to love?"

"It goes away. I don't know why." Wade put his hand on Ayden's leg.

"I don't want this love to go away."

Wade smiled at him sadly and held his hand as he drove them home.

~

Wade cooked up sea scallops as Ayden made salad with at least a dozen fresh vegetables they had picked up from the market. Mellow music on in the background, Wade snapped off the stems of the asparagus to steam. He glanced at Ayden as Ayden sliced cucumber and peppers, and tossed them into a large bowl. "You okay?"

"Huh?" Ayden looked up.

"You've been very quiet since we got home from the gym."

"I'm okay. I like making dinner. Mom always did, and when I tried to help her, I got teased for doing 'woman's work.'"

"That's absurd. Do you know how many top chefs are men?"

Ayden shrugged, getting back to his salad preparation.

"So, look, tomorrow...I head out at around eight. I could leave you my cell phone."

"No. I'm good. I was going to look up more comic book submission sites on the computer and do some more drawings for my portfolio."

"Check to see what each publisher requires. I'm sure each company has its own set of rules."

THE FARMER'S SON

"I noticed that. That's why I need to revise some of my sketches. Oh, and they say not to send originals."

"We'll get quality copies made."

Ayden nodded, washing and trimming radishes.

Then he got quiet again.

Wade wiped his hands on a dish towel and headed to the cabinet. He removed a bottle of whiskey and poured two small glasses, placing one near Ayden and sipping his, trying not to be concerned.

"Thanks," Ayden said, then asked, "What is it?"

"Whiskey."

Ayden's nose curled in reaction.

"I thought it might relax you."

"Fucking you will relax me." Ayden smiled.

"Okay, babe. That's our dessert."

Ayden dumped the sliced radishes into the bowl and wiped his hands on a towel. "That's everything."

"Looks awesome." Wade put the glass he was holding down. "Just set it on the table and I'll get the scallops baking." He placed the small casserole dish into the oven and turned the burner on the stove to steam the asparagus.

Once he made sure Ayden had everything he needed, Wade joined him at the dining table and scooped out the salad for each of them. He knew something was bothering Ayden, but didn't want to pester him. Leaving the family orchard and coming to LA was a big change for Ayden, and Wade knew it would take time for them to adjust to each other, and the circumstance.

But in Wade's opinion? It was going better than he expected. Ayden was so easy going, he just couldn't foresee a problem.

~

Ayden ate the light meal, devoid of heavy creams, mass carbohydrates and butter. He was aware his mother's home-style cooking was high in calories but he and his brothers burned it off quickly with the physical labor. When he stood to help Wade clear the table and wash the dishes, he could hear his father's degrading words in his head but ignored them.

Washing dishes did not make him less of a man. That was insane. Ayden tried not to become preoccupied with what he had left behind, but the longer he was away from it, the worse it became, not better. There were too many unanswered questions and bad feelings. And he missed his granddad, terribly.

When the kitchen had been placed in perfect order, Wade reached out his hand to Ayden and beckoned him to the bedroom. After dimming the light, Wade undressed and turned down the bed, climbing in and waiting for Ayden.

Ayden folded his clothing up neatly and crawled in beside Wade in bed. Instead of them going into a heated passionate act, Wade drew Ayden close, holding him, comforting him, as if he sensed Ayden's mood.

Ayden curled around Wade, closing his eyes, suddenly fighting back emotions he never expected to hit. Wade kissed his head and stroked his hair lovingly.

"It's okay, baby. It's okay."

At the sympathy, and the telepathic way Wade knew, just knew, the state Ayden was in, Ayden hid his face in Wade's neck and hot tears rolled down his cheek.

"We'll work everything out. You just give us some time." Wade squeezed him, kissing his hair.

Ayden didn't know if he believed he and his family could ever work this out. But the sense of grief at losing them, as if they had all died suddenly, was killing him.

"Don't worry." Wade rubbed his arm warmly. "Somehow we'll work it out."

Ayden nodded against Wade's neck, but he doubted it. Very much.

The Farmer's Son

Chapter 17

Monday morning Wade entered his office, greeting people as he did.

"Hello, handsome!" Abby approached him, a cup of coffee in her hand.

"Hey, sweet-cheeks. How was your weekend?"

"Eh. How was yours? Did your brother get parole?"

"No. He did not. And I missed the damn hearing." Wade entered his office and turned his computer on.

Abby stood at his office door. "No. I'm sorry, Wade. What happened? Did you get caught in traffic?"

"No. My navigation system screwed up and I ended up on a muddy road in a ditch."

"I've heard of that shit happening. I hate those things. You can't trust them. Oh well, life sucks, then ya die." She sipped her coffee.

"Hey, Abbs, you know of any publishers of gay comic books?"

"Huh? Gay comic books? I haven't a clue. Why?"

"Can you ask around for me? I wish I knew someone in the biz." Wade picked up his coffee mug with the intentions of filling it in the lounge.

Abby backed up to allow him to leave the office so he could. "I'll ask around, but this company is full of dweebs and geeks. No one is that cool that they would be into something like that."

"Heck, doesn't hurt to ask." Wade headed down the hall.

"Wait!"

He spun around.

Abby approached him. "*Judas' Rainbow* is located in this office building."

"The gay mag!" Wade smiled. "Do you know someone from there?"

"Not personally. But why don't you just go up and talk to the editor?"

"That's not a bad idea." Wade grinned at her. "Smart." He tapped his head. "See? That's why I asked you."

"Love you too!" Abby spun around and headed to her desk.

Wade forgot about magazines. It was at least a starting point.

He brought his coffee back to his desk and sat at his computer, looking up the magazine information. The senior editor's name was Sigourney Edina, and indeed she did work in this office building. He jotted down the floor and suite number and checked his watch. "No time like the present."

He took a sip of his coffee, straightened his tie, buttoned his suit jacket and headed to the lobby. As he left he told the receptionist, "Be right back. Just stopping at another office in the building."

"Okay, Wade." She nodded at him and got busy with her phones.

Leaving the office, Wade waited for the elevator to go up four floors. He looked at the number he had written down and stuffed the note into his jacket pocket. He wasn't too familiar with the magazine, but had read it before. It was an eclectic array of fashion, political commentary, and pretty model pictures. No comics. But that didn't mean he couldn't get some much needed guidance.

Stepping into the elevator, which was full since it was Monday morning and everyone was arriving for their nine to five

The Farmer's Son

job, Wade stood patiently as people exited and finally stopped at the correct floor. He stepped out and read the numbers on the doors, walking down the carpeted hall and paused at a door that had the magazine's rainbow logo on the glass.

He opened it and entered a brightly lit reception space with a rectangle couch and coffee table, which had the magazines displayed on it.

"May I help you?" a young woman asked.

"Yes. My name is Wade Reed and I was wondering if I could speak to Sigourney Edina?"

"Do you have an appointment with her, Mr Reed?"

"No." He smiled and approached the young woman's desk, seeing behind her employees all busy tapping keyboards or speaking on phones. "This is kind of a bizarre request."

"She's used to those!" The woman laughed.

"My partner draws gay superhero comics, and I have no clue how to help him get published. The internet was a quagmire, and to be honest, a straight-domain, if you know what I mean."

"I do. Superheroes and sports heroes. Gay? No way!" She waved her hand dismissively. "Let me call her. She is in." The woman picked up the phone on her desk.

"I don't mean to bother her."

She held up her finger for Wade to wait.

"Sig? I got a man here, Wade Reed, and he says his partner draws gay superhero comics. How cool is that?" She winked at Wade and bit her lip as she listened to the reaction on the phone. "No. He's just lost and needs a little of your superwoman advice. Can I send him back?"

Wade investigated the action behind the woman, seeing a nice diversity of employees. Ayden would fit in so well at a place like this.

"Sure. Okay. Thanks." The woman stood and said, "You've got her curiosity piqued."

"Do I?" Wade smiled happily.

"Yup. Follow me."

He ran his hand over his hair and walked behind the petite brunette, catching the eyes of the other employees who looked up from their computers to watch him walk passed. He smiled amiably and stood waiting as the young woman used her knuckles to tap an office door.

"Come in!" was called from within.

She opened the door. "Wade, this is Sigourney."

"Thanks. I can't tell you how much I appreciate it." Wade held out his hand to the woman in charge.

"Good luck!"

"Thanks, Dixie!" Sigourney said as she stood from her chair.

"My pleasure, boss!" the young woman left.

"Come in. Close the door. Sit."

Wade closed the door behind him. "I just want to say thank you. I can't imagine how busy you are."

"No, you can't." She laughed and gestured again to a chair in front of her desk.

Wade unbuttoned his jacket and sat down, seeing this woman was around his age, and sensing pure business and no nonsense from her. Awards hung on the walls and she had a shelf of magazines and books behind her. "I work in the building as an environmental planner. My receptionist reminded me your magazine is...well...right here."

"So, your partner draws gay superheroes? Is he any good?" She sat down and interlaced her hands on the desk.

"He's unbelievable. He draws in pen, no preliminary sketches. And the comics are really hot."

"Does he have a website?" She turned to her computer.

"Not yet."

"A social network page I can see them?"

"Uh no."

THE FARMER'S SON

Sigourney tilted her head suspiciously. "Is he eighty?"

Wade laughed and covered his mouth to stop the hilarity. "No. He's a farmer's son. Not a hick, but, well, he grew up in the great valley on an almond orchard."

"Shut up!" She laughed loudly. "That's already a human interest story for my mag. Are you kidding me?"

"No. I'm not. He's twenty-two and—"

"Twenty-two? You're either one lucky stud or crazy."

"Both. Anyway, I really want him to get a chance at something great. He's got so much talent..." Wade shook his head as he thought about it. "If you watch him draw, you'd really be amazed he can just create these characters from thin air. Oh, and one is Neo Magnay, an anagram for One Gay Man, and the other is Boovery, Lover Boy."

Sigourney broke out into hysterical laughter, dabbing her eyes. "I have to see this stuff! Get him the hell in here!" She tapped a button on her phone and said, "Mason, get your ass in here. I have someone for you to meet."

"Okay," a man's voice came over her speakerphone.

"Call your man!" Sigourney gestured to Wade. "I'm dying to see his work."

Wade took his phone out of his pocket, pumped as hell, and dialed his home number.

~

Ayden was seated at the dining room table, pads and drawings sprawled all over the top, the heel of his hand blue from his ink, and new panels of heroic storylines flying from his head through his hand to the pad.

When the phone rang he jumped and held his heart, then put his pen down and leapt up to grab it.

"Babe?"

"Hi, Wade." Ayden rubbed his nose, then looked down at his inky hand in dismay.

"Look, I have great news!"

"Yeah?"

"A woman I work with reminded me there is a gay magazine publisher right here in my building. I'm talking to the senior editor now, and she's dying to see your work."

"Are you kidding me?" Ayden's heart beat faster.

"And she even loves the human interest story about you coming from the family orchard and drawing the gay heroes. She's all over this idea. Look, can you come now?"

"Yes! Of course!" Ayden danced around. "I drew up a whole bunch more."

"Awesome. Grab a pen, write down the directions to get here."

"Cool!" Ayden spun in a circle and raced back to his work. He picked up one of his drawing pens and didn't want to write on any of his good paper. "Uh."

"Ready?"

"No. Shit." Ayden began opening drawers in the kitchen and located a pad. "Okay. Go." Wade gave him directions from their home to his office.

"I should have left you my cell phone, Ayden. You see? If you get lost you won't be able to contact me."

Ayden looked at the directions. "You're right off the freeway. How can I get lost?"

"Okay. See you soon. Come to my office and we'll go to meet the editor together."

"I can't believe this, Wade!"

"Well, don't get too excited yet. She has to see your work, you know."

"Thank you." Ayden wanted to kiss him so much.

"You're welcome. Oh, and dress decently."

"You got it! Let me go. I'm going nuts!"

"Bye."

The Farmer's Son

Ayden hung up and did a happy dance, pumping his arms over his head and shuffling his feet. "Yes! Yes!"

He loaded all his artwork into a cardboard portfolio and raced to the bedroom to change and wash up.

With his artwork on the seat beside him in the truck, Ayden had the directions in his hand and headed for the highway via Santa Monica Boulevard. This was it, right? His big break? He could actually draw comics and make money?

"Yes! Yes!" Ayden grinned and stopped for a traffic signal, checking the directions he'd written, headed to 101 South.

When the light changed, the cars in front of him began to crawl through the intersection. Ayden heard a blip of a police siren and looked into his rear view mirror. He pulled over to allow the cop to go by and when the patrol car did not pass him, but followed behind him, Ayden was confused. He certainly was not speeding and had stopped for the traffic light.

Once there was no doubt he was indeed the target of this LAPD cop, Ayden put the truck in park and waited for the officer to approach to let him know what he had done wrong.

The cop did not walk up to his car, but Ayden could see him on his police radio, his overhead lights were flashing and occupants of cars were staring at Ayden as they passed.

"What the...?" Taking off his seatbelt, Ayden opened the car door, intending on asking the cop what was going on. Through a loud speaker, he heard, "Get back in your car! Now!"

Ayden jumped out of his skin and closed his door, suddenly breaking out in chills of terror.

"Put your hands where I can see them!" was the next order over the PA system.

"What?" Ayden held his hands over his head as out of thin air he was swarmed with patrol cars, front, sideways and two behind. He nearly peed his pants in fear.

With their guns drawn and pointed towards him, they all appeared to get into a battle position.

Ayden began huffing for air and had no idea what on earth was going on.

"Step out of the car!"

That was the last thing Ayden wanted to do. He kept his right hand up, and opened the truck door.

"Get out!"

Cops all around him were crouching behind their patrol cars, aiming their weapons at him as traffic was diverted.

Shaking like a leaf, Ayden got out, hands over his head, looking directly down several gun barrels.

"Turn around! Face away from me!" was ordered by the cop who had made the original stop. The cop was standing outside his patrol car, door open, the microphone to his mouth while still pointing his gun at him.

Ayden turned around, very slowly, looking at several other black and white patrol cars, their overhead lights spinning and now he heard a helicopter overhead. He didn't dare look up.

"Get on your knees! Hands interlaced behind your head!"

What the fuck? What the fuck? Ayden couldn't conceive of what he had done to deserve this. He slowly got to his knees, and nearly fell over, interlocking his hands behind his neck. He heard fast approaching footsteps behind him.

"Don't move!"

Ayden wouldn't dream of it.

He was pushed to the ground face first, his cheek against the tarmac, and his hands were jerked behind his back and locked in handcuffs. He was so stunned he couldn't think straight.

He was rolled side to side and hands ran up and down his body and along his belt. "Get up."

Ayden was hauled painfully to his feet as two other cops, still pointing their guns, looking into the truck. "Clear!" one shouted.

THE FARMER'S SON

Weapons were holstered and Ayden was pushed against his own truck hood and his wallet was removed. He pressed his cheek against the running hot hood and tried not to cry.

"Ayden B. Solomon...fourteen, one, nineteen-ninety-one."

Hearing his name and date of birth, Ayden shivered in terror.

"Copy."

The interior of the truck was rifled through, the glove box opened, his portfolio set on the truck's hood. One said, "He's got keys. The ignition's not punched."

Finally a cop turned him around and met his eye. "Who owns this truck?"

"My family." Ayden's eyes ran with tears and he tried to wipe it on his shoulder.

"Who is your family?"

"Solomon Orchards."

"This truck was reported stolen."

Suddenly Ayden got it. He sank against the truck and his knees went weak.

Two cops conferred and another approached, one with chevron stripes on his shoulder.

"Sarge, his last name is the same as the registered owner. He said it's the family's truck. And he's got keys."

Ayden shook his head in agony thinking of his father reporting the truck stolen and doing this to him.

"Put him in the back of your car. Get this truck hooked and we'll figure it out at the precinct."

"Okay."

Ayden asked through his tears, "Can I have my artwork?"

One of the cops pointed to his portfolio. "That thing?"

Ayden nodded.

The item was taken from the truck hood and brought with Ayden to the patrol car. After another very thorough pat-down, he was placed in the backseat and had to sit sideways so the handcuffs didn't bite his wrists.

His artwork was tossed into the trunk of the patrol car and he was driven away from the pickup truck and the scene.

Ayden closed his eyes and died inside. Never in his life had he been so terrified and humiliated. Never.

~

Wade checked the time. He called home again and got his answering machine. He said to himself, "I knew you'd get lost." He was at his desk, keeping busy, anxious to get Ayden and his artwork to Sigourney while she was interested. Knowing most of the world had ADD in some form or another, Wade didn't want to get the woman pumped about the comics and then suddenly not show. It was simply bad business and this was a huge favor to ask.

A half hour turned into an hour, and Wade had no idea what to do. Half of him was worried, the other, annoyed. With no way to communicate, and simple directions, Wade figured Ayden had indeed taken a wrong turn. And that truck didn't have a navigation system, so he hoped Ayden was the type of guy who could pull over and ask directions.

When an hour turned to two, Wade began to get a nervous feeling in his chest. He couldn't work, paced his office and wrung his hands.

Where the fuck are you? Wade kept checking his watch and stood by his office door, then the receptionist's desk.

"Still waiting for Ayden?" she asked.

"He has to be lost. Or got into an accident. This is absurd."

"What can I do?"

"I'm about to drive the route to my house. I really have a bad feeling."

"Go."

"Damn it!" Wade took his key out of his pocket and left.

Ayden was taken to a holding cell area that stunk of BO and piss and was filthy. His pockets were emptied and his wallet was placed into an envelope with his name written on it. His portfolio was brought with him and one of the cops opened it and looked inside. He glanced at Ayden. "Did you draw these?"

Ayden nodded, still an emotional wreck.

"Nice. Huh." The cop closed the folio up and they placed all Ayden's belongings into a locker. His name was written on a clipboard sheet and finally the handcuffs were removed.

Ayden rubbed his raw wrists and brushed off his dirty knees from kneeling on the street.

"Go have a seat in that cell." One of the cops pointed to a nasty looking cubicle with an iron door.

"Can I call someone?"

"Soon."

Ayden went into the cell and stood by as the door closed, locking him in. The claustrophobia sensation was instant. He watched out of the thick glass-wire mesh tiny window as two cops stood talking. He could not hear what they said, but saw one shaking their head as if either annoyed or frustrated.

Ayden used the backs of his hands to wipe his eyes, knowing how filthy everything was that he was touching.

Why, Dad? Why?

Ayden slumped against the scarred wall and hung his head. "I would have brought it back. You didn't have to do this." He dabbed at his eyes with his shirt sleeve and battled hard with his tears.

After what felt like an eternity, someone opened his cell door.

"We have your father on the phone." The man with the chevrons on his shoulder gestured for Ayden to follow him. Ayden was brought out of the stinky cell and to a desk inside a small room. He was handed a phone.

"Dad?"

"Where the hell did you go with my truck?"

"With Wade. I tried to tell you. Why did you do this to me?" Ayden looked into the eyes of the officers. There was one other cop with the man with the chevrons on his sleeve. The one who had originally stopped him.

"You took that truck without permission!"

"I didn't steal it, Dad! They took me out of it at gunpoint! I was handcuffed! Do you know what they did to me?" Ayden welled up again and tried to face the wall.

"You had no right taking that truck."

"That's all you care about? The truck? Really, Dad? Not me? Not what they did to me on the streets here in LA?"

"You made the decision to leave, not me."

"Dad...am I going to jail?" Ayden checked the eyes of the cops in the room. They gave him a poker face.

"I haven't decided."

"You haven't decided?" Ayden sobbed. "Dad!"

"Let me talk to the police."

"Can I just talk to Mom? Or Granddad? Please?"

"No."

Ayden handed the phone off and dropped down on a metal chair, feeling sick.

"Okay," the one with the stripes on his shoulder nodded as he spoke on the phone. "Fine. I agree. I think it's for the best. The truck is up here in a tow yard."

Ayden wondered if Wade thought he fell off the face of the earth. *Now I'm like your brother. A fuck up. Don't go to jail. I remember you saying that to me.* "Oh, God." Ayden moaned and asked the second cop, "Can I use a phone? Please?"

"Hang on." He nodded to the other officer who was still on the phone, indicating for Ayden to wait.

The Farmer's Son

"Okay. I will. Thank you, sir." The man with the chevron stripes on his shoulder hung up. "Your father said he won't press charges."

"Wouldn't hold up in court anyway," the second cop said softly. "Here." The cop pushed the phone towards Ayden. "Dial nine first. We'll be right outside."

"I need my wallet for a phone number." Ayden bit his lip to try and stop feeling emotional.

"Hang tight." The cop left the room.

Ayden looked at the man with the stripes. "My own dad did this to me."

"I'm sorry. I know families can be really screwed up."

"I was on my way to show my artwork to a magazine editor."

"You'll be okay."

"No. After this? I won't be."

The man put his hand on Ayden's shoulder. "Life moves on, kid. Believe me."

The door opened and Ayden was given his wallet and his portfolio.

"Thanks." He searched for Wade's cell phone number.

"Like I said, we'll be right outside." The two cops left the room, closing the door.

Ayden's hand shook as he read the number, trying to dial.

~

When his cell phone rang Wade had already made the round trip home and was on his way back to the office, furious and worried sick. He grabbed it and saw it was from a blocked number. Almost letting his service pick up, he answered. "Hello."

"Wade."

"Where the hell are you? I'm looking for you! I've driven all over the goddamn place!" Wade pulled over and threw the car in park.

"Wade...I was..."

"Was? In an accident? What?"

"No. You see..."

"Ayden! Spit it the fuck out!"

"Dad reported the truck stolen. I was fucking taken out of it at gunpoint! I was handcuffed. Wade! They threw me in a fucking police cell!"

A flood of memories from Cole washed over Wade and his temper rose. "Please do not tell me you are in jail."

"Not jail. A police station."

Wade counted to ten and wondered why he constantly got saddled with losers who got arrested!

Ayden said, "Hang on. I don't know where I am. Let me ask."

While Ayden did, Wade screamed, "Fuck!" and punched the steering wheel with his palm. He ran his hand through his hair and lost a whole day of work with this bullshit, probably lost his 'in' with *Judas' Rainbow*, and now he had to go to pick Ayden up from a police station? *I'm going to kill someone.*

"Wade?"

"Still here." He snarled and had no patience left.

"North San Vincente Boulevard."

"Fine."

"Wade?"

"What?"

"Are you mad at me?"

"Goodbye, Ayden." He hung up and headed to the police station, so angry he was about to explode. "What the fuck? Huh? *What the fuck!*" He brooded, thinking of his fucked up brother, and made his way in the traffic.

The Farmer's Son

Chapter 18

Wade parked on the street and had to find change to feed a meter. He stormed to the police station and walked through the doors to see a line formed and one cop working behind a counter. Looking at the caliber of 'clientele' that was waiting to be assisted, Wade was about to turn around and leave, but kept trying to calm down and wait. The lobby was so small he heard every word said to the cop, who appeared either to have had a lobotomy or was being punished and stuck where he was, in hell.

After forty minutes Wade stood before the man. "I'm here to pick up Ayden Solomon."

"What's he in for?" the man tapped a computer.

Wade cringed and said quietly, "Stolen truck."

The cop nodded and then got on the phone. "Some guy's here to pick up Ayden Solomon. Okay." He hung up and said, "He'll be right out."

Goody. Wade nodded and stepped aside, trying not to touch anything since the room appeared filthy and the steady stream of odd people coming in was slightly unnerving.

A door opened and Ayden stepped out, holding a black cardboard portfolio. Ayden didn't look up as he walked through the lobby. Wade followed him outside and before Ayden headed off in the wrong direction, Wade grabbed his arm. "How about, hello? Or thank you, Wade?"

Ayden faced him, showing his teeth in fury.

It was then Wade could see how red his eyes were, his soot stained cheeks from his tears.

"I was at gunpoint! I had to kneel in the street like a thug!" Ayden choked up on his sob. "My dad…" Ayden started crying.

Wade's anger vanished and he embraced Ayden.

"My dad did this to me." Ayden cried. "He reported the truck stolen. He put me through this."

"Where's the truck now?"

"In some tow yard. I don't know."

"Come on, baby. Come home."

"No! I want to show my art to that editor." Ayden wiped his face with his sleeve.

"Ayden."

"Please! Oh, God, please!"

Wade checked his watch. It was nearly two, and he had spoken to Sigourney at nine.

"Wade, please."

What was he going to say? No? He led Ayden to the BMW and they climbed in. Ayden put the portfolio down at his legs and sank in the seat.

Wade took a tissue out of a pack on the console and wet it with a little spit, then tried to wipe Ayden's grimy cheek.

Ayden flipped down the visor, as if he had no idea what he looked like and took the tissue, trying to clean his face. "Oh, Christ…oh, Christ…" he whined.

"We'll stop at the men's room at the office, and you can clean up."

"A week in a hot shower won't clean me after that disgusting experience." Ayden pushed the visor back up and used the tissue to wipe his eyes.

"Are you sure you're up for this meeting?"

Ayden's expression was so desperate, Wade started the car and headed to the office building, hoping for the best.

The Farmer's Son

~

Ayden hated to admit he was numb, but he had to function or he'd crawl into a hole and die. Wade walked with him into an office building, a tall skyscraper like the kind that Ayden had only seen on TV and in movies. Glass, concrete, twenty stories high...perfect landscaping, perfect interior design...perfect-perfect...*and then there is me. Sad fucker.*

Wade held Ayden's elbow and walked with him to the elevator. Without Wade's touch, Ayden would probably just stand still and stare at nothing.

Inside the elevator they rose to a floor. Ayden didn't pay attention which. He was escorted out of the elevator and brought down a hall to a men's room. Wade took the portfolio and nudged Ayden to the sink and mirror.

When he looked at himself Ayden fell apart, and held onto the sink for balance. His eyes were red-rimmed and puffy and his face smeared with dusty soot and bruised and scratched from hitting the street when he was handcuffed.

Inhaling for courage, Ayden washed his face and hands then used the paper towels to dry off. With a damp paper towel, he wiped at his knees and made sure his pants were clean of street dirt. Then he tried to tame his hair. "Hopeless."

"No. It's not. Come on. We've come this far." Wade handed Ayden the portfolio.

"Hang on." Ayden walked to a urinal and relieved himself, trying to stop self-destructing.

Behind him Wade washed his hands and wiped his face with a paper towel, then straightened his tie and suit jacket.

Ayden finished at the urinal and washed his hands again, checking his appearance. "Day from hell."

"Indeed."

"Nothing to lose." Ayden took the portfolio.

"Nothing." Wade led the way out and down the hall. He allowed Ayden a moment to gather himself and then opened a door with the logo of a rainbow on it.

Ayden stepped inside and immediately could see a busy office, with employees on the phones, typing on computers, and a wall of offices lining the back wall.

A woman approached. "Well! Better late than never."

"Sorry, Dixie. We had a little snag." Wade brought Ayden forward. "This is Ayden Solomon. He's the artist."

Ayden extended his hand. "I am so sorry I'm so late."

Dixie studied him carefully and Ayden knew she could see he'd been through something…something rough.

"No problem. We get waylaid all the time. Sigourney is very cool. Not to worry." Dixie walked them to an office along the far wall.

Wade was behind him, and Ayden wondered if he was too numb from this ordeal to function. This was an important step towards him getting his work out here. Was this smart? Doing it now? When his brain was fried?

Dixie knocked on the door. "Madam?" she said playfully, "Your artiste has arrived."

"Come in! Get Mason too!"

"Will do." Dixie opened the door. "Go on in. Do you need anything? Coffee? Water?"

"Water? Please?" Ayden tried to keep it together.

Dixie smiled warmly and walked off.

"Well!" Sigourney stood from behind her desk. "You sure know how to be fashionably late."

"Forgive me. I am so sorry." Ayden stood near the chair, holding his portfolio, trying to stop his hands from shaking. The stress had taken its toll.

"Don't worry. Life happens." Sigourney gestured for them both to sit down. A man appeared from behind them and walked near Sigourney. He extended his hand. "I'm Mason Bloomfield. I handle the lifestyle editing for the magazine."

Ayden shook the man's hand and tried to stand.

"Sit." He gestured for Ayden to not get up.

Dixie brought in a few bottles of water and then shut the door behind her as she left.

Ayden placed the portfolio on his lap and opened a bottle drinking thirstily. He noticed Sigourney meet eyes with Wade, but had no idea what was said previously that he was not privy to. Ayden capped the water. "Sorry."

"No need."

Mason pulled over a chair from the side of the office to join them.

Wade nudged Ayden. "Show them your work."

Ayden tried to set the bottle of water on the desk, and it tipped but he caught it, righting it. He felt clumsy and stupid.

Wade moved the bottle for him and Ayden cleared his throat and placed the portfolio on the desk, opening it. Mason shifted closer first, getting a look. "May I?"

"Yes. Of course." Ayden sat back in the chair, nervous as hell.

Wade reached for his hand and squeezed it for reassurance. Ayden appreciated it but was drained to the point of dropping dead.

"You did these freehand?" Mason held up a sketch, one Ayden had done this morning, on heavy quality paper. It was a comic strip with ten panels on one sheet.

"Yes." Ayden watched Sigourney leafing through the pages as well, then opening the pad. "Ayden, you are amazing."

"Thank you." Ayden felt some of his stress leave.

"Think of it, Sig." Mason said, holding one of Ayden's works. "We can showcase him in the lifestyle section, show off his best comics, and then see how the readership responds. My guess is it would be great fun to feature him in each issue, next to the back page, as a bonus comic for the fans."

"Love it!" Sigourney read the panels of the sketch pad drawings and laughed. "Oh God, Mason, look at the cocks. Is that you?" she teased.

Mason laughed. "In my dreams." He said to Ayden, "What was your inspiration? What started you on this path?"

"Boredom and I guess the need to explore my gay side."

"Neo Magnay and Booverly." Mason tilted his head curiously as he read the names.

Sigourney explained, "Anagrams for One Gay Man and Lover Boy."

Mason coughed and laughed in a robust laughter, delighted. "Amazing! Oh, God, I love it. The artwork, the storyline…"

Ayden glanced at Wade. He appeared to be lost in his head, but he acknowledged Ayden's gaze with a slight smile.

"Look, Ayden," Sigourney leaned on the desk. "Can we do a feature on you first? Non-paying? Just to test the water? I'd love to do a story on your background. You know, how you managed to get from A to B."

"I'm still getting to B." Ayden tried to smile but couldn't. "Yes. Anything will be fine. I don't expect to make millions."

"You won't at first, but this kind of thing will catch on and go viral." Mason took the pad from Sigourney and flipped pages, reading more comics. "Priceless." He looked up at Wade. "Is this Neo-guy you?"

Wade chuckled. "It is now."

"Ayden, the comics are both hilarious and very supportive of the community. And…there's a huge vacuum when it comes to gay superheroes and comics. It's still a battle we've yet to gain ground on." Mason leafed through the newer drawings. "So, these are originals."

The Farmer's Son

"Yes." Ayden was beginning to feel completely drained, trying to focus.

Wade said, "We don't want to leave them. I can get copies made and bring them here tomorrow."

"Get them scanned onto a high definition hard drive or DVD," Sigourney said, gathering the drawings. "Mason will write up an interview with questions for Ayden, and Ayden can answer them on paper or through an email file." She asked Ayden, "Do you have an email address?"

"He doesn't yet. Send it to me." Wade took a business card out from his wallet and handed it to her.

"Okay." She read it.

"Thank you." Wade stood and reached out his hand.

"My pleasure. Thanks for thinking of us. I'm thrilled to have *Judas' Rainbow* show off this new talent." Sigourney shook Wade's hand.

"Thanks," Ayden said, "and I'm sorry I was so late."

Mason stared deeply into Ayden's eyes. "It's okay. Don't worry."

Ayden felt the care from him and nodded, having a feeling they suspected something bad had happened and it wasn't from carelessness or neglect.

Ayden folded his portfolio and fastened it, taking the water bottle with him as they left. Wade walked him out of the office and they waved goodbye to Dixie.

As they stood at the elevator, Ayden said, "Can I walk home from here?"

"No. It's way too far. And today is shot." Wade checked his watch. "Let's head to a print shop and then home."

Ayden nodded, tucking the portfolio under his arm and drinking the water thirstily. All he wanted to do was lie down.

~

Wade sensed Ayden's distress and exhaustion, because he felt the same way. He stopped at a print shop before heading back to the condo and he and Ayden, although they were weary, managed to get Ayden's comics on disk, a hard drive, and fabulous prints. But it took over an hour and Wade could see the stress was making them both anxious to be home.

Once he and Ayden were through with copying Ayden's artwork and walking to the car in the parking lot, Wade checked his phone and noticed missed messages since he had shut it off during the meeting with Sigourney and forgotten to turn it back on. He read a text from Simon asking him and Ayden out to dinner, ignored it, and listened to a voicemail from his brother.

'*Wade, I need a few things. Clothing and food. Can I borrow some money so I can order them from the Walkenhorst catalogue? Please? You owe me since you didn't show.*'

Wade stuffed the phone into his pocket. *Owe you? I don't fucking owe you.* He pointed his key fob at his car to unlock his doors and climbed behind the wheel as Ayden sat beside him after putting the plastic bags of their purchases in the back seat.

Ayden slouched low and stared out of the window looking forlorn and depressed.

Wade didn't comment, letting Ayden alone, and drove home. He wished he had a private Jacuzzi, not wanting to use the one for the complex. The last thing he wanted was meaningless chitchat from a neighbor.

"It's been a really long day." Ayden rubbed his face.

"Oh, babe. You said a mouthful." Wade stared at the heavy traffic he was hitting on 101 and sighed.

The Farmer's Son

Chapter 19

Ayden entered the condo, placed his portfolio and packages from the print shop on the coffee table in the living room and headed directly for the bedroom. He stripped off his clothing and stood near the shower stall in the bathroom, waiting for the water to heat up. Once it had, he stepped into the tub, faced the spraying water, and pressed both palms on the tiled wall, letting the water cleanse and soothe him. He was heartbroken. Devastated.

Even with the hope and promise of something good coming out of his comics, he felt as if he had so much unfinished baggage to deal with back at the orchard, he couldn't move on or function until he found closure. If he ever could. But avoiding it, not confronting his family head on? That was the coward's way out. And Neo and Boo were not cowards.

Ayden scrubbed his skin with the coconut scented soap and shampooed his hair, resolved to not run away from his problems. No matter the cost.

~

Wade undressed, taking his suit off and hanging it in the closet, trading it for a pair of soft sweatpants and a T-shirt. He heard the shower running in the bathroom and was torn between going in and trying to comfort Ayden or giving him time to think and decompress on his own. He didn't understand Ayden well enough to know which Ayden preferred.

But after picking Ayden up from the police station, Wade was preoccupied with bad feelings about Cole, and maybe the way he and his family were treating his incarcerated brother.

But it wasn't fair to compare the two men. Ayden did not commit armed robber for drug money. Although, maybe it was time Wade forgave his brother. Time Wade's whole family had.

He walked to the bathroom doorway and looked in, seeing Ayden rinsing behind the frosted glass.

The way Ayden's family treated Ayden, wasn't too far off from the way Wade's family was treating Cole. And he could see the anguish in his lover. Was he willing to open up and understand Cole's heartbreak too?

The water shut and Ayden stood still, dripping.

Wade picked up a towel and waited, beginning to empathize with Ayden and Cole's agony. Life sometimes dealt you bullshit, and you coped the best way you could.

But not supporting a man in need? A man you are supposed to love? That has to be the ultimate cruelty.

Ayden rolled back the sliding door and spotted Wade there.

When their eyes met, Wade melted. Yes. He loved Ayden. So much. Holding the towel up for him, Wade approached, standing near, feeling the steam and damp heat rushing out of the stall.

"Wade." Ayden's eyes teared up.

"Baby." Wade hugged him with the towel, closing his eyes and squeezing Ayden so tightly he wanted them to be one.

"I'm sorry." Ayden rested his head on Wade's shoulder.

"You have nothing to be sorry for. Nothing."

"I love you. I love you…" Ayden held Wade close, kissing his neck and hair.

"Oh, my baby-doll. I love you too. We'll be okay. Everything will be okay." Wade kissed his lips and tried to dry Ayden, rubbing the towel on his chest and hair.

Ayden's jaw twitched like a live wire, as if he were trying to keep himself together emotionally.

"Are you hungry?"

Ayden took the towel and stepped out of the tub. "I feel sick to my stomach but I should eat."

"Yes. You should." Wade stepped back as Ayden dried his long muscular legs and groin.

"Wade."

"Yes, my love?"

"I…I need to go back home. I need to get this worked out. Even if it's to be told I'm disowned or banned from the farmhouse. I have to."

Wade nodded. "I know. I've been thinking of what I did to Cole. Maybe I need to talk to my parents and see if I can convince them to go see him. But, like you, I need to go visit him myself. I think we both have unfinished business in the Great Central Valley."

"Thank you." Ayden's blue eyes were so beautiful. Like a summer's day.

Wade drew him to his lips and kissed him. "For you? Anything."

Ayden went limp in his arms as Wade held on tight. "What would I do without you?"

"Well," Wade smiled sadly as he said, "You'd be back with your family, not on the outs with them, and certainly have not been held at gunpoint by the LAPD."

"Oh, that."

Wade actually heard a smile in Ayden's voice, so he drew back to see it. And there it was. "You'll be okay. You know that, right?"

"With my Neo by my side, I can battle anything."

"That's my Boo." Wade smiled and gave him another quick kiss. "Let me see what I can cook for dinner."

"Okay." Ayden rubbed the towel over his hair.

Wade peered back at him as he left the room, and made for the kitchen, trying to figure out how to convince his parents to see Cole.

~

Ayden blew his hair dry and stared at himself in the mirror's reflection. What would Neo do?

"He'd face his demons head on." Ayden left the bathroom and dressed in a pair of faded comfortable jeans and an old soft flannel shirt. He smelled onions cooking and followed his nose to the kitchen. An iced beer mug was waiting for him on the kitchen counter, and Wade was at the stove with a wooden spoon in his hand.

"That for me?" Ayden pointed to the beer.

"Yup."

"Thanks." Ayden picked it up and drank down a gulp in thirst. He stood behind Wade and looked into the frying pan. "Mm. What are you making?"

"Sausage, peppers and onions over pasta."

"Damn. Sounds great. What can I do?"

"Sit. Do nothing but relax." Wade pointed his wooden spoon at the dining room chair.

Ayden sat and turned to face him. "Listen, uh, Wade?"

"Yes?"

"I really need to face my family. Like ASAP. Should I rent a car so I can go tomorrow?"

Wade met his gaze. "You don't have to rent a car. You can either use mine or we can go together. I need to head back to the prison and see Cole."

"When?"

"Does it have to be tomorrow? Is Saturday soon enough? Or do you want me to take time off?" Wade stirred the pasta into boiling water and set a timer.

"Okay. Saturday will work. It'll give me time to come up with a good way to get my foot in the door without getting beaten up."

"Christ." Wade shook his head, then it appeared an idea hit him. "Would you like to meet my parents?"

"Huh? Sure. Would they like to meet me?" Ayden drank the rest of the beer.

"Yes. They don't have any issue with me being gay. And, they'd really like you."

"Do they live in LA?"

"They do."

"Okay. May as well. I don't have parents now."

"Yeah, uh, look, speaking about coming up with a way to get a foot in the door..."

"Yes?" Ayden was confused but gestured for Wade to go on.

"I want to use you to get them to see Cole."

"How?"

"By showing them how hurtful it is when a family abandons their son."

"Oh. May work. But...I'm not in jail." Ayden frowned. "I mean—"

"Let's not go there. There's no comparison between you and Cole. And...don't even mention the incident to them. Okay?"

"Okay." Ayden's stomach grumbled. He stood and looked over Wade's shoulder again. "Can I get another beer?"

"It's your home. You don't have to ask. You can do whatever you like."

"Do you want one?" Ayden opened the refrigerator door.

"No, but I'd love a glass of scotch."

"You got it." Ayden grinned at him. "Anything for you."

Wade chuckled at hearing his own line and poured the pasta into a colander in the sink. "Dinner's done."

"Good. I'm starving and it smells great." Ayden poured a glass of scotch for Wade and then brought both that and his beer to the table. As Wade put the pasta into a big ceramic bowl, Ayden set the table. "So, you want me to be brutally honest with your parents about how I feel about my family?"

"I do. Brutally." Wade brought the bowl to the table, and stuck a serving spoon in it. He took parmesan cheese out of the fridge and sat down as Ayden began spooning out servings.

"Strange, huh," Ayden said.

"What is?" Wade sipped his drink.

"How me being shunned may help your brother."

"Life's weird that way."

Ayden sprinkled the cheese onto his food. "It may not work. And I mean both, me trying to get someone to accept me, or your parents visiting your brother."

"Odds are it won't."

Ayden tasted the food. "Mm. My mom would love this. If we ever do get to talk to her, I'll let you exchange recipes."

Wade laughed and ate his food, smiling at Ayden.

Ayden enjoyed the meal, knowing he had to mentally prepare himself for the worst. But all he and Wade could do was try.

~

Wade and Ayden cleared the table and Wade started the dishwasher. They relocated to the living room and Ayden sat with the laptop on his legs, propped up on the sectional with his legs on the hassock, searching for ideas for more submissions for his cartoons. Wade held his phone as he sat beside him and then said, "Look up gay magazine websites. May as well see if we can go non-exclusive with Judas."

"Okay." Ayden tapped keys.

Wade pushed a few buttons on his phone and put it to his ear.

"Wade?"

"Hi, Dad."

THE FARMER'S SON

Ayden glanced at him and then continued to work.

"What's up? Everything okay?"

"Everything is fine. I wanted to know what you guys were doing for dinner tomorrow?"

"Tomorrow? It's Tuesday. Nothing. Why?"

"I want to take you out. I would like you both to meet my new boyfriend." Wade felt odd saying that. The last and only man he introduced to his parents previously was Simon. They did like him and no comments were made on the age gap.

"Wouldn't you rather do it this weekend?"

"No. Ayden and I are busy this weekend. Look, if you don't want to—"

"No. It's fine. Just tell us where to meet you."

"I know you guys like Spago's."

"Are they even open on a Tuesday?"

"Dad." Wade began to lose his patience.

"Okay. What time?"

"Seven."

"See you there."

"Bye." Wade disconnected the phone call and set the phone on the side table.

"Always bullshit," Ayden said.

"Yup. I can't complain. They accepted me as gay."

Ayden sneered at Wade. "What's to accept? I hate that. Why is it conditional?"

"You're right. Love shouldn't be. That's the argument I am going to try and use for Cole."

"Maybe your mom and dad can talk to mine."

"Hm. Maybe." Wade put his arm around Ayden and looked at the computer. "What magazine is that?"

"Something in the UK." Ayden handed Wade the laptop and went to stand.

"Where you going?"

"To write it down."

Wade hit print and gestured for Ayden to sit. The sound of the printer working in the spare bedroom was heard. Ayden looked at Wade.

"Wireless." Wade shrugged.

Ayden dropped back to the couch and said, "I am so far behind."

"Not true. Considering how little practice you said you've had on computers, you're amazing."

"You are so good for my ego."

"You took the words out of my mouth." Wade kissed him. "Okay, let's set you up an email box, baby."

"Cool."

THE FARMER'S SON

CHAPTER 20

Ayden worked on new cartoons all day while Wade took the hard drive, prints, and disk with him to work to give to Sigourney. He had to get used to Wade being gone nine to five, more like eight to six, and keeping busy. But the adjustment was not easy.

Once again, his sketches laid out all over the dining room table, Ayden began to make up more complex storylines for his characters, in case he could actually publish an entire comic book, not just a panel or strip.

His hands covered in blue ink, Ayden heard the home phone ring and put his pen down and tried to wipe at the stains on his fingers as he walked to where the cordless phone was. "Hello?"

"Ayden, it's me."

"Hi, Wade."

"Mason sent the interview questions to my email box and I forwarded them to yours. Are you in front of the laptop?"

"No. I was drawing. I can get it." Ayden walked to the living room where the laptop was from the night before.

"My password is saved if you just want to get into mine. So just log in and open the email from Mason. You can just type your answers directly on the email and hit reply."

"Okay. Should I do it now?"

"I would."

"Okay." Ayden brought the laptop to the dining room and cleared a space for it.

"I got the disks and hard drive to them. Ayden, they seem very eager to help you out."

"Good, because being cooped up all day here is going to make me lose my mind. I need to get out and work."

"Uh, I have news for you, Ayden, your work is not going to consist of chainsaws anymore. If anything it will be learning a computer graphic program and sitting on your ass all day."

"Yeah. I'm getting that feeling. No wonder you go to the gym. This kind of sucks."

"Oh? You want to go back to the orchard?"

"I miss the physical labor and being outside. Am I nuts?" Ayden opened the laptop and booted it up.

"No. You've been working on the orchard since you could walk. Believe me, I get it."

Ayden logged onto his own email box and spotted the only message, opening it. "Wow. There are a ton of questions."

"I saw that. Look, do your best. If you want, when I get home, I can review them."

"With the gym and seeing your parents? When?"

"Before we go to bed. Don't worry. There's no deadline on it. It can be done Thursday or something. Please don't stress."

Ayden rubbed his face then looked at his stained hands. "I'm nervous about meeting your parents."

"Don't be. They really are nice people. And they will love you."

Ayden sat up and felt a rush of calm. "Love me?"

"Yes, Ayden. They seem to have a lot of love in them. I just have to get them to give some of that to Cole."

"We will, Wade. We will."

THE FARMER'S SON

"Okay. Let me get back to work. I'll see you at around six and we'll head to the gym for a quick workout, then go straight to meet my folks."

"Okay."

"Love you."

"Love you too." Ayden disconnected the call and put the phone down, looking at the number of questions in the interview. He scooted the chair closer and began answering them.

~

By five Wade was in his car, battling the traffic home. Too tired for the gym, Wade wondered if skipping it was an option, but knew he'd been more exhausted than this and still managed a workout. After fighting the snarls on the LA freeway, Wade drove under the complex to park in his garage. He reached into his coat pocket and removed two wrappers from protein bars. How they were still in his pocket was beyond him. As he headed to the lobby door, he closed the garage with a remote and tossed the wrappers into the garbage pail near the lobby door. That night. That crazy night.

Wade turned his master key in the security lock and stood at the elevator, hoping everything worked out. Wouldn't it be nice if families could support each other? Not judge?

But most were dysfunctional messes, and his was nothing less.

As he rode the elevator to the fifth floor, Wade wondered which was worse? His or Ayden's family. It wasn't as clear cut as he thought.

They were all screwed up.

He walked down the hall and stood in front of his door, trying to psych himself up for the gym and then dinner. When he opened the door he stopped short. A man was standing, hands on hips, in his living room, a towel pinned around his neck like a cape, wearing nothing but black briefs, and dark sunglasses.

Wade cracked up with laughter and shut the door. "Hello, Boo."

"Been waiting for you, Neo."

Wade took off his wool coat and hung it up, trying not to take his eyes off Ayden. "I can see that. Nice hard-on. Did your artwork get you horny?"

Ayden puffed up his muscular chest and arms, closed the gap between them and picked Wade up, tossing him over his shoulder.

Wade's eyes sprung open at Ayden's strength. "I take that as a yes."

"Yes. Been drawing men with hard dicks all day." Ayden dropped Wade on the bed with a bounce and began undressing him, starting with his shoes and socks.

Wade removed his tie, sliding it from his collar. "We really need to get costumes. Seriously. How much fun would role playing be?" He shimmied out of his jacket and began unbuttoning his shirt as Ayden opened Wade's belt and slacks.

"Too hot." Ayden tugged Wade's trousers and briefs off, then stood like a superhero again, admiring him.

Once Wade was naked, he made sure the condoms and lubrication were within reach, then bent his knees and pulled on his own cock as he stared at Ayden. "So? Did you draw your supermen fucking?"

Ayden tossed the sunglasses on the nightstand and leapt onto the bed, between Wade's legs, nuzzling his crotch.

"Can't wait to see your new comics. They get me as hot as they get you." Wade dug his fingers through Ayden's hair. "You realize if we get into a good bout, we'll have to skip the gym to meet my parents on time."

"If we fuck for an hour, we'll burn calories." Ayden took Wade's cock into his mouth.

The Farmer's Son

At the wet heat and pleasure, Wade relaxed on the bed. "Sold." He stared down at the act and watched Ayden release his own cock from his briefs, giving it a tug and then resuming his focus on Wade. Wade reached for the 'cape' and carefully opened the safety pin, removing the towel and dropping it onto the floor.

Ayden scooted lower, holding Wade's cock in one hand while he lapped at Wade's balls.

You wanna fuck me. I know you do. Wade had only let one man screw him. He was in high-school and it was the first time he had done anything that heavy with another man. All he recalled was it hurt, and he didn't want to do it again.

"Lube." Ayden reached out his hand.

"What are you going to do with it?"

"You said you like a nice rub. So?" Ayden knelt upright and pulled on his own cock while he stared at Wade.

Wade handed him the bottle, losing his erection.

Before he took it from Wade, Ayden noticed. "Wow. That bad?"

Wade sat up and tackled Ayden, rolling over so he was on top. "You said it wasn't an issue."

"It's not!" Ayden gripped Wade's shoulders. "I just want to please you."

Wade turned Ayden over, face down on the bed and spread Ayden's legs. *Will you get curious and find a man to fuck?*

Knowing Ayden was a virgin, Wade didn't need this to add to his worries. This was the problem he had with several past men, them wanting to either share the act or exclusively be top.

The debate made Wade lose interest in the sex. He sat on his heels and checked the time wondering if they could still make it to the gym.

"Wade?" Ayden looked back over his shoulder. "What the hell just happened?"

Wade felt guilty and rubbed his face tiredly. What was he supposed to do? Tell Ayden he could never feel penetration except in a mouth?

Ayden rolled to his side slowly, having lost the momentum as well. He tucked a pillow under his head and said, "I can't do anything right."

"It's not you."

"Have you turned off me since yesterday? You said never to go to jail."

Wade lay beside him and caressed Ayden's face. "It's not that."

Ayden waited to see what it was about, but Wade didn't say anything else. "Fine." He rolled off the bed. "Are we going to the gym?"

"Ayd."

Ayden lowered his head and didn't look at Wade. "I can't handle not knowing why. I can't. Not now. I only have you."

"Come here."

At the soft words, Ayden looked over his shoulder. Wade was reaching out his hand. Ayden lay with him on the bed and Wade held him in his arms, pressing his mouth to Ayden's ear, which always gave Ayden chills.

In a deep whisper, Wade said, "I'm afraid if I don't let you top me, you'll cheat."

Ayden shook his head adamantly.

"Yes. That you weren't given the choice of what you wanted, and haven't fucked a man."

"Wade..."

"Ayden, I see how much you want to dominate me."

"I'm playing. I told you I'll have sex however you want me to." Ayden backed up to be able to see Wade's light eyes. He ran his knuckle against Wade's coarse shadow. "You're my Neo. You're the main man."

"Are you sure?"

"Yes!" Ayden felt his cheeks blush and his cock swell. "I love you fucking me."

This time Wade pinned Ayden to the bed, knelt up and began fisting himself to get hard.

Instantly Ayden's blood rushed to his groin as he watched.

"Lube." Wade reached out his hand this time.

Ayden smiled and picked up the bottle, pouring some onto Wade's fingers. As he did he spread his legs, giving Wade a mischievous grin. What had left was back. Ayden's cock was stiff and bobbing between his thighs and so was Wade's.

When Wade touched Ayden's rim with his slick fingertips, he dropped his head onto the pillows and closed his eyes, ready for the wild ride.

While Wade gave Ayden's balls and rim a good massage with the slick gel, Ayden moaned and held his knees, offering himself, loving their coupling.

He was penetrated with Wade's fingers, gently, pushing in and corkscrewing. The rush to the tip of Ayden's cock was intense and he began to seep pre-cum.

Wade placed the condom on and resumed what he was doing, his fingers inching inside Ayden as Ayden's body craved the climax. Wade held the base of Ayden's cock and licked at the drop at the slit, making Ayden open his eyes to watch.

After sucking the head of Ayden's dick, Wade found Ayden's internal sweet spot and began rubbing hot friction over it.

Ayden's hips jerked upright in reflex and he gasped at how intense the sensation was. Did he have complaints about their lovemaking? *No!*

"Wade! God!" Ayden released his knees and gripped the bed, strangling the blanket as the intensity rose.

"That's it, baby." Wade pushed Ayden's right leg to rest against Ayden's chest, keeping up the internal massage.

As Wade worked in deep and fast, Ayden's groin began to rush with chills and his cock dripped with pre-cum so heavily, Ayden again wondered if he was climaxing. Seeing it, Wade pulled out his fingers and thrust his cock deep, then he grabbed Ayden's at the base with his slick fingers and began jerking it in time with his hip-thrusts.

Ayden threw back his head and choked on his grunt of ecstasy. Knowing he was coming now, since his chest was spattered with creamy spunk, which kept spraying as Wade pulled on it. Wade groaned in pleasure and pushed deeply inside Ayden, so deep, Ayden felt every pulsating beat of Wade's cock.

Shaking his head side to side in absolute awe, Ayden's body reverberated with the shocks as Wade milked him gently and pulled out.

"Oh, God..." Ayden breathed loudly. "And you think I don't want sex like this? Are you out of your mind?"

Wade released Ayden's cock and huffed air as he recuperated. "Holy Christ, it's so good."

Ayden cupped his softening cock and closed his eyes. "So good. I have no complaints, Wade...believe me."

"That's all I want to hear." Wade managed to get off the bed. "Now we have to shower and act civilized for my parents."

"Augh..." Ayden splayed out. "Sleep. Need sleep."

"I hear ya. But no. Come on, young man. If I can motivate myself, you can."

Ayden opened his eyes and reached for Wade's hand, allowing Wade to haul him off the bed.

~

Wade checked his appearance in the mirror, seeing the gray at his temples and thinking of his father. His uncle on his dad's side

The Farmer's Son

was snow white by fifty, so Wade wasn't sure what the outlook was for him. And was he ready to be a silver-haired man?

No.

But the thought of dying his hair made him cringe. Just as concept of aging entered his mind, Ayden stepped behind him in the bathroom and asked. "Do I look okay?"

Wade spun around and had a look at Ayden's shirt and slacks. Wade took a brush to Ayden's hair and fluffed his chocolate-colored locks up so he looked gorgeous...*more* gorgeous, and then kissed his lips.

"I'm nervous." Ayden backed out of the bathroom.

"Don't be."

"Can I wear that leather jacket?"

"Sure. Keep it. I never wear it." Wade checked his pocket for keys, phone, wallet...

"Thanks." Ayden put it on and untucked his hair from the back collar. "What should I call your mom and dad? Mom and Dad?"

Wade laughed. "Yeah, try that. That's fucking hilarious." He opened the door and shut the light before walking to the hall.

"I can't imagine you calling my mom Helen." Ayden stood by as Wade dead-bolted the door. "She's just 'Mom'."

"After we get married I'll call your mom, Mom." Wade smiled and walked down the hall to the elevator.

"Married? You want to marry me?" Ayden jumped into the air in little hops of excitement instead of walking beside Wade as they made their way.

"I was joking. Kind of." Wade pushed the elevator call button.

"Married. Huh. I would love to get married." Ayden stuffed his hands into his jacket pockets. "Do you want a big affair? Or to elope?"

"I was kidding." Wade gestured for Ayden to enter the elevator first, then pushed the lobby floor button.

"Would you be the kind of guy to get down on one knee and propose?"

"Uh oh. Did I open a can of worms?" Wade assumed he'd never marry, since most men strayed. Didn't they?

"No." Ayden appeared shy. "I guess I could see getting married. I mean, I am a one-guy kind of guy. I don't want to date around."

Wade stared at him in disbelief. "You've just had me!"

Ayden's eyes lit up and he hugged Wade, pushing him against the elevator wall and grinding on him. "Have I ever!"

"You're worse than a woman when it comes to falling for your first fuck." Wade couldn't be more flattered.

"Yeah. I am." Ayden kissed Wade.

Wade knew he was full of bullshit. He'd marry Ayden in a heartbeat if he didn't know him for such a short time. As the elevator stopped at their level, and the door opened, Wade spotted an older couple waiting to get on.

He parted from Ayden's amorous kiss and didn't meet their eyes, walking passed them to the parking garage. He heard Ayden's shy, 'Hello,' and had no idea if he got a smile or a scowl in return, not caring.

The garage door elevated with a touch to a button on his key chain and he sat behind the wheel and felt Ayden's nervous energy. "They'll love you. But they'll hate me for the guilt trip I'm going to lay on them." He started the car and fastened his seatbelt.

"I got your back."

"Thanks, Boo." Wade leaned over for a kiss and pulled out of the garage.

~

The Farmer's Son

Since it was a Tuesday, the evening traffic was light on their drive to Beverly Hills and the parking easy. Wade didn't even bother with the valet. They walked hand in hand to the entrance of the restaurant and Wade opened the door for Ayden, allowing him to pass first, and they approached the hostess together.

"I'm meeting my parents here," Wade said, looking down at her seating chart and then out into the restaurant's main dining area.

"Are you Mr Reed?"

"I am." Wade smiled. "I take it they're here."

"Yes. They said they wanted to wait at the table for you." She picked up two menus and added, "Follow me."

Wade put his hand on the small of Ayden's back and looked for his mom and dad in the sparsely occupied restaurant. The aroma of roasted meat and garlic permeated the air, and although Wade knew tonight would be a struggle, it hadn't affected his appetite.

He spotted his mother in the well lit room and she waved at him as she noticed him as well. A smile lit up her pretty plump face instantly.

The hostess escorted them to their white linen-covered table, and placed menus down. "I'll send the waiter right over to get your drink order."

"Thank you." Wade took off his jacket as his dad stood, waiting for an introduction.

"Dad, this is Ayden Solomon. Ayden, this is my mom and dad, Pat and Doug."

Doug shook Ayden's hand. "So nice to meet you, Ayden."

"You too, sir." Ayden removed his jacket and hung it on the back of the chair. The table was for four, and his parents were adjacent to each other, not across, so Ayden and Wade sat the same way, next to each other.

Wade was facing his dad, and Ayden, his mom.

Seeing his parents had already ordered drinks, Wade opened the menu to have a look. "What would you like to drink, Ayden?"

"Anything."

"Beer?"

"Sure."

"They have an extensive list." Wade looked up and noticed Ayden fidgeting, running his hand over his hair nervously. Wade smiled and patted his leg. "I'll order for you."

"Thanks."

Pat sipped a glass of wine and addressed Ayden. "Wade hasn't told us much about you."

"We just met." Wade looked up as a waiter approached.

"What can I get you to drink?" he asked.

"The Belgium white beer for my partner, and for me, I'll have a martini."

"Excellent. Can I get either of you a refill?" he asked Wade's parents. Both declined and he left.

"We've already decided on what we're going to order," Doug said, "Maybe before we get into a conversation, you can too."

"Okay, Dad." Wade looked over the menu. After he'd decided he glanced at Ayden. "Any idea?"

"Huh?" Ayden looked at Wade and then back at the menu, chewing his bottom lip as if he were undecided or nervous.

Wade whispered in his ear, "Need help?"

Ayden whispered back, "I'm safe with the steak, right?"

"Yes." Wade tried not to laugh.

"Good. Seeing octopus, I kind of got worried."

"What are you two saying?" Pat said, smiling.

"He just wants to order something he'll enjoy, Mom." Wade leaned on Ayden's leg with his hand and pointed to the item he was ordering. "Chicken breast. Also safe."

Ayden blew out a breath of relief. "Yes. Please."

THE FARMER'S SON

"You trust me on ordering for you?"

Ayden met his eyes. "You know I do."

Wade winked at him and Ayden closed the menu. He looked at his mom, she was smiling sweetly. His dad as well. "So..." Wade wished Ayden's parents could get over the same sex thing. His had. Now if he could work his magic on the prison issue, all would be right with the world.

The waiter brought a tray with two glasses of water, a beer, and a martini shaker and glass, as well as a basket of rolls. He placed them down, filled both Ayden's iced mug, and his martini glass, then asked, "Shall I come back, or do you know what you'd like?"

"Mom?" Wade gestured for her to go first.

After his parents ordered, Wade said, "Two of the chino salads, and jidori chicken breast."

"Very good." He took the menus and left.

"How did you two meet?" Doug asked.

"I got lost on the way to Cole's parole hearing, and stuck in the mud." Wade sipped his drink. "You have any idea how bad Tule fog really is?"

Ayden chuckled and sipped his beer.

"Ayden's parents own an almond orchard. He was kind enough to save my freezing ass."

"How interesting." Pat picked up her wine glass. "Have you been to LA often?"

"No. Never." Ayden eyed the rolls.

Wade held out the basket. "Stop being shy and eat one."

After he took one out of the basket, Ayden's cheeks went red from being bashful.

Wade also placed a roll on his plate and spread butter on it. "He draws comic book heroes. Gay ones."

"Do you? Have you been published?" Pat asked.

"Not yet. We gave them to a magazine editor today who seemed interested," Ayden said, then tore the roll in half and ate it.

"Are you out to your parents, Ayden?" Doug asked.

And Wade was very glad he did. "He came out when he left for LA with me." Wade waited to see his parents' reaction. "They chased after us with pitchforks and torches."

Pat immediately cringed and his father appeared grim.

Ayden added, "I have three older brothers. They wanted to pummel me."

He knew his parents would be upset. His mother was a member of PFLAG. Wade just wished her kindness extended to incarcerated sons as well as gay ones.

"I'm sorry, Ayden." Doug leaned his elbows on the table. "I know it's hard for some families to accept a gay child."

"Why?" Ayden asked simply. "Why is it hard? I'm still me."

"Have you tried to talk to them since you left?" Pat asked, drinking her wine.

Ayden shook his head and ate the second half of the roll. "My father reported the truck I was driving as stolen. I was pulled out at gunpoint yesterday, handcuffed and taken to the police station."

"No!" Pat cringed. "Why did they do that?"

Even though Wade asked Ayden not to mention it, it seemed to have a desired effect. So he said, "Some parents can't love unconditionally." Immediately he got a reaction from them. They knew where he was going.

"Don't even try to compare Cole to you or Ayden." Pat set the glass down and dabbed her lip with the cloth napkin.

Ayden said, "I was arrested. Should you hate me too?"

"You weren't dealing drugs and robbing people to support your habit." Doug shifted in the chair.

The Farmer's Son

"He was twenty-two, Dad. Cole's thirty-eight now. Sixteen years you've neglected him."

"When did this discussion become about Cole?" Pat asked, appearing upset.

"Neglected him?" Doug sneered. "He's a convicted felon."

"He made a bad decision. Please. He's so let down by all of us. He's still our blood."

When his parents looked indignant, Ayden said, "Yeah. That's how it's going to be for me. I know no matter what I do to try and change it, I'm going to be dead to them."

Pat's expression altered drastically.

Wade glanced at Ayden as Ayden dabbed the corner of his eye. Wade caressed Ayden's hair to comfort him. "We'll try our best, Ayden. You never know."

"Are you going to see your folks, Ayden?" Doug asked.

"I am. Wade and I are going to drive there Saturday. I can't deal with it at the moment." Ayden used his napkin to wipe his eyes. "Shit. You said not to mention it. I'm sorry, Wade."

"It's okay. Don't upset yourself, baby." Wade scooted his chair closer to Ayden's and put his arm around his shoulder. He looked at his mother and said, "This is how Cole feels."

His parents exchanged glances.

Wade rubbed Ayden's back. "Calm down. It's going to be okay."

"No, Wade. It isn't. I know how it's going to be. I miss them. I miss my mom, my granddad." He stood from the table, nearly toppling his chair. "Where's the men's room?"

Wade pointed to the corner of the room.

Ayden hurried towards it.

Before he chased after him to make sure Ayden was okay, Wade said, "Picture that as Cole. Will you? Yes, he made a mistake sixteen years ago. But he's stuck alone now. No one but me even goes to the hearings, and I don't do enough for him either. What are we doing to him?"

Pat took a tissue out of her purse and dabbed her nose.

"Excuse me. I have to make sure Ayden is okay." He put his napkin on the chair as he stood and headed to find him.

~

Ayden hid inside a stall in the men's room, trying to compose himself.

"Ayden?"

Inhaling deeply, Ayden said, "In here."

Wade opened the stall door and peeked in. "Baby. I had no idea talking about this would hit you so hard, or I never would have done it."

"I'm sorry. You said not to tell them. I did. I don't know why. I'm so ashamed."

Wade reached for him. "It's okay. Come 'ere."

Ayden fell against Wade and Wade rocked Ayden in his arms. "Do you want to leave?"

"No." Ayden felt better in Wade's embrace. "I just wish my mom and dad could be cool with us. Like yours are."

"You can't change people. Believe me. I know." Wade cupped Ayden's cheek and made Ayden look into his eyes. "You're not driving. If you want to do a couple tequila shooters, go for it."

Ayden laughed and it felt good. "That's all you need. A drunk farm boy."

"My farm boy." Wade drew Ayden to his mouth and kissed him.

It was so hot, not to mention, two men kissing in a public place? It made Ayden's toes curl. "Better stop or I'll be on my knees."

Wade smiled and rested his forehead against Ayden's. "Let's eat. You're going to love the food."

THE FARMER'S SON

"Okay." Ayden nodded and followed Wade out, straightening his posture and trying to keep strong.

When they returned from the men's room, Ayden could see their first course had been placed on the table. Wade waited for Ayden to sit down, helping him scoot the chair in, and then he picked up his napkin and took his seat.

Immediately Pat reached out her hand to Ayden and said, "If you want me and Doug to go with you to talk to your parents, maybe make them aware of PFLAG, a group for parents of gay children, we can."

Ayden brightened up and looked at Wade. Wade shrugged. "Up to you."

"Yes! Thank you!" Ayden was stunned and knew with Wade's parents with them, there was no way anyone in the family would react strongly. They'd be too embarrassed to.

Wade picked up his fork and said, "Hmm. Corcoran prison is so close to Ayden's family's orchard."

Doug cleared his throat. "We know. We figured that was coming next. Your mother and I had a chat while you were gone. You're right. Sixteen years is a long time to hold a grudge against Cole. We should at least see how he's doing."

Wade sat back in his chair and gaped in amazement.

Ayden said, "Neo and Boo triumph once more."

"Who?" Pat asked.

"Ayden's comic book heroes." Wade began eating his salad. "Yup, Boo, they did." He reached to squeeze Ayden's hand. "Thank you."

"No! Thank you!" Ayden smiled in delight. "And you're right. The food is good." Ayden was surrounded by laughter and smiled shyly.

Chapter 21

To say Ayden was nervous was an understatement.

Seated in the passenger's side of Wade's BMW headed north to his family's orchard, was making his hands clammy. *Isn't it odd I am more nervous to see my flesh and blood than to meet strangers?*

It was eight in the morning on Saturday, and the highway was free of congestion. Even the fog had lightened up, and the forecast was for a clear but cold day.

Wade's parents, seated in the backseat, were silent for the most part. Ayden knew this was going to be challenging for them all. But slight progress had already been made for Wade's brother, Cole. A care package of clothing and food was in the trunk. It seemed as if Pat and Doug had decided to not only stop ignoring their youngest son, but to offer him help.

Ayden crossed his fingers he was as lucky. But Ayden knew at least his parents and his brothers would not react violently in the presence of Mr and Mrs Reed. In front of Wade, maybe. Not his respectable parents. No way.

After two hours of driving Wade asked, "Anyone need a break?"'

Ayden didn't. All he wanted to do was get this meeting over with and figure out if he was an outcast or…?

"We're good," Doug replied. "Three hours isn't that long a drive, son."

THE FARMER'S SON

"I know. I just figured I'd ask."

"Ayden?"

"Yes, Pat?" Ayden tried to turn around in the front seat to see her.

"Do you want me to talk privately to your mother about how we feel about having a gay son?"

"If she's open to it, yes. I have a feeling she'll be taking cues from my dad."

"I just wanted your permission to have a little girl talk."

Ayden glanced at Wade, who returned the gaze, looking very serious.

"Mom's the only woman in a house of six men. I bet she'd like that."

"Wow. And I thought I had it bad with four." Pat chuckled.

"Then you two can relate." Wade reached to touch Ayden's hand. "How're you doing?"

Ayden didn't know. "I think I'd be better if Dad didn't report that truck stolen. That's a sticking point in my head that I keep going over."

"You may have to let it go."

Ayden stared at the open highway as they passed a semi-tractor trailer, cruising at about seventy-five on the freeway. "Not sure I can."

"This is going to take compromise on both sides."

"I know."

An hour later, Ayden pointed to the correct private road leading to his home. On the entrance to the property was a sign which read, '*Solomon Orchards, Almonds for America*', in fancy scrolling letters and a logo of their label, which was a blooming tree and their name in an arching line above it against the American flag.

Ayden grew even tenser and checked the time. It was eleven thirty, and that meant everyone would be inside the farmhouse for their afternoon meal.

Wade slowed the car as the gravel crackled under his tires.

"Oh, Ayden, this is lovely," Pat said as they drove between lines of trees that seemed to go on for miles.

"It is beautiful." Wade held Ayden's hand tightly.

Doug leaned closer to the front seat. "How're you doing, Ayden?"

"Scared, Doug."

"Don't be. We're here for you."

"Where do you want me to park?" Wade asked.

"Just pull right up to the main house." Ayden pointed. Ayden could see several pickup trucks on the driveway, including the one he had taken last weekend. He ground his jaw in rage and blew out a loud exhale.

Wade parked and shut off the engine. He looked at Ayden before he got out. "Looks like they got the truck back."

"Yup." Ayden clenched his fists.

"Calm down before you head in." Wade rubbed his leg.

"They're going to come out if we don't go in. They'll have heard your car." Ayden opened the door and stood outside it, closing it as he faced the front of the house.

All four of them exited the vehicle.

Before Ayden had even made it to the front door, he spotted Levi peek out the front window, then appear to shout something over his shoulder—a warning to the rest.

With his mini army behind him, Ayden walked to the front door and opened it. It was never locked.

As he entered, one by one his family left the kitchen to stand in the living room to see him.

The Farmer's Son

Ayden allowed Wade and his parents inside, and closed the door behind them. The minute Ayden spotted his grandfather he rushed him. "Granddad!"

Tony opened his arms and welcomed his embrace. "I missed you, Ayd."

"Missed you too." Ayden's eyes teared up and he hugged his grandfather and kissed his cheek.

Josiah asked, "Are you going to introduce us to these people?"

Ayden released his grandfather and dabbed at his eyes. "You met Wade, Dad. This is his parents, Doug and Pat."

"Would anyone like coffee?" Ayden's mother asked, trying to be polite in an awkward situation.

Immediately Pat took the opportunity. "I would love some. Let me help you." She began taking off her coat and boldly walked right through the line of men—Ayden's brothers—who hadn't done so much as shift their nasty sneers.

"So," Tony asked Ayden, "what have you been up to in the big city?" Tony, apparently the only male with civility in the room, gestured to Wade and his father. "Take off your coats. Have a seat."

Jacob snarled in irritation and he and Jeremiah returned to finish their lunch, vanishing from the living room. Levi gave his father a gesture which read to Ayden as, *'you're not going to do anything?'*

Ayden's dad ignored Levi and stood where he was, acting like a voyeur and not a host.

Levi joined his brothers in the kitchen.

Ayden was too nervous to sit. He could hear his mother and Pat speaking quietly as the noise of dishes and silverware clicked and tapped. "I..." Ayden tried to pay attention to his grandfather. "I submitted some of my drawings to a magazine. They're going to do an article about me."

"What for?" Josiah asked bitterly.

Wade replied, "It's a human interest story about Ayden growing up here on the orchard."

Tony appeared pleased. "I can tell them some stories, Ayden."

"I know, Granddad. I think your stories are wonderful." Ayden sat beside him, knowing he had one ally whose love was truly without condition.

Wade spoke to Ayden's dad. "Why don't you join us?"

Josiah appeared about to object when Doug said, "How long have you been in the almond business?"

Ayden could see his father soften considerably at the question, liking talking about how hard everyone had worked. "It was handed down generation to generation."

Doug nodded and tilted his head to the sofa, indicating Josiah should sit beside him.

When he did, Ayden nearly fell over from the shock at seeing his dad give in.

Doug continued to show a genuine interest in the family business and Ayden's dad appeared to be calm as he spoke about it.

Ayden checked on Wade, giving him a curious glance as Tony entertained Wade about the 'ole days'. Wade shot a very brief smile Ayden's way, indicating his hope for the best.

Ayden stood and walked to the threshold of the kitchen doorway, seeing his three brothers eating their afternoon meal. Pat and his mother were standing near the counter, chatting quietly, cups for coffee laid out near the coffeemaker as it dripped and filled the carafe sending the scent of perked beans though the air.

Ayden's mother met his gaze. The sadness in her eyes nearly killed him.

"Hi, Mom."

The Farmer's Son

"Ayd." Helen walked towards him. "We need to talk."

Ayden looked at Wade's mother and saw her supportive smile. When Helen approached him, Pat walked boldly over to the three farm boys and said, "So, tell me about what you boys do all day here at the orchard."

Even Jacob perked up and smiled at her interest.

Helen hooked Ayden's arm and they walked down the hall to Ayden's old bedroom. Once they were inside, she closed the door for privacy. "Sit."

Ayden looked around his old room. It felt cold and alien to him after sleeping with Wade for a week in his posh condo. He sat on the bed and folded his hands on his lap.

"Wade's mother told me how difficult it was for her to accept Wade as gay."

Ayden flinched and couldn't meet her eyes.

"I've thought about you so much this week, of what happened last weekend, of the way you were treated."

"Mom..." Ayden couldn't take it.

"You're my son. You will always be my son."

He looked up at her. "Who is my dad?"

She seemed to collapse inside and sat down next to him. "I hoped you'd never find out. Never."

"Did you cheat on Dad?"

"We...we separated for a year, Ayden. We went through a very rough patch."

He nodded. Never had his mother told him anything personal about herself before. He reached for her hand and she seemed surprised but returned the clasp.

"I lived at your Aunt Rose's place at that time. Your brothers stayed with your dad and granddad, just for the weekdays, and with me and your aunt on weekends." She inhaled for strength and looked into space. "I thought your father and I were through, but we never applied for divorce papers. Maybe waiting to see if we should or not." She squeezed Ayden's hand and seemed to gather up the courage to tell him this story.

"During this separation from your father, I met my old high-school sweetheart at the local movie theater one night. Rose and I were going to see *Father of the Bride*." She smiled sadly as if remembering the night.

Ayden tried to digest this story and believe it. So far it was as alien to him as his comics.

"Well, who was there with his friends? None other than Jay Baher. Imagine how I felt seeing my first love again after nearly two decades."

Ayden looked down at his mother's hand, at her wedding rings.

"We reminisced about old times…I never stopped loving him. I know your father knows that. But Jay wasn't the type to settle down."

"So, you made love to him?"

"I did. Not that night, but we went out for coffee a few days later…and…"

"And."

"Ayden, I never thought I'd get pregnant after one night of passion with Jay."

"What happened then? Why didn't you and Jay stay together?"

Helen's expression hardened. "Because to him it was just some trip down memory lane. He was already with another woman the next time we ran into him…only a week later."

"I'm sorry, Mom."

Inhaling and straightening her back, setting her shoulders as if she were resolved, she said, "Well, after that, I got to thinking about your father, and how maybe what we had wasn't perfect but he's a good man, solid, trustworthy." She tucked back a wisp of hair behind her ear. "I came back home the next day, and we tried to put the separation behind us....then I realized I was pregnant."

"So, Dad knew?"

"I didn't lie. Yes, Ayden. He knew."

Ayden released her hand and rubbed his clammy palms on his jeans. "He's hated me from the day I was born."

"No, Ayden. He's hated me. Not you."

Ayden looked into her light eyes. Her hair had gotten so gray, even more so in the week he had been gone, he wondered if worry did indeed have an effect on her.

She gave him a sad smile. "So, who am I to judge you? I'm the last one."

"I won't apologize for who I am. I won't say I'm sorry. Because I'm not."

"You have no reason to. You are who you are."

Ayden's mouth dropped in surprise. "Thank you."

"Don't thank me. No need."

"Mom?"

"Yes, Ayden?"

"Is there any way I can contact Jay? Does he know about me?"

"I did tell him, yes. And you know what he told me?"

"No. What?"

"That I was a liar. That he was sterile, and that he wanted nothing to do with me, or you... Rose tried to find him a few years after you were born, but his mom said he'd moved out of the state, and no one had any information about where to find him."

"Oh." Ayden nodded.

"I'm sorry, Ayden. But Josiah has tried to be a dad for you. He didn't do so badly."

"He never hit me."

"No. He never hit you." She caressed Ayden's hair.

"Will he get over the fact that I'm a gay man?"

"Well, even if he doesn't, you can count on me and your grandfather."

Ayden kissed her cheek and smiled.

When he and his mother returned to the living room, Ayden heard laughter. He stopped short at seeing his brother Levi, standing in the middle of the rest of family members, being animated in his description of some event.

"…he's way up on the cherry-picker!" Levi said, "…can't get the controls to work."

Jacob teased Levi, "I said I knew how! You just didn't believe me that it was stuck up there."

Ayden glanced at Wade. He had a cup of coffee in his hand and was smiling at Levi and Jacob's retelling of their mishap.

Pat stood from the sofa and approached Ayden. "How are you, my lovely boy?"

"Uh…stunned?" Ayden looked around the living room. His dad was sitting beside Doug, chatting about business, his brothers were telling Wade about their antics on the orchard, and Granddad was nodding off in the chair.

Helen asked, "Would anyone like a refill on their coffee?"

A few empty mugs were raised in response.

She smiled and left the room.

Jeremiah said to Ayden, "Wade tells us that your stupid drawings may be published."

"Maybe." Ayden hadn't shown any of the homoerotic art to them, but they all knew he drew superheroes.

"I can't believe that." Jacob shook his head. "You can really make a living doing that?"

Wade said, "He can. And he's so good he will."

Ayden tried to read his father's reaction to all of this. Doug caught Ayden's attention, and smiled.

THE FARMER'S SON

As if finally knowing what he'd done, Josiah said, "I'm sorry I put you through that stolen truck ordeal, Ayden."

Ayden's knees actually felt weak. His dad was apologizing?

Doug said, "I don't think your father realized just how traumatic being held at gunpoint in Los Angeles really is."

Ayden was speechless.

Jacob asked, "Were you really pulled out of the truck at gunpoint by cops? I watch that show, COPS, and seriously thought about being one."

"Good luck." Wade shook his head. "I wouldn't want that job."

"You want to be a cop?" Levi asked. "Great. Another one bailing out on the orchard."

Helen brought out a tray of a fresh pot of coffee, the cream and sugar, and homemade almond banana bread.

As the intermingled families passed their mugs, Pat refilled them.

"Ayd."

Ayden turned to look at his father. Josiah stood and gestured for him to come closer so they could speak quietly. Ayden did, stuffing his hands into his pockets, feeling anxious.

"I'm sorry for judging you. Wade and his family are very decent people."

Thoughts of how this man had taken back his wife, after she became pregnant with another man's child, ran through Ayden's mind. He had to admit, he had a lot of respect for his dad after not blowing his top and divorcing her. The man could have made it difficult for her see her other three sons again as punishment for her deed, but he didn't. He took her back.

"I didn't do anything to hurt anyone, Dad. I just want to be happy."

"We want that too. It's just that it came out of the blue and no one understood what happened. You vanish overnight, show up with a man we'd never met, and then you took off without warning, without even asking for the truck."

"I did. But I thought my brothers were going to beat us up." Ayden turned around to see Wade and Jacob laughing together as they ate the banana bread. Ayden was beyond stunned that the meeting of families was going this well.

"We all needed time to adjust. And..." Josiah nodded to the group. "This. We needed this."

Tony woke with a start and said, "Did I ever tell you the story about the day I was in the trenches?"

In harmony, Jacob, Jeremiah and Levi said, "Yes, Grandpa," and then laughed.

Doug perked up. "I haven't heard it."

"Uh oh." Levi cracked up. "Granddad's got a new person to tell his war stories to."

Ayden looked back at his father, seeing him smile. Smile!

He spotted his mom and Wade's mom, standing together near the kitchen. Pat said, "It's called PFLAG. I'll send you all the brochures."

"How amazing there's a group of parents like that."

"Oh, yes. You'd be amazed at how enormous it is, coast to coast. You and Josiah should come to LA for a weekend. Stay with us. We can take you to some great restaurants and if you'd like we can plan it on a weekend with a meeting."

Ayden's jaw dropped and he caught Wade staring at him. Ayden made a comic gesture to him, opening up his palms and mouthing, '*What the fuck?*'

Wade stood from his spot on the sofa as Tony elaborated on his experiences in the war to an eager Doug.

Wade asked, "You and your mom talk?"

"Yes. But..." Ayden gestured to the room. "Am I dreaming?"

The Farmer's Son

"I think your family and mine are good people. Maybe you and I threw something at them they just couldn't handle in one day."

"Dad apologized!" Ayden whispered excitedly into Wade's ear.

"Good." Wade turned to look at the group.

"And..." Ayden made sure no one was listening. "She told me about my real dad."

Wade paid careful attention.

"She said she and dad split up for a while. This guy, my dad, Jay is his name. She said he was her first love in school and when they reconnected, they, well..."

"Reconnected?" Wade did not smile. Neither of them thought of it as a joke.

"Yeah. She said she just had sex with him once, but who knows. Anyway, the guy was a fuck-up and she saw him with another woman right after...and he left the state and no one knew where he went. So..." Ayden again made sure no one was overhearing them before he continued. "So she went back to Dad. When they figured out she was pregnant, both of them knew it was Jay's. But Dad didn't kick her out. That has to mean something."

"It means your father really loves your mom, no matter what."

Ayden thought about it and looked at his parents through different eyes now. With more compassion.

Wade gave him a one arm hug in support.

Pat said, "Don't they make a handsome couple?"

"Mom," Wade replied, "Really?" He narrowed his eyes at her, scolding.

"They do." Helen smiled.

"Who are you people and what have you done with my real family?" Ayden coughed on his shock.

"Aww, go draw a cartoon, super-boy," Jacob teased.

Ayden shook his head in amazement. "I love you all. Do you know that?"

He got a reaction of silly noises from his brothers, playfully mocking him, and a wink from Pat in adoration.

~

As the afternoon crept up on them, and the end of visiting hours at the jail loomed closer, Wade and his family stood to say their goodbyes at what turned out to be a few hours of a very pleasant visit.

Wade hugged Ayden's mother warmly, thanking her, and went around shaking the hands of the male members of the Solomon family, who smiled at him and seemed to get over their homophobia.

"Sir." Wade held out his hand to Tony. "A pleasure to see you again and to listen to your incredible stories."

"The pleasure was mine as well. You have a wonderful family, Wade, and I hope we can see each other again soon."

"Count on it." Wade hugged the old man and then found he was face to face with Ayden's father. His smile fell and he reached out for a shake.

Josiah clasped Wade's hand. "Take care of my boy."

"He'll be treated like a king."

"Don't spoil him." Josiah frowned. "Just make sure he stays out of trouble."

"I'll do both." Wade was shocked when Josiah hugged him. He patted the man's back and parted from him, seeing the older man slightly misty-eyed. "He's a phone call away," Wade said softly. "And he'd love it if you called...a lot."

"We will."

Wade joined his mother and father at the doorway as they waved and everyone was laughing and talking about seeing each other for family outings. It made Wade shake his head in wonder.

Ayden made the rounds as well and after what felt like a long goodbye, they climbed into the Beamer, and kept waving as Ayden's family stood outside the picturesque farmhouse and waved back as he drove away.

"Well!" Pat exclaimed happily. "You have a lovely family, Ayden."

"Am I awake?" Ayden asked Wade, "Did that just go as well as I think it did?"

Doug chuckled.

"I doubt it would have gone that well without you guys," Wade said as he looked into his rearview mirror. "Thanks. You have no idea how hard this would have been for me and Ayden to battle on our own."

"Even my brothers were cool?" Ayden sank in the seat. "I am stunned!"

"I had no idea the almond business was such a lucrative field, Ayden," Doug said, "Your family has worked very hard, and are incredibly successful."

"I'll say!" Pat replied, "What a beautiful home. And look at all this land. It's such a wonderful place to live. So peaceful."

Wade glanced at Ayden, happy to see him smile. "So. Are we ready for prison?"

The backseat grew quiet.

"Hello?" Wade tried to see his parents in the rearview mirror.

"Yes, Wade," Doug answered quietly.

Ayden spun on the seat to face them. "I feel sorry for Cole. He won't be able to come to any of our family outings. I can't imagine how hard that will be for him."

Wade was waiting for his father to make a snide comment about Cole committing armed robbery, but he didn't. He was also stunned to see how he had missed the turn off last weekend by a mere two miles. Fog and a bad navigator had done him in, but…brought him an amazing man.

As they drove closer to the prison, the inside of the car got as quiet as a tomb. No one wanted to be there, especially Cole.

They passed through a checkpoint with a guard and gate. Wade was the only one who had been through his before, but he had a feeling this was torture on his parents.

Knowing you have an incarcerated son and seeing him in jail, were two different things. And they had not seen Cole in sixteen years. Wade wondered if they would even recognize him.

They were allowed through the barrier and Wade parked, shutting off the car. After opening his seatbelt he asked, "You ready?"

"Will they let me in?" Ayden asked. "Since I'm not related?"

"Yes." Wade opened his car door. "Come on." He popped the trunk and picked the box up that they had prepared for Cole and carried it to the visiting area. With Ayden at his side, his parents lagging behind, holding onto each other as they walked, Wade felt like he was going to a funeral, not a visit.

They entered a room and the box was immediately requested and opened. Wade took off his coat and they passed through a metal detector, like in an airport, and a guard used a wand to wave over them for weapons.

The room had a half a dozen rectangular tables with inmates receiving visitors, and several guards standing by.

Wade could hear Ayden's gulp of anxiety from where he stood, and wondered if his experience in handcuffs gave him an even greater sense of fear here.

They were shown to a table and all four of them were asked to sit on metal chairs on the same side. The guard placed the box on the floor after it had been thoroughly inspected. "No contact. No passing anything."

"Okay." Wade nodded in reply as everyone else appeared too petrified to respond.

"I can't believe my son is in this place." Pat looked furious.

Ayden put his arm around her shoulder and held her. "Imagine how it is for him."

Wade immediately saw the expression change on her face to sympathy.

After a few minutes, Cole appeared, wearing a pair of jeans and a sweatshirt. He was led by a guard to the seat opposite all of them, and asked to sit down. He too was told, "No touching, no passing of anything."

"I know." Cole moved away from the guard in annoyance.

Wade watched his parents' reaction as this man—a man who was thirty-eight, no longer twenty-two, and been through hell—sat at a table with them.

"Don't I even get a hello?" Cole asked in exasperation.

"My God. I wouldn't recognize you," Pat said.

"Whose fault is that!" Cole reacted.

Wade tried to calm them down. "Okay. No fighting."

"Who are you?" Cole asked Ayden.

"He's my partner." Wade checked Ayden's expression. His gaze was riveted to Cole.

"Still like 'em young, eh, big brother?"

"Yup."

"We brought you some things." Doug gestured to the box.

"What?" Cole went for it, digging in it.

Wade half expected he'd be stopped by a guard, but the items had already been checked out.

"Good. I need clothing. Thanks for the food as well." Cole sat up and ran his hand through his hair. "That's what I was going to order through the Walkenhorst's catalog."

Wade thought Cole looked like his older brother, not younger, he was so thin and worn, with a closely cropped beard.

The growth just as dark as Wade's but longer. Designer stubble? In jail? Ironically, Cole would be the better looking of the two of them if he wasn't so rough and haggard.

"I'm sorry, Cole." Pat reached out her hand but a guard stepped up so she retracted it. "Sorry we neglected you."

"I fucked up. You don't think I know I fucked up?" Cole said, "But not having any of you at my parole hearings? That tells the judge a lot, believe me."

"We'll be here from now on." Doug interlaced his fingers on the table.

"Thanks. So? What the hell is it like in the fucking outside world?"

Ayden asked shyly, "How...how much more time do you have to do?"

"Four years if I don't keep screwing up inside."

"Ouch." Ayden flinched.

"Did sixteen. *Ouch!*" Cole sneered then his pretense dropped. "Sorry. You play you pay."

"Cole..." Pat teared up and dabbed her eyes with a tissue.

"It's okay, Mom. I get it. I was a fuck up."

"What will you do when you get out?" Doug asked.

"How do I know?"

"Are they training you for anything?"

Wade could see this visit was killing them all. No one knew what the future held for Cole. But did any of them know?

"I can landscape or something. They let me do it here." Cole rubbed his face and checked a clock on the wall. "Will you guys call me once in a while? Or can I call you?"

"Yes. I'm sorry, Cole."

"Mom, stop crying. Okay?"

"I was held at gunpoint." Ayden sniffled sadly.

Cole looked at him. "By whom?"

The Farmer's Son

"The LAPD cops. My dad reported the truck I was in as stolen."

"Fun, huh?" Cole smiled sadly.

"No. Not fun."

Wade wondered if Ayden was trying for some common ground and to show his empathy. It didn't do much to sway Cole. Wade knew one day in cuffs did not translate to sixteen years in prison.

"We'll come down every other weekend," Pat said.

"It's okay. Once a month is fine. I know it's a long trip."

"Whatever you want, son."

By his father's body language, the clenching of his hands, Wade could see his dad wanted to touch Cole.

The guard began to call 'time' and the family members around them stood up.

When Cole did, Pat reached for him to embrace and she got a good hug in before the guards parted them.

Cole's eyes were red from his emotions. "Love you guys." He picked up the box and was led out of the room.

Ayden bit his lip as he watched, and Wade knew his parents were about to lose it.

"Bye!" Pat waved, "Bye, baby!"

"Bye, Mom. Dad....Wade." Cole paused and said, "Ayden, no more cops with guns."

"No. No more."

They waited until he was led off and then Wade touched his mother's back gently. "It kills me each time."

"Oh, God. Look at him. He's aged so much." Pat dabbed her eyes as they walked to the exit.

"I wouldn't have recognized him if we met on the street, Wade." Doug held the door open for them and Wade gazed at the late sunshine and knew it would be dark by five.

He noticed Ayden straggling behind and put his arm around him as they walked to the car.

"Poor Cole." Ayden pouted.

"Maybe if we all show up for the next hearing, he'll get out sooner." Wade used the fob to open the doors of his car.

They dropped in heavily and Wade started it, getting the heat going since the temperature had plummeted with the setting sun.

"Ready to head home?" Wade asked.

"Yes." Ayden slid low in the seat. "I'm exhausted."

"You okay to drive, Wade? We could say at a hotel, have a nice dinner." Doug leaned closer to the front seat.

"No one brought an overnight bag. No. Let me get us home." Wade put the car in reverse and backed out of the spot. "Mom? You want me to stop for a meal on the way?"

"Whatever you want."

Wade knew this would be hard on them, and also understood it was why they didn't make the effort for so long. The pain at seeing their youngest son look like a ragged old man.

"Okay." In a car of preoccupied people, Wade drove them off of the prison premises, and headed back to civilization. He put on a soft music CD and imagined stopping for dinner once they were closer to LA.

The Farmer's Son

Chapter 22

By the time he and Ayden walked through the door of the condo unit, it was nearly ten. A twelve hour day. They hung up their jackets in the closet and removed their shoes. Ayden continued on to the bedroom as Wade went through first his mail, then his missed calls and text messages while standing in the kitchen. After he separated bills from junk, he then read his text messages, all the while contemplating booze.

He sent Simon a text since he asked how the meeting between families had gone. During the week he had been in touch with Simon, but hadn't seen him since the gym on Monday.

He wrote, *'things went well with Ayden's family, but tough on mom and dad with Cole.'* After he sent it he placed his phone on the counter and poured a glass of whiskey for himself, standing in the darkness of the kitchen sipping it.

Ayden appeared, topless, wearing sweatpants. "You coming to bed?"

"I am. Just taking the edge off." Wade held up the glass.

Ayden approached and reached for the glass. Passing it to him, Wade watched as he sipped it, then Ayden shuddered and made a face of disgust. "Yeck."

His reaction was so cute it made Wade smile. He put his arm around Ayden and walked with him to the bedroom. "It's an acquired taste."

"Must be. Blah. Now I have to brush my teeth again."

"Well, with a minty mouth, no booze will taste good." Wade put the glass down and began undressing.

"Oh. I didn't think of that." Ayden dropped back on the bed and stared at Wade while he undressed. "What a day."

"I know. Right? Good thing we can sleep in tomorrow." As Wade tossed his clothing into the hamper, he noticed Ayden with his hand down his sweats, playing with himself as he watched.

Wade shook his head. "My horny man." He picked up his glass to take another sip as he looked at Ayden. Ayden flipped his stiff dick out of his pants and was showing it off, pushing it up and down, laying it flat against his sweats.

Wade stared at Ayden's sculpted chest, his six pack abs and then that lovely cut cock and small pubic bush. After finishing the booze he pointed to the bathroom. "Be back. Don't go anywhere."

"Where'm I going?" Ayden smiled, watching him.

"Don't come without me."

"Nope. I wouldn't do that."

Wade closed himself into the bathroom and peeked at his reflection. All in all, though stressful at times, it had been a decent day. Followed by an even better night. The dinner with his parents had helped him and Ayden decompress completely. They spoke about both the meeting with Ayden's family and Cole, knowing with time, things would improve.

He washed up for sex...and bed. Wade's trust in Ayden and this relationship had taken a huge leap forward after today. The uniting of their families, the positive interactions from both sides, and peace made on all fronts? Wade couldn't have wished for anything better.

He met his own blue eyes in the mirror and whispered, "Ya got a good one, ya fucker."

~

THE FARMER'S SON

Ayden removed the lower half of his clothing and bent his knees, staring at his own cock as he ran his hand over it. He peeked at the nightstand, rolled over and removed the condoms and lubrication from the top drawer, noticing the dildo selection. He picked up a small egg shaped one curiously, which had a wire and a small box with a switch. He turned on the switch and the little egg buzzed in his hand. "Hmm." He peeked at the bathroom door and heard the water running in the sink.

Using lubrication, Ayden made the little egg slick and reached between his legs to push it inside himself. It went in easily since it was quite small. Holding the tiny box in his hand, he turned it on. The minute the egg vibrated, Ayden melted and closed his eyes. "*Ohhh,* yes." He spread his legs, bent his knees tightly and rested the tiny box on his pelvis.

The door opened and Ayden looked under heavy lids at Wade. "You're spoiled."

"Am I?" Wade noticed what Ayden had done.

"Yes. If I had these toys on the orchard I wouldn't need you."

Wade laughed and laid down across the lower half of the bed, looking at Ayden's ass. "It is nice, that one. I like it because it's small…but effective."

"Man, so soothing."

Wade slid closer, touching Ayden's balls gently.

"Yes. That's nice. Do something wonderful to me, then fuck my brains out."

"I think I can do that." Wade put the little box on the bed between Ayden's legs and scooted higher, nuzzling against Ayden's balls. As Wade began to use his mouth and tongue, Ayden started to go into a sexual swoon. Wade pushed Ayden's knees to the bed, making Ayden nearly perform a split and his cock point straight up. Wade opened his lips and drew the head into his mouth slowly, sinking Ayden's entire length into wet heat.

Ayden closed his eyes and began to rise to a climax. As the urge to come increased, Ayden needed something more in him, not the little egg. He went reaching for it.

Wade sat up. "What?"

"Need something bigger in me...like your dick."

"Do you?" Wade purred and ran his tongue around the head of Ayden's cock.

"Your big, Neo-rod."

Wade chuckled. "Don't start making me laugh." Wade removed the little egg and pushed it off the side of the bed. He knelt up and rolled on a condom, jerking his cock to get it harder.

Ayden shivered in anticipation. "I love you in me!" He grabbed his knees and offered himself. Wade inched closer, pointing his cock at Ayden's rim. The minute Ayden felt the head of Wade's cock penetrate and the sense of being filled completely, he whimpered and licked his lips.

Wade entered Ayden gently, allowing him to relax until their bodies met. With complete penetration, Wade cupped the back of Ayden's head and drew him to his lips. At the contact of their mouths and tongues, Wade began to thrust into Ayden. Ayden's cock was trapped between their bodies, so he locked his ankles around Wade's hips and humped him for that friction and amazing sensation of being stimulated inside and out.

Soon the heat and intensity got Ayden crazy. He parted from their kiss, needing deep breaths of air. Ayden fucked Wade from below, ramming his hips upward. He grabbed Wade's hips, hammering against him, feeling their skin begin to dampen with sweat and Wade's cock growing harder inside him.

He opened his eyes to see Wade's gaze on his expression and as they locked stares, Ayden went into a strong climax. He vocalized the intensity with choking grunts of pleasure and Wade pressed deeper inside Ayden and came, his cock pulsating in time with Ayden's own. Sticky cum sealed their hot skin and Ayden kept rocking against Wade for the aftershocks, rubbing his cock between the slickness of their slippery skin. Wade braced himself on his arms, lowering his head as he caught his breath.

Ayden released his ankles from around Wade's hips and placed his feet on the bed, panting, sweating and so sated he could close his eyes and sleep. "Love you."

"Love you too, my beautiful man." Wade kissed his slack lips and pulled out.

"Can't move."

"If I can, you can." Wade reached out his hand and Ayden was hauled to his feet.

"Sleep." Ayden scuffed into the bathroom to clean up. "Need sleep."

"Sleep." Wade agreed.

G. A. HAUSER

San Diego
Six months later…

Wade showed his pass at the side entrance and he and Ayden were allowed into the enormous hall. "I cannot believe I am doing this."

"Yes! Yes!" Ayden had a look around the booths and pumped his fists into the air.

"There's Mason." Wade spotted the man from the magazine at a huge booth, surrounded by life-size cutouts and banners of Neo Magnay and Booverly, the only gay superheroes taking part in Comic-Com this year.

"Look at you two!" Mason cracked up with laughter. "Those costumes are fantastic!"

Ayden spun around, flexing his muscles and showing off his utility belt.

"He can pull this charade off. Look at that chest." Wade pointed to his sidekick. "I need padding."

"Nope. You can too, Neo." Ayden embraced him and began rubbing his hard cock on him.

"No way. Ayden, calm down." Wade backed up and looked around nervously.

"Don't worry. We're not in the macho wing." Mason pointed to several rainbow decals at neighboring booths. "They placed us with the gay friendly pack."

Ayden picked up a comic book and held it up like an award. "We have a comic! We have a comic!" he sang happily.

"First edition." Mason straightened the stack. "Soon to be a collector's item. Bet on it."

Wade touched his mask and felt silly. "I look awful, right? Mason, be honest."

"You look fucking hot. Is that all you?" He pointed to Wade's groin.

"Yes! I didn't stick a sock in it!"

"Damn." Mason shook his head.

"Mm!" Ayden went for a grope.

"Calm down, Boo-boy. This joint is about to open to the public. How on earth did I get talked into this?" Wade tried to control his excited man's hands as they went for a grope of him in tights.

"Because this is you!" Mason pointed to the cardboard figure of Neo.

"I'm insane." Wade looked around in paranoia, then down at his groin. "You do realize my parents are coming."

"And mine," Ayden said, checking out all the Neo and Boo literature, including little plastic action figures.

"You guys are going to make a real mark on this convention. Word is everyone wants the first edition, even the straight dudes, because they know how ground breaking it is." Mason playfully slapped Ayden's hand away from messing up all the neat rows of boxes.

"Hey!" Another man from *Judas' Rainbow* showed up, wearing a Comic-Com ID badge on a lanyard around his neck. "It's about to open. It's such a zoo outside! Sorry I'm late. Parking after I dropped you off, Mason, was a bitch."

"Hi, Parker!" Ayden posed for him, fists on hips, showing off. "I'm Booverly!"

"Look at you two. Growl!" Parker Douglas stepped back as if getting a good view. "Photo op." He raised his camera phone and signaled for Wade to get closer to Ayden.

Ayden grabbed Wade by the shoulders and yanked him close roughly.

"Smile, Neo." Parker cracked up.

Wade was tugged into place and peeked at Ayden. The grin on Ayden's face was priceless. Wade smiled and the camera flashed.

An announcement came over the loud speakers. "We're open, ladies and gentlemen! Have fun!"

"Yes! Yes!" Ayden jumped into the air and danced around.

Wade caught sight of Ayden's semi-erect cock. "Uh, Boo, calm down or you're liable to cream your tights."

"Can't!" He raised his hands over his head in triumph. "I'm at Comic-Con!"

The noise hit before the rush of bodies. But soon they were overwhelmed with crazy people in costumes waving cash to buy up their merchandise.

Ayden's thrill was contagious and Wade fell into the silliness and posed with hundreds of fans and admirers. It was insane, but what the hell.

~

Ayden signed autographs for his fans, and watched Mason and Parker taking cash for their comic books and posters. A young man, appearing shy, seemed to be waiting for his chance to speak to Ayden. Ayden managed to make his way over to him and asked the young man, "Do you want an autograph?"

"Yes. Please." He handed Ayden a pen and the comic book he bought. As Ayden signed it, the young man said, "To Jason."

"Okay."

Jason spun around as if wanting Ayden to use his back as a writing board. Ayden did, signing the comic and handing it to Jason.

The young man took back his pen. "I just wanted to say thanks."

"You're welcome."

"No. A special thanks. Not just for the autograph."

Ayden tilted his head. "Oh? For?"

"For giving me courage. Because of Neo and Boo, I'm not afraid anymore."

The Farmer's Son

Ayden's jaw dropped. He grabbed Jason and hugged him, enveloping the young man in his arms. When he released him Jason staggered back and was flushed bright red. "Wow!"

"You're welcome!" Ayden beamed at him.

"Ayden!"

Ayden looked up to see his family rushing over to him. "Hey! You guys found me!"

"It wasn't easy. What a mob!" Jacob shook his head then looked at Ayden's outfit. "You're a dork."

"I know." Ayden giggled. "Hi, Mom. Dad."

"Look at you!" Helen's eyes widened and she covered her laughter.

"Check out Wade," Ayden said in a conspiratorial whisper, pointing him out as he signed comics for fans.

His brothers roared with hilarity making Wade look up, and frown in embarrassment.

Ayden kept laughing too as Wade made his way over.

"I know. I look like an idiot." Wade shook his head and crossed his arms.

"You look very handsome," Helen said.

"Granddad!" Ayden rushed to him and hugged him. "I didn't think you'd come."

"I wouldn't miss my grandson as a superhero."

"Dad, take a picture! Wade, get on the other side of my granddad." He held onto the old man and smiled.

Wade did too, waiting as Josiah took a photograph.

"This reminds me of a story." Tony looked from Wade to Ayden.

His brothers rolled their eyes and began investigating the booth, and just as Ayden was about to hear something about the war, Wade's mother appeared from the crowd, rushed them, and gave them both a hug.

"Wade!" Pat said, "It took us forever to find you. Even with this map!" She held up the guide.

Ayden spotted Doug and watched his reaction to Wade's get-up.

"Dad"—Wade held up his hand in a gesture to stop him, anticipating the teasing—"don't start."

"Uh…" Doug gave Wade a once-over. "I can see why gay men would be drooling. You guys aren't ashamed to show it all."

"Christ." Wade covered his groin in embarrassment.

"Should we buy an ugly Ayden doll?" Jacob held up a plastic box with Booverly in it.

Ayden chuckled, knowing this time, the teasing was good-natured.

"I would," Parker said, "In ten years you can sell it for a couple hundred on eBay."

"Damn!" Jacob didn't appear so smug suddenly.

Tony tapped Ayden to get his attention.

Ayden and Wade both stopped what they were doing to listen.

"Did I ever tell you the story about the farmer's son?" the old man asked.

Ayden tried not to laugh and shook his head, keeping a straight face.

Tony's eyes gleamed. "Well, there was this man from LA who got lost in the fog…"

Wade couldn't hold it in and started laughing.

"…and this young man who thought he could pull the city slicker out of a ditch." Tony kept tapping Ayden to keep his attention, though Tony was smirking as he did.

"Did they live happily ever after, Granddad?" Ayden asked, feeling giddy.

"Why, I think they did." Tony laughed.

THE FARMER'S SON

Ayden glanced at Wade to see his smirk. He lunged for him and picked him up off his feet in his embrace. The fans around the booth began to whistle and chant, "Boo! Boo!"

"I'll never live this down," Wade said, still laughing.

"And you'll never forget this day either." Ayden cupped the back of his head and kissed Wade.

A chorus of cheers went up around them.

Ayden set Wade back on his feet and looked around at all the cameras flashing.

Wade held Ayden's waist and whispered in his ear, "The city slicker and the farmer's son. I think that's a joke I've heard years ago."

"It's not a joke anymore, Neo. It's a love story." He smiled at Wade.

"Yeah. It is." Wade kissed him again.

The End

G. A. HAUSER

ABOUT THE AUTHOR

Award-winning author G.A. Hauser was born in Fair Lawn, New Jersey, USA and attended university in New York City. She moved to Seattle, Washington where she worked as a patrol officer with the Seattle Police Department. In early 2000 G.A. moved to Hertfordshire, England where she began her writing in earnest and published her first book, In the Shadow of Alexander. Now a full-time writer, G.A. has written over ninety novels, including several best-sellers of gay fiction. GA is also the Executive Producer for her first feature film, CAPITAL GAMES. For more information on other books by G.A., visit the author at her official website. www.authorgahauser.com
www.capitalgamesthemovie.com

G.A. has won awards from All Romance eBooks for Best Author 2010, 2009, Best Novel 2008, *Mile High*, and Best Author 2008, Best Novel 2007, *Secrets and Misdemeanors*, Best Author 2007.

The G.A. Hauser Collection
Single Titles

Unnecessary Roughness

Hot Rod

Mr. Right

Happy Endings

Down and Dirty

Lancelot in Love

Cowboy Blues

Midnight in London

Living Dangerously

The Last Hard Man

Taking Ryan

Born to be Wilde

The Adonis of WeHo

Boys

Band of Brothers

Rough Ride

I Love You I Hate You

Code Red

Marry Me

Timeless

G. A. HAUSER

One Two Three

The Farmer's Son

Three Wishes

COPS

L.A. Masquerade

Dude! Did You Just Bite Me?

My Best Friend's Boyfriend

The Diamond Stud

The Hard Way

Games Men Play

Born to Please

Of Wolves and Men

The Order of Wolves

Got Men?

Heart of Steele

All Man

Julian

Black Leather Phoenix

London, Bloody, London

In The Dark and What Should Never Be, Erotic Short Stories

Mark and Sharon

The Farmer's Son

A Man's Best Friend
It Takes a Man
Blind Ambition (formerly The Physician and the Actor)
For Love and Money
The Kiss
Naked Dragon
Secrets and Misdemeanors
Capital Games
Giving Up the Ghost
To Have and To Hostage
Love you, Loveday
The Boy Next Door
When Adam Met Jack
Exposure
The Vampire and the Man-eater
Murphy's Hero
Mark Antonious deMontford
Prince of Servitude
Calling Dr Love
The Rape of St. Peter
The Wedding Planner
Going Deep

G. A. HAUSER

Double Trouble

Pirates

Miller's Tale

Vampire Nights

Teacher's Pet

In the Shadow of Alexander

The Rise and Fall of the Sacred Band of Thebes

The Farmer's Son

The Action Series

Acting Naughty

Playing Dirty

Getting it in the End

Behaving Badly

Dripping Hot

Packing Heat

Being Screwed

Something Sexy

Going Wild

Having it All!

Bending the Rules

Keeping it Up

Making Love

Men in Motion Series

Mile High

Cruising

Driving Hard

Leather Boys

Heroes Series

Man to Man

Two In Two Out

Top Men

G.A. Hauser
Writing as Amanda Winters

Sister Moonshine

Nothing Like Romance

Silent Reign

Butterfly Suicide

Mutley's Crew

THE FARMER'S SON

Other works by G.A. Hauser:

I LOVE YOU I HATE YOU

Parker Douglas started his new job at *Judas' Rainbow* as a sex and style columnist for the LGBT magazine. After one week he was learning the office politics and gossip. It didn't take long to figure out two of the men who worked beside him were having an on-again-off-again, fiery relationship.

Forty year old group advertising manager, Mason Bloomfield always had bad karma for being attracted to Mr Wrong. It seemed to Mason, no matter how hard he tried he was drawn to very young pretty men who treated him badly, and the hunk, Dack Torington, was no different. Mason was smitten by the twenty-six year old man's looks and physique, but inevitable, Mason was let down, again and again.

When Valentine's Day hits the couple hard, and thirty-five year old Parker witnesses some firsthand drama between the two men. Parker's impulses are at first to stand clear of the mess- but his second thought was...complete empathy for Mason, who is clearly the loser in the scenario.

Can the end of one relationship signal the beginning of a new one? Or are love and hate truly tied together like a bow on a box of Valentine's chocolates?

I Love You I Hate You!- Parker knew which emotion he preferred, and soon it became clear to Mason, Hate was not a virtue, nor did it have a place in a healthy relationship.

Code Red

Thirty-five year old, African American Noah Hopkins loved his job as a nurse. He worked late nights and long hours, so that wasn't conducive to meeting and dating. But inevitably on his shift, the paramedics from the Los Angeles Fire Department would bring in victims from accidents or illnesses to their trauma center and the female nursing staff would put out the alert. 'Code Red'. It was a silly phrase they used when a hot fireman would be spotted in the ER. And everyone who worked at the LA Medical Center knew, fire-fighter Keegan Vance was 'Code Red' indeed!

Noah had to tolerate the female staff circling Keegan like buzzards when he showed up, and Noah and Keegan were always friendly and professional to each other when they met.

Tough, masculine, Keegan Vance was ex-army, and in a career where homophobia was rife, the LAFD, so he kept his private life private. He was not out to anyone, not even his family. Only one person knew his secret, his housemate Karen. But there was a man he kept meeting at the ER who had already captured his heart.

Seeing the care and professionalism Noah used with everyone he contacted, Keegan was already smitten with the handsome nurse. But he had no idea how he was going to date him without the gossip and information getting out and making his life miserable.

It was a risk Keegan would have to take if he took the leap and wanted a man in his life. A man as incredible as Noah.

Both men were used to trauma and high stress on the job, thought they could handle anything. But when it came to love, it was anything but easy. It was 'Code Red' all the way, and the two men had to handle putting out the fire or learn to enjoy the burn.

The Farmer's Son

BOYS-

BOYS WHO LOVE BOYS WHO LOVE GIRLS

Twenty-five year old Jag Huntington loved straight men. He couldn't help it. Something about their macho-allure intrigued him. But Jag had never even managed to have a straight man as a friend.

His best friend Tyson Hopper, and Tyson's boyfriend Howard Steinman invite Jag out for a night with the gay-boys and Howard's sister, Virginia.

When Virginia brings her straight boyfriend, Carson Phelps, Jag's attraction to the thirty year old stud was instant. But there was not mutual attraction, not even curiosity.

It wasn't until Virginia insinuated that Jag and Carson should be friends, 'close' friends, that Jag began to wonder if he had a chance.

Carson liked hanging with gay men. They were fun. His straight buddies didn't get into dancing, music, or anything he really wanted to do. The idea of having a great gay friend appealed to Carson. Self-assured, Carson didn't flinch at the racy conversation nor sexual overtones of his gay companions' conversation. He liked it.

There was something which intrigued both men into crossing the line of friendship into a physical relationship, but for Jag, it was devoid of any emotional attachment, which he craved from Carson.

Would Jag and Carson's friendship ever evolve into anything more than a couple of friends; one gay and one straight?

Or was there really something extra special about a boy who loves boys, who loves girls?

G. A. HAUSER

BAND OF BROTHERS

Two young men in their early twenties, Austin Shelby and Henry 'Woody' Woodcliff, had somehow lost their way. Living in Albuquerque, petty thieves, neither man had family or hope of becoming anything more than inmates in the county jail.

Orlando Ancho had other plans. Working in his family restaurant, going to med-school, Orlando meets the two young men one night when they come to the restaurant for a meal. Immediately Orlando suspects they are living on the street, and may dine and dash. But what Orlando doesn't expect, is to find a common bond with these men.

Being deep in the closet, living with a brother who was a harsh critic of Orlando, and extremely homophobic, Orlando had no intention of coming out. Hiding from intimacy, Orlando led a lonely life. When Austin and Woody, exchange a 'blood' vow with him one night, Orlando admits his sexual attraction to the fair-haired Austin, craving his love and touch.

But jealousy and violence becomes inevitable, and disaster strikes one of the trio.

What had begun as a friendship between three very different men, turns into a journey for this Band of Brothers; blood brothers…who are put to the ultimate test of trust and loyalty.

The Farmer's Son

ROUGH RIDE

In this sequel to *Cowboy Blues*, we find out about the sexy but proud gay rodeo star, Dean Houston. Though Dean came across as a larger than life superstar, immersed in both gay porn and one of the big players in the Tex-Ass Rodeo league, at thirty-one, Dean is nearing the end of both his careers, and struggling to accept the changes that are coming in his life; no longer being the prime star of the rodeo and top dog of the gay porn circuit.

And Dean was going to be handing his rough stock bull riding crown over to the new stud in town; Clint Wolcott.

To everyone around him Clint looked like the next big sensation of the gay rodeo scene, but his partner Cheyenne Wheeler and close friends, Rob Grafton and Victor Sarita knew his secret.

Will the end of the line for Dean be the beginning of a new life with a potential new partner?

And will the beginning of Clint's career and stardom end with disaster?

Whichever way they boys get bucked, its going to be a Rough Ride.

G. A. HAUSER

COWBOY BLUES

Gay cowboys? Gay rodeos?

Rainbow Rough Riders Rodeo, is a small, newly formed group made up of a diverse selection of gay men who each have their own reasons for wanting to compete in the rodeo challenges and enjoy the fun of the celebration of the wild west.

Follow three couples; Ken Marsh, the forty-one year old founder of the group, his forty-five year old country music singer lover, Lyle Jackson; the two bearded cuddly bears who are the perfect couple, Rob Grafton and Victor Sarita, and the youngest of the bunch, Mike 'Clint' Wolcott and the object of his desire, Cheyenne Wheeler.

Six men, three complicated relationships, and all the thrill and hardship that goes with life on the road, moving town to town, riding bareback and enjoying a good hard buck! And that doesn't even include the rodeo competitions!

Cowboys. The new macho sex symbols, or maybe not 'new', maybe just the sexiest men around. But being a cowboy sometimes is a hard road, and even Cowboys get the blues.

The Farmer's Son

Midnight in London

Thirty-one year old Ted Mack, the high-school 'geek', was on the cusp of developing the next mega social-network-for-one. His group of techno-philes worked day and night to create a unique computer network that would astonish the world.

Twenty-three year old Kevin Moore, Jeremy West's straight roommate from the novel 'Teacher's Pet', has graduated college with honors and is now working on his own creating websites. His idol? Ted Mack.

When the two meet during an IT convention in London, the connection between the handsome college jock and the geek is electric. With the chiming of Big Ben signaling the midnight hour in the background, Ted and Kevin kiss, altering their lives from that moment on.

Can that one moment in time make a connection that will last a lifetime? Or will their colliding worlds pull them apart?

Both Ted and Kevin knew their relationship would not be easy. And if it fell apart? They always had Midnight in London.

G. A. HAUSER

Happy Endings

Twenty-seven year old, Kelsey 'Kellie' Hamilton was caught up in the economic housing disaster. Losing his home, his job, and having to reinvent himself, Kellie went back to school for his certificate in massage therapy and is hired by an elite spa in West Hollywood. Though Kellie had experienced 'happy endings' in the past while getting massages from older men, he was going to abide by the rules and not get sexual with his clients.

Montgomery 'Monty' Gresham, ex Navy SEAL plans to open up a SEAL training boot camp for civilians, and decides getting referrals from a celebrity club in LA would be a perfect idea. While Monty recruits members to his military training center, he meets the handsome massage therapist, Kellie Hamilton.

The contact between Kellie and Monty while Monty is on the massage table instantly sends both men into a state of pure sexual arousal. In this heightened state, where two opposites certainly are attracted, Kellie needs to decide if the tough thirty-eight year old ex-military man will be his Happy Ending, or if living happily ever after is just a fairy tale.

THE FARMER'S SON

The Crush

Straight thirty-two year old Cooper McDermott knew marrying an eighteen year old pageant queen was a mistake. And after two years, his young wife began a spree of cheating on him, breaking his heart.

Newcomer from New York City to the Los Angeles area, Blair Woodbury joins the staff of the law office where the stunning Cooper McDermott works. Blair considers himself 'bisexual', but has just ended an affair back in New York with a man. It didn't take long for Blair to get a full blown crush on Cooper, especially when he was asked to represent Cooper in his divorce. Blair knew getting emotionally involved with a man on the heels of a bad breakup was bad enough, not to mention the object of Blair's desire was straight-

As their friendship grew and they became best buddies, Blair's crush on Cooper became extreme. When Cooper agrees to go for a 'boy's' weekend in Las Vegas, as his sexual curiosity began to emerge, Blair knew he was in for a wild ride!

Can Blair convince Cooper that his feelings for him are real? Or will this fantasy of Blair's be simply just a crush on his co-worker. All Cooper kept hoping was that what happens in Vegas stays in Vegas!

G. A. HAUSER

Lancelot in Love

Still working through an upset of a romance gone bad, thirty year old Lancelot Sanborn escapes to an old haunt; the bungalow colonies of the Catskill Mountain Resort. As a child Lance remembered the comfort and simplicity of his summer vacations, lazing by the lake and enjoying everything upstate New York had to offer. A stark contrast from his hectic life in the Big Apple.

Twenty-three year old Keefe Hammond and three of his friends from Rutgers decide to rent a cottage at the resort for a Labor Day weekend of non-stop partying. Keefe was deeply in the closet and had no intention of stepping out. Until...

The two men meet as they became temporary neighbors in the bungalow resort and soon Keefe began testing his own desires for sex with a man, against his terror of revealing who he is to his friends.

One place Lancelot never expected to find true love was during a retreat to escape from it.

In the end, love always finds a way and for Lancelot, he finds the love of his life in a young man named Keefe.

The Farmer's Son

Capital Games

Let the games begin…

Former Los Angeles Police officer Steve Miller has gone from walking a beat in the City of Angels to joining the rat race as an advertising executive. He knows how cut-throat the industry can be, so when his boss tells him that he's in direct competition with a newcomer from across the pond for a coveted account he's not surprised…then he meets Mark Richfield.

Born with a silver spoon in his mouth and fashion-model good looks, Mark is used to getting what he wants. About to be married, Mark has just nailed the job of his dreams. If the determined Brit could just steal the firm's biggest account right out from under Steve Miller, his life would be perfect.

When their boss sends them together to the Arizona desert for a team-building retreat the tension between the two dynamic men escalates until in the heat of the moment their uncontrollable passion leads them to a sexual experience that neither can forget.

Will Mark deny his feelings and follow through with marriage to a woman he no longer wants, or will he realize in time that in the game of love, sometimes you have to let go and lose yourself in order to *really* win.

Capital Games- soon to be a full length feature film

G. A. HAUSER

Secrets and Misdemeanors

When having to hide your love is a crime...

After losing his wife to his best friend and former law partner, David Thornton couldn't imagine finding love again. With his divorce behind him, he wanted only to focus on his job and two children. But then something happened, making David realize that despite believing he had everything he needed, there was someone he desperately wanted—Lyle Wilson.

Young and determined, Lyle arrived in Los Angeles without a penny in his pocket. Before long, however, the sexy construction worker nailed a job remodeling the old office building that held the prestigious Thornton Law Firm. Little did Lyle realize when he gazed upon the handsome and successful David Thornton for the first time that a door would be opened that neither man could close.

Will the two men succumb to the tangled web of societal pressures placed before them, hiding who they are and whom they love? Or will they reveal the truth and set themselves free?

The Farmer's Son

Naked Dragon

Police Officer Dave Harris has just been assigned to one of the worst serial murder cases in Seattle history: The Dragon is hunting young Asian men. In order to solve the crime it's going to take a bit more than good old-fashioned police work. It's going to take handsome FBI Agent Robbie Taylor.

Robbie is an experienced Federal Agent with psychic abilities that allow him to enter the minds of others. You can't hide your secrets and desires from someone that knows your every thought. Some think what Robbie has is a gift, others a skill, but when the mind you have to enter is that of a madman it can also be a curse.

As the corpses pile up and the tension mounts, so does the sexual attraction between the two men. Then a moment of passion leads to a secret affair. Will their love be the distraction that costs them the case and possibly even their lives? Or will the bond forged between them be the key to their survival?

G. A. HAUSER

The Kiss

Twenty-five year old actor Scott Epstein is no stranger to the modeling industry. He's done it himself between acting jobs. So when his sister, Claire, casts him in a chewing-gum commercial with the famous British model, Ian Sullivan, he doesn't ask any questions. He's a professional. He'll show up, hit his mark, say his lines, and collect his paycheck. Right?

Ian Sullivan is used to making heads turn. Stunningly handsome, he's accustomed to provocative photo shoots where sex sells everything from perfume to laundry soap. Ian was thrilled when Claire Epstein cast him in the new Minty gum commercial. He has to kiss his co-star on screen? No problem. Until he finds out Scott is the one he has to kiss!

Never before has a commercial featured two men, kissing on screen. Claire knows that the advertisement will be groundbreaking, and Scott knows that his sister needs his performance to be perfect. As the filming progresses and the media circus begins around the controversial advertisement, the chemistry between Ian and Scott heats up and the two men quite simply burn up the screen. Is it all an act? Or, have Ian and Scott entered into a clandestine affair that will lead them to love?

THE FARMER'S SON

For Love and Money

Handsome Dr. Jason Philips, the heir to a vast fortune, had followed his heart and pursued his dream of becoming a physician. Ewan P. Gallagher had a different dream. Acting in local theater, the talented twenty-year-old was determined to be a famous success.

As fate would have it, Jason happened to be working in casualty one night when Ewan was admitted as a patient. Jason was more than flattered and surprisingly aroused by the younger man's obvious attraction to him. The two men entered into a steamy affair finding love, until their ambitions pulled them apart.

Now, one year later and stuck in a sham of a marriage that he entered into only to preserve his inheritance, Jason is filled with regret. Caught between obligation and freedom, duty and desire, Jason finds that he can no longer deny his passion. He plans to win Ewan, Hollywood's newest rising star, back!

G. A. HAUSER

The Vampire and the Man-eater

Love at first bite!

Stock broker Brock Hart's idea of fun was playing at the local gay nightclub every weekend with someone new. He imagined the Rules of Relationships didn't apply to him, and his best friend thought his nonchalant attitude towards sex was crazy. Until one night his playboy image was put to the test.

Spying Brock in a crowded club, Vampire Daniel Wolf sets his sights on the handsome 'man-eater' businessman. Sparks literally fly, between the two, and with one bite from the sexy vamp Brock is hooked.

Never did Brock ever imagine falling for anyone, especially not a man from Sixteenth Century England! The only problem is, he's a vampire. Can love conquer all? It will be a challenge, but one Brock is up for, in so many ways.

THE FARMER'S SON

Murphy's Hero

Sometimes...being a hero isn't about putting on a cape.

Alexander Parker has always been painfully shy and his job at the British Museum keeps him busy. Dedicated and serious, no one is more surprised than Alexander when the replica of a Greek warrior's helmet he impulsively places on his head suddenly transforms him from mild-mannered clerk into something else entirely.

Adrian Mackenzie, the editor of a famous erotic gay magazine, is about to get the scoop of the decade. The crime ridden city seems to have a savior, a mysterious man who is righting wrongs, protecting innocents, and as luck would have it… is extremely hot.

When Adrian happens to stumble upon the Good Samaritan in action he falls hard and fast discovering love *and* Alexander's true identity. Now, if he can only get Alexander to come out of the closet. But is the world ready for a gay superhero?

Let bestselling author G.A. Hauser take you on an unforgettable fun-filled adventure and discover the story that inspired Ewan Gallagher's famous movie roll in G.A.'s *For Love and Money.*

Exposure

Exposure...the truth will set you free

In politics for twenty years, Senator Kipp Kensington knows that even a whisper of suspicion about his sexuality could jeopardize his aspirations for the Presidency. Kipp thought he could be content living a lie in a marriage of convenience. Then he met Robin Grant.

Leather-clad, motorcycle riding Robin isn't accustomed to hiding what he is or denying himself who he wants. The instant he meets Kipp, the sparks begin to fly and what started as a chance encounter soon turns into a full-blown affair of sizzling proportions.

When the contract Kipp has had for nine years with his now alcoholic, bitter wife begins to crumble and he's threatened with blackmail, the senator needs to make a decision. Should he hide who he really is in order to avoid losing his career, or reveal the truth and set himself free?

Mile High
Book One in the Men in Motion Series

Divorced accountant Owen Braydon spends his weeks working in Los Angeles and his weekends in Denver with his daughter. Straight-laced and mild mannered, he normally looks at the weekly flight to and from Denver as an opportunity to get some extra work done. But then he found himself on the same plane as the luscious Taylor Madison.

Texas-born Taylor is from Denver, but for several months he's been flying back and forth to Los Angeles where he works as a project manager on a major construction job. Charismatic and confident, Taylor is a man who knows what he wants and isn't afraid to go after it. The second he lays eyes on bi-curious Owen, he knows he wants him.

What starts out as a smoldering no-strings-attached initiation into the Mile High Club quickly turns into a weekly ritual that both men look forward to over all else. Soon their desire for one another deepens and both men find themselves wanting and needing more.

When a possible change in work assignments threatens to end what they have, both men are faced with a decision. Can the heights they soared together in the air be maintained on the ground? Only if Owen and Taylor are willing to cast aside their doubts, open up their hearts, set aside all inhibitions, and go the extra mile.

G. A. HAUSER

Cruising
Book Two in the Men in Motion Series

Brodie Duncan expected to be taking a week-long Alaskan cruise with his girlfriend. But when she ended their relationship just moments before boarding, he ended up on the ship alone. Determined to make the best of a bad situation, Brodie considers a no-strings-attached fling. What he didn't bargain for was a man as appealing as Julian Richards. Trapped in his own bad relationship with a selfish woman he was starting to resent, the charismatic Julian is shocked by his reaction to tall, dark, and handsome Brodie. Instantly attracted to each other, the men create enough heat on their trip to the Inside Passage to melt the Glaciers in the bay.

In the end, on a vacation full of surprises, Julian and Brodie discover that not only do they have strong feelings for one another, by *Cruising* they just might have found their soul mates.

The Farmer's Son

Driving Hard

Book Three in the Men in Motion Series

They met on the highway. It was the beginning of ride they'd never forget...

Texan Jude Rae Clark hit the road in his pride and joy, a jet black International big rig, searching for a new life after his divorce. Unfortunately the long, lonely hauls provided little comfort until just outside Houston on Interstate 10 a blue-eyed stranger asked for a lift.

Yale Law School graduate, Logan Bleau, set out to explore America and escape his past by hitching his way across country to San Francisco. When he meets up with a handsome stranger in his eighteen-wheeler, a physical attraction blooms and the two men end up taking a detour.

When what began as sexual exploration on the open road turns into something deeper, the pair find themselves reevaluating their lives and Jude is faced with a decision. Give up his career of cruising the highways or pass up on the love of a lifetime.

G. A. Hauser

Leather Boys
Book Four in the Men in Motion Series

Start your engines, mount up, and get ready for the ride of a life-time...

Sexy gay fiction author Devlin Young donned his helmet, black leather jacket, and jeans. Then he mounted his Kawasaki and set off for what he anticipated would be a wild ride to Sturgis.

There were thousands of motorcycles, thousands of men, but only one Sam Rhodes. When web-designer Sam Rhodes joined a local group called The Leather Boys, he wasn't quite sure what to expect, but he knew what it was he wanted. Amidst the decadence and insanity of the monster event, all Sam could think about was what it would be like to share an erotic experience with the deliciously naughty Dev Young.

Never one to apologize for who he is, or who he desires, Devlin doesn't understand Sam's reluctance to openly explore their relationship or his wish to keep their liaisons confined to the darkness of their tents while at the rally. Then he crosses swords with a tough-as-nails biker who both taunts and tempts him, unleashing a potentially dangerous craving and pushing Dev to make a choice.

The Boy Next Door

Brandon Townsend and Zachary Sherman were best friends and next-door neighbors. Growing up together in a cozy suburban town in New Jersey, they were inseparable and thought nothing could tear them apart. Then one night something happened between them, something that brought them even closer together…

They didn't anticipate that what began as youthful sexual experimentation would lead them into an affair of the heart that would rock them to the core. Nor did they expect the danger of being discovered and separated by their families. At the time, neither Brandon or Zach realized that life would give them another opportunity.

Now, ten years later, a chance meeting brings them together again. Let best-selling gay fiction author G.A. Hauser take you on an unforgettable journey. A coming of age story about faith, about courage, and about trust…you'll never forget The Boy Next Door.

G. A. HAUSER

When Adam Met Jack

Attorney Jack Larsen may not have everything he wants, but between his successful career and best friend Mark Richfield, he's content. But when Mark comes out of the closet only to declare his love for ex-LAPD officer Steve Miller, Jack is devastated. Months later and still wounded, he's not looking to be swept off his feet, but it's hard to say no to handsome

Hollywood hotshot Adam Lewis. Adam Lewis has made a name for himself representing some of today's brightest stars. But when his business partner is accused of unethical behavior, he finds himself in need of legal advice. When Adam walks into the law office of Jack Larsen, it's strictly business until he sets eyes on the powerful and sexy hero that's about to rescue his reputation.

When Adam Met Jack is an amazing new novel by Amazon best selling gay fiction author G.A. Hauser featuring characters from Love you Loveday, For Love and Money, and Capital Games. It's got the glamour of the entertainment industry, the drama of the courtroom, and the amazing passion that you've come to expect from every G.A. Hauser book.

The Farmer's Son

Love you, Loveday

Angel Loveday thought he had put his life as a gay soft-porn star of the 1980's behind him. For seventeen years he's hidden his sexuality and sordid past from his teenage son. But when someone threatens Angel's secret and Detective Billy Sharpe is assigned to his case, he finds himself having to once again face them both.

Since his youth Billy Sharpe has had erotic on-screen images of Angel Loveday emblazoned in his mind. Now Angel is there in the flesh, needing his protection and stirring up the passionate fantasies that Billy thought he'd long ago abandoned.

As the harassment continues and the danger grows, Billy and Angel become closer. What began as an instant attraction turns into an undeniable hunger that unlocks Angel's heart. It's a race against time as Billy tries to save the man of his dreams from a life without love and the maniacal stalker hell-bent on destroying him.

G. A. HAUSER

To Have and to Hostage

When he was taken hostage by a strange man Michael never expected he'd lose his heart...

Michael Vernon is a rich, spoiled brat with a string of meaningless lovers and an entourage of superficial friends. With no direction in life, he wastes his days spending his father's money and drowning himself in liquor...until he crashes into a man even more desperate than himself, Jarrod Hunter.

Jarrod Hunter grew up on the wrong side of the tracks. Out of work, about to be evicted, and unable to afford his next meal, Jarrod thought he'd reached the end of his rope and was determined to take his life. Then fate intervened delivering him

Michael Vernon. Why not take him home, tie him up, and hold him hostage to get the money he needs?

Two men from two different worlds...one dangerous game. Trapped together in close quarters, Jarrod and Michael find themselves sharing their deepest thoughts and fighting an undeniable attraction for each other. As the hours tick by, the captor becomes captivated by his victim and the victim begins to bond with his abductor. This wakeup call might prove to be just what Michael needs to set himself free. To Have and to Hostage...sometimes you have to hit bottom before realizing that what you need is standing right in front of you.

The Farmer's Son

Giving Up the Ghost

The visit from beyond the grave that changed their lives forever...

Artist Ryan Monroe had everything he wanted and then in a blink of an eye, he lost what mattered most of all, his soul-mate, Victor. Tortured by an overwhelming sense of grief and unable to move on, his pain spills out, reflected in the blood red hues of his paintings.

Paul Goldman thought he'd found the love of his life in Evan, his beloved pianist. Their mutual passion for music was outweighed only by their passion for one another. They were planning a life-time together, but then one fateful night Evan's was taken. Drowning in sorrow, unable to find solace, the heartbroken violinist has resigned himself to a life alone.

Now it's two years later and something, someone, is bringing them together. Two men, two loves, two great losses... and one hot ghost. Giving up the Ghost by G.A. Hauser, you won't be able to put down!

G. A. Hauser

Made in the USA
Lexington, KY
04 November 2013